EMPTIES

Jay Caselberg

White Cat Publications

FIRST EDITION
10 9 8 7 6 5 4 3 2 1
ISBN 978-0-9882446-1-0
Published in September 2014
Printed in the U.S.A.

White Cat Publications, LLC.
33080 Industrial Road, Suite 101
Livonia, MI 48150

www.whitecatpublications.com

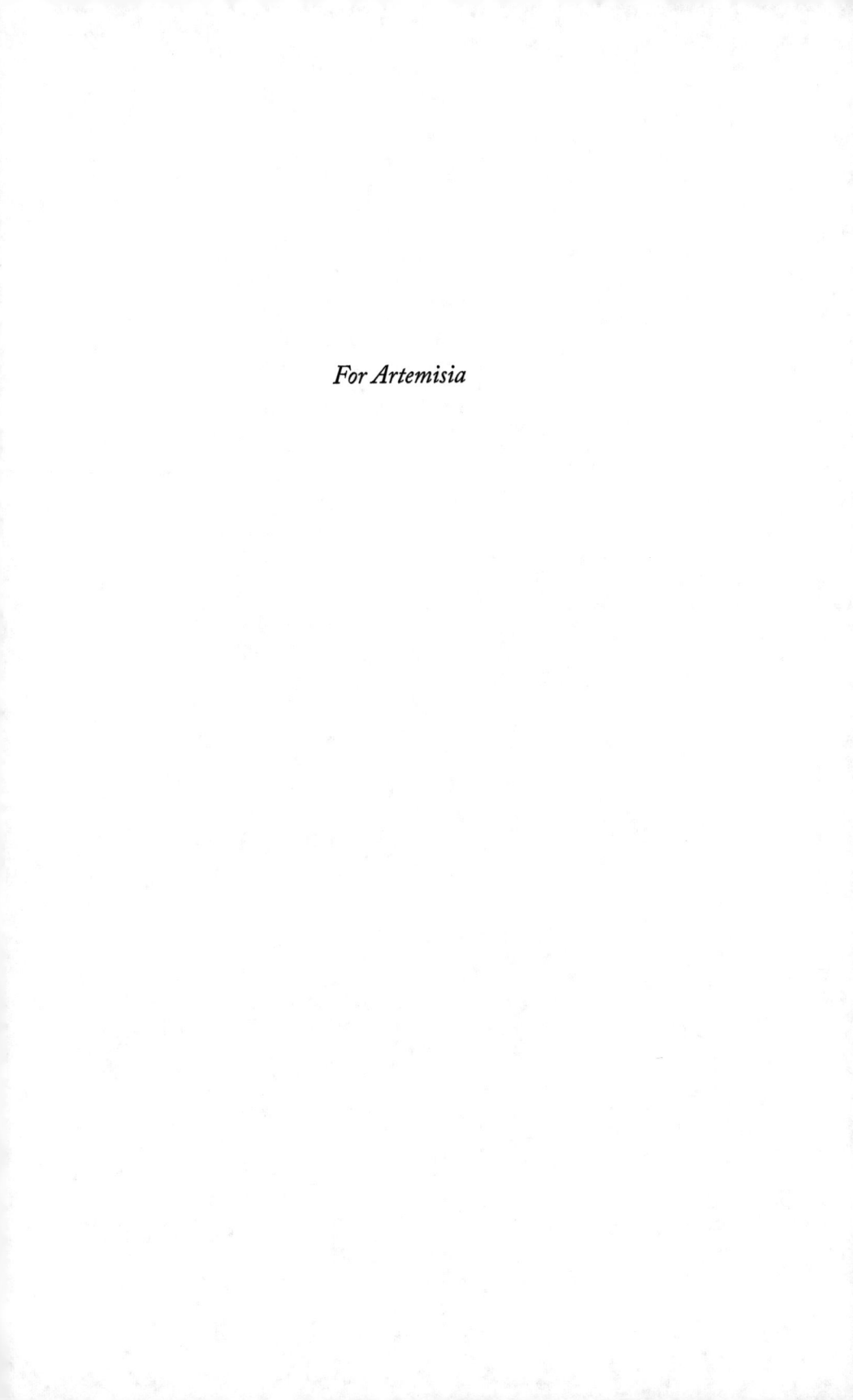

For Artemisia

Between the conception
And the creation
Between the emotion
And the response
Falls the shadow

—T.S. Eliot

CHAPTER ONE

SPACE

Sometimes it's hard to know whether it's a man thing or a woman thing. Perhaps it's neither, that impossible distance from reality, that hollow inability to touch feeling. You might notice it after a while, as you get older, as the world creeps up and assaults your inner senses. How exactly does it manifest? As a void inside? As a gap stretched from wall to wall of the inner self?

Imagine, if you will, a sheet of thick plastic, draped, like on the inside of a building site, suspended like a parachute or tent just above your head and hanging down around you. You can see the impression of faces and noses pressed against the sheet beyond—sometimes, pale palm prints marked out in the dust. Behind this formless definition lies truth. The problem being, that in reaching for that truth, you risk suffocation. To get close enough to see clearly, you have to press your face hard against the sheeting, and that cuts off your ability to breathe.

And so it is inside.

Chris first noticed his own sense of removal in his late twenties. Palpably, tangibly, the gap from reality began to grow inside, stretching across the dusty space of his inner walls. What once had been a mere footstep had become a leap, a bound—to step impossibly across a yawning void. How was he to know or suspect that it was preparation? How was he to know where that understanding might lead him?

He'd been married for about four years when he first really noticed the distance. Anastasia and Chris got on well. They got on like a house on fire. Though they had differences, in the things they liked and the things they found interesting, difference was a healthy thing. There were those tiny shreds of interaction that held them together and made the relationship what it was: the half-startled expression she seemed to get when she looked up and saw him; the vague quirk of her lips that showed something he had said had sparked something inside. He found them all appealing. Somehow, he stirred her, and she stirred him in return.

"Stase," he'd say to her. "What would my life have been without you?"

He simply couldn't imagine it. She'd smile and get that stupid grin, and he'd know that what he'd said had touched her. She'd run her long fingers through her hair and look away, still with that half smile upon her lips.

Then came work, and the mortgage, and the bills, and gradually, over time, that smile faded. They never got around to having kids. The time was never right, or their position wasn't secure, or there were things they had to achieve with their lives first. So many things stood in the way. Perhaps if they'd managed it, the kids would have brought them together, strengthened the glue between them. Perhaps.

All relationships go through their transitions, growing, shaping, morphing into places where they had never been before, or where you might not have expected them to go. Once in a while, that path takes you to a locale not seen in your imaginings, nor mapped out in those fragile hopes and dreams that make up your wished-for future. Stase and Chris were no different.

The night he slapped her, when her fingernails scored his cheek, dragging clear lines into his flesh, he knew the void had grown too great. He pulled his hand away from his face and looked dumbfounded at the pale-brown blood stripes across his palm. He lashed out, shocking himself by the action. Where had the violence and hollow lack of feeling come from? He looked at her then with narrowed eyes. They say the eyes are the windows of the soul, but all he saw in hers was dark emptiness, the softness gone hard. Perhaps there should have been tears, but there weren't.

They half made up—a tension-filled truce—but the damage had been done and they knew it without saying a word. The secret knowledge of what lay between then now lived silently within the both of them.

When he walked out of the house the next morning, he understood that a bridge had been crossed, but even though there was no going back, knowing it wasn't enough. He had a life like any other—streets, and buildings, and offices, and all the other rituals of adulthood. There was the daily trek to work, the obligatory drinks at the end of the week, and all of the pseudo-social engagements that come with the network that supports life. And with it came the work colleagues that became part of your existence whether you wanted them to or not. He was forced to use her foundation to cover the marks, dabbing lightly with one fingertip across the ridged lines on his cheek, working it palely across the intervening skin as he leaned across the bathroom sink close to the mirror, the slightly perfumed scent filling his nostrils. As he pulled the door shut behind him on his way to work, Chris was concocting stories in his head.

He didn't know what made him take the alternative route to the office. Perhaps it was an urge to shield his wounded pride, avoid the crowds. As he walked, he struggled with the compulsion to lift his hand and hold it to the side of his face, shielding his indignity from the world. He needn't have worried. That morning, hardly a soul trod the roads he traveled, but he was painfully conscious of the marks and his awareness walked with him, prompting him to be vigilant for passers-by.

Halfway along Sydney Street, on a grassy verge, lay a man, his pale, distended half-moon belly pressing towards the sky. Some drunk, was Chris's first thought, catching a blessed few moments of unconsciousness. The man wore jeans and running shoes, silver stripes against black. His maroon tee shirt had ridden halfway up across his middle, exposing pale, flabby flesh. The man's head was turned away from him and Chris couldn't see his face, only stringy hair flopping across a balding pate.

Looking at the figure lying there, he had second thoughts and he stopped. Everything looked too new—none of the stains, or the soiling, or the greasy disheveled aura that hangs around the itinerant alcoholic like a bedcover. He waited, watching, looking for some sign of life, going through that internal debate about whether he should see if the guy was all right or simply walk away, pretending he hadn't seen.

The man didn't move. Not even the slightest stir to show he was breathing.

After a while, Chris shook his head and moved on, feigning the fact that he hadn't seen the man at all, even though there was no one to see, but as he neared the corner, he glanced back with a tinge of guilt. The guy was still lying there. A large white truck was just rounding the corner at the other end of the street, so he quickened his pace so as not to become involved.

His workday went as any other, and he forgot about the guy in the street. He spent most of it huddled over his desk, his head angled to conceal the telltale marks on his cheek, avoiding the inquiring glances. On public show, he had far more important things to worry about than some unconscious derelict on the street. He finally made up some story about a tree branch in the garden, though he knew the marks were spaced the wrong distance apart, and he tried uneasily to ignore the knowing glances that passed between his co-workers.

The uncomfortable day drew to a close and he returned home by his normal route. He needn't have bothered. He was back to a Siberia of silence and avoidance of eye contact. The walls of their mutual lack of conversation sparked and shorted in the air between them. Eventually Stase went upstairs and closed herself in her room—her room now—leaving Chris slumped in front of the television in the steel-blue semi-dark. That night, just like the previous night, he slept on the couch, the television voices intruding into his unconsciousness, whispering things to him in the colored darkness and populating his dreams. He was up early and gone before she rose.

It was a full three days before another word passed between them.

He was tired and snappy at work, and he felt that hollow space grow and echo within. Stase, in her silence, expressed her tension by the set of her shoulders and the stiffness of her back. He wished he could get inside her head for just a few moments. In the end, it was a household account that drew the first words.

"Yes, I'll look after it," he told her, short and clipped.

They were bonded then by their domesticity. Words passed between them, but they were hollow, utilitarian. The hollowness was a whisper of that which had taken up residence inside them.

Another week crawled by and the marks on Chris's face faded daily. It was then that he saw his second. It was a Saturday, leaden gray and filled with an opalescent chill. He'd gone out to get the newspaper, and Stase was still in bed. They were still sleeping in separate rooms. He'd tried on the previous evening to start a conversation, but she wasn't interested—almost as if she just didn't have the energy to bother. As he walked to the store, he bunched his coat around him; protection from the cold or the way his life was going, he didn't know.

He almost didn't notice the woman lying at the bus shelter as he passed. She was young, dressed in a long coat, her hair shining in the morning light. A wave of blonde strands draped across one cheek and her blue eyes stared straight ahead, out into the road. One leg was exposed where the coat had fallen away. He hesitated, remembering the fat man on Sydney Street. There was nothing there to say that there was anything wrong with the girl, but he stopped anyway. After a few moments, standing there and staring, he walked in front of her. There wasn't a flicker of recognition from her eyes—nothing to say she even saw him. He walked back in front of her, looking for some sort of reaction, then stood at the side of the bus shelter, debating. Nothing moved, not her chest, her eyelids, nothing. A slight flurry of breeze lifted a screwed-up piece of paper and dragged it scraping across the gutter.

He crouched down in front of her.

"Are you all right?" he asked.

Nothing. It was cold and she seemed to be wearing very little under the coat. She kept staring, straight ahead, right through him. If it hadn't been for the crisp cold and the color in her cheeks, he could have thought she was dead. He'd seen a dead man, pale, chill. You know when they're dead. The color's different, the skin waxy. You know when they're dead.

Still crouched in front of her, Chris looked up and down the street, but there was no one in sight. He waved a hand in front of her face, but there was nothing, not even a flicker. Hesitantly he reached out with one hand and touched her cheek. It was warm, barely, but warm.

"Hey," he said. He stood staring down at her. Maybe she was on something.

Hesitation. Lack of involvement. Safety.

There was nothing he could do for her, was there? If she was still there when he got back from buying the paper, then he'd call someone. That would be the right thing to do, he told himself. So he headed away from the bus shelter and up the road. Secretly, he was hoping she'd be gone by the time he got back. It wasn't his problem. Let it please be someone else's. Or that's what he told himself.

On the way back, as he neared the shelter where she'd been lying, he could see she was gone. Inside himself, Chris was relieved, but he was struck by a sense of wrongness. He hadn't a clue what had happened to her. Perhaps someone had come past and had the goodness to do something. It had only been twenty minutes. How long did it take for an ambulance to arrive and depart? Was twenty minutes long enough? He didn't know. He felt the guilt all the same.

He was chewing it over all the way back to the house. The fact that he'd walked away, just left her, and was filled with a callousness of action that surprised Chris, a something he had trouble recognizing in himself. He didn't think he'd always been that unfeeling. What had happened to him in the intervening time? He wondered if it was a symptom of the general emptiness he'd been experiencing, of the deterioration of his relationship and everything else. It was almost as if life conspired to drain you of the capacity for anything but numbness, assaulting you at every turn with images and pictures that filled your head until one became indistinguishable from the other.

He slipped inside the front door, still thinking about it, wandered in from the hallway and tossed his keys and the paper onto the kitchen table. Front page was a story about ethnic cleansing and the associated atrocities, all in lurid color. He barely glanced at it. Stase was already out of bed, sitting hunched in her robe and sipping at a cup of tea. She didn't look up and he avoided looking at her. Instead, his head was full of the too-still woman at the bus shelter. If he hadn't seen her, he wouldn't have thought about the man on Sydney Street. He wouldn't have made the connection. But once the connection was made, it was there for him to hold on to and for it to hold on to him.

"Stase," he said. "Can I talk to you about something?"

"Yeah, what?" she said, without looking up from her tea.

"I saw something on the way to get the paper."

"And what might that be, a lonely future staring you in the face?"

"Yeah, right," he said, holding back the urge to snap with difficulty. "Not quite."

Chris wondered for a moment how far she was from the truth, and a hollow nestled inside. "There was this woman. She looked like she was dead, but she wasn't. She was just lying there staring into space."

Stase looked up from her cup then. Her face was stony. "What do you mean, she looked dead but wasn't? What, like us, you mean?"

"Cut it out," he said with a heavy sigh. "I'm being serious."

"So am I," she said quietly, drawing the moment out. "So did you do anything?"

"I thought about it, but by the time I got back she was gone."

"What, you just left her there? Typical." She pursed her lips, shook her head, then stood and carried her cup to the sink. That was it. She left him standing there, looking at the empty chair where she'd been.

What like us? he thought.

That was the extent of their interaction for the rest of the weekend. He felt the ringing space solidify inside and between them. But what she'd said had started him thinking.

Like us.

Knowing there was little he could do to address it then, until he'd worked out what was happening between them, he turned his attention to other things, to the mystery of the girl at the bus shelter, to the fat man on Sydney Street. At the start of the following week, he started watching, looking for other examples, trying to see if the suspicion he was feeling was mere imagination, or maybe something else

Both of them, the young woman at the bus stop, the man on Sydney Street, they were the same, and in some strange way, deep in his guts, he knew it. It was as if life had drained all the identity from them—just worn it away. In the back of his mind, he was aware that there was an echo there in what he was seeking. There was a strange parallel with what seemed to be happening in his own life, but he tried very hard to dismiss that particular connection as imagination.

So he started watching for signs. He looked in doorways and bus shelters, in the hollow, shadowed places beneath subway steps. He didn't go out of his way to search for them; he just kept himself aware. That awareness paid off, and one by one, he started to find them.

The next one he found was sitting inside a doorway. A down-and-out, he thought. Then he looked closer and saw the blank gaze, the slack face, simply staring into nothingness. Chris stood in the middle of the commuter crowd, fascinated as people passed, their eyes averted, denying that they had even seen the person hunched in the doorway. It was so easy for him to go unnoticed. It was as if he didn't really exist at all—invisible. But Chris saw.

He crossed the road and took up position on the opposite side of the street, propping himself against the low window ledge of a huge department store. The occasional bus or truck slid past, obscuring the man briefly from his view, flashing advertising images and clever graphics in slipstream motion past his eyes, but he refused to be distracted. If this one was going to disappear, he wanted to see how. Maybe he should have crossed the street and gone to help him, but he didn't know if there was anything he could have done. Passers-by strode past, studiedly oblivious.

At long last, his patience and fascination were rewarded. A white van slowed in front of the doorway and stopped. Chris leaned forward, trying to catch a good look between the passing pedestrians. There were two men in the van. They looked like workers from some benevolent society or mission: neat haircuts, clean-shaven, clean unremarkable features. They walked over to the building and bent down in front of the man slumped in the doorway. There were a few moments of consultation between the two, then one of the men crossed to the van and opened the rear doors before returning. Together, one on each side, they got a grip under the man's armpits and hoisted him to his feet. He sort of half walked, almost stumbling, a few paces between them. Slowly, they steered him across the pavement, up into the back of the van, then closed the doors and drove away. That was it. They were gone. The rest of the world strode past, uncaring.

Chris leaned back against the store window, staring thoughtfully at the place where the man had sat. Somehow, these guys in the van, they'd known he was there ...

That would have been the end of it. He had his answer about where they went, in part. It didn't matter how those faceless others knew. There was someone who came and took them away. That truly would have been the end of it, except that he saw the man from the doorway three days later.

He was dressed just as Chris had seen him and he walked past him in the street, semi-blankness on his face. Chris stopped and stared after him, tracking him through the crowd, uncertain. People flowed around Chris as he stood in the middle of the rush-hour throng. Finally, Chris shook his head and went on his way. He must have been imagining it.

CHAPTER Two

VISITORS

A couple of days later, Chris had his true confirmation. There was a small café he frequented on the way to work and he'd stopped for a cup of coffee. He was casually scanning the other patrons when he noticed her. It was his girl from the bus shelter. He'd been close when he'd seen her then—right up close. He remembered her hair and her pale white features touched with pink. He remembered the flaxen tress falling across her cheek. There was no mistaking her for someone else.

She was in an animated discussion with a friend at the next table over. He stopped with his cup halfway to his lips and stared. After a few moments, she caught his gaze, frowned, and leaned closer to her friend to say something. The friend looked over her shoulder and gave him a look filled with hostility. Carefully, Chris placed his cup back down. They were leaning close together, still talking in low tones. The young woman, his girl, shot a brief glance in his direction and frowned again.

He debated; then, plucking up his courage, he pushed back his chair, stood and walked over to their table.

"You don't remember me, do you?" he asked. "The other day at the bus shelter."

She looked up, her face hard and unfriendly.

"I don't know what the hell you're talking about," she said. "I don't know you. Now leave us alone."

It was the same girl, all right. He thought perhaps that mention of the bus shelter would have sparked something.

"Are you still here?" said the girl's friend.

Chris mumbled apologies and backed away. He knew it was the same girl. He sat and watched until eventually his continued scrutiny became too much for them and they left. She sneered and gave a toss of her head as she walked out the door, half-glancing in his direction. As the pair walked up the street, their heads were close together. He could almost hear her saying, "Can you believe that guy?"

For the first time in weeks, he felt as if something mattered. Suddenly, here was something he could hold onto and do something about. He had to find out what was happening with these people.

He chewed it over for two days before he decided he'd broach the subject with Stase. He had to talk to someone. They'd talked about things in the past. He waited until they were both sitting quietly in front of some cop show in the middle of an ad break.

"Stase?" he said.

"What is it now?"

"You know that girl I saw at the bus shelter a couple of weeks ago ...?"

"Yes ... that again."

"Well, I saw her today."

"And ..."

"There was nothing wrong with her."

"So?" She crossed her arms and stared at the screen as the ad light flickered across her face. Comedic music and a cleaning product washed across his awareness with a man standing there wearing a stupid grin on his face.

He grabbed the remote and killed the sound. "Will you listen to me?"

She sighed and looked over. "What do you want me to say?"

"Well, there's definitely something strange going on."

"The only thing strange going on is you." She stood, and started walking past him, back to the bedroom. He pushed himself up from the chair and grabbed her arm.

"Just listen to me," he said.

She wrenched her arm free of his grip. "I don't care about what's going on in that fucked-up head of yours," she said. "Now let me go, will you?"

"What's your problem?"

"You're my problem," she said flatly. "We've got nothing to say to each other." The truth of what she was saying slammed into him, then exploded into anger and resentment.

"If you feel like that, why don't you just get out?" he yelled.

"Yeah, right," she spat back. "Why don't you?" He could see the hollowness there, the lack of feeling. She pushed past and strode into the kitchen, away from him. Chris followed, spinning her round to face him in the middle of the small kitchen.

"Why are you doing this? Jesus, you're just so fucking stupid sometimes," he muttered between tight lips.

"I am not stupid!"

Her hand flashed towards his face, nails curled, and he reacted. Chris pulled back his arm as if to strike, but something stopped him. Everything faded into slow motion. He watched her hand approach his cheek. Her lips were slightly parted, the tip of her tongue resting wetly in the corner of her mouth. A slight contact of her fingers, but no more. The ends of her nails rested on his skin, claws in the dust of what they had become. What was she waiting for? Her breath came in short shallow gasps, then nothing. Blankness filled her eyes and she crumpled to the floor.

He stood over her, his arm still half-raised, prepared to force the blow that would never come, his anger transferring into shame. He stood like that for almost a minute, wondering at this new game she'd invented.

"Stase," he said. "Cut it out."

She lay there, not moving, her eyes staring straight ahead across the lines of wooden floorboards.

"Stase?"

She wasn't breathing. He lowered his arm and stared. He stooped and gently pushed her shoulder. When that brought no reaction, he crouched in front of her.

"Stase?"

He reached for her neck and felt for a pulse. It was there, low and slow.

He'd seen that look, that lack of being, before—at least three times over the past few weeks. Strangely, he couldn't feel anything. Slowly, Chris lifted himself to a chair. He sat like that for the rest of the night, just watching. From time to time he'd crouch down in front of her to look, reach out to touch the warmth of her face, then ease himself back up into the chair. He didn't even think to call anyone.

He was still sitting there the next morning, numb and staring, as the world grew lighter outside the window. He barely noticed when the doorbell rang. The second time it rang, it was long and insistent. He shook himself and stood, tearing his gaze away from Stase's still form and stumbled to the door. Two men, clean-cut, smiling, stood there.

"Yes?" he asked, barely registering what was happening.

One nodded and gently pushed past him into the house.

"Hey, what are you doing?" Chris asked.

The other man gently took his shoulders and moved him out of the way, then also stepped past and disappeared inside.

A mix of emotions ran through him, but somehow dulled. It never got to outrage. He mentally shook himself and followed them inside.

"What do you think you're doing? Excuse me?" he called from the kitchen door.

They stood in the room's center, Stase's still form between

them at their feet, staring down at her. One of them glanced at Chris, held the look, then looked over to his companion and gave a brief nod. The look he gave Chris, though it was full of nothing, pinned him there in the doorway, any further questions driven from him, powerless. He didn't understand. How could the guy do that? It was just a look. It was as if Chris had lost all will to move.

Still without a word, they stooped, lifted Stase from the kitchen floor and carried her out between them.

Just before they lifted her, there was a moment of hesitation. They looked at Chris again and then at each other, an unspoken consultation passing between them. Then one of them shook his head. His companion gave a slight nod and stooped to help with lifting Stase's still, quiet shape. The second man looked at Chris long and hard as they maneuvered past him and carried her out the door.

He stood at the front door watching as they shut the rear doors of their big white van, clambered up front, and then drove away. The guy in the passenger's seat was still watching him from the window as they pulled away and he stood there staring after them.

CHAPTER THREE

THE DEAD ACTRESS

Chris stood at the doorway, looking out onto the street. He turned, closed the door and went back inside the house. He stood in the center of the living room for about ten minutes, just staring into nothing, feeling like crap. He'd been up all night for some reason, he had a full eight hours of work ahead of him and he didn't quite know how he was going to get through the day. His eyes were sensitive and watery, his back ached and he was feeling kind of strung out, thoughts skittering across the surface of his brain with no real form or substance to them. What he needed was a shower and a cup of coffee, not necessarily in that order. He thought about switching on the news, but couldn't be bothered. He decided he didn't really need the noise right now. Every morning they had the breakfast news program, chirpy happy faces as they gave words to what was going on in the world, however grave. It was part of Stase's ritual, and she'd clearly already left for work without saying a word. Not that that was so unusual these days.

Briefly, he considered calling in sick, but they had a current project that really needed his attention; despite the state he was in, it would be better to be there, in among the semi-friends and colleagues you accumulate in the workplace—the little faux community. Glancing at the clock, he realized he had maybe enough time to get ready, but only if he hurried. The shower and coffee would have to be quick.

Both coffee and shower done with, in that order, he headed to work. The habitual walk along familiar suburban streets, squinting through the morning sun, his shoulder already aching with the weight of his bag, and a few minutes later, he reached the bus stop. A line of fellow commuters already stood waiting, and he grimaced. Normally, he tried to get in a lot earlier to avoid the crowds. That way he could be assured of a seat and the vague chance of immersing himself in a couple of chapters before having to wrench himself back to the day-to-day mundane. That was the good thing about books—the magic. You could immerse yourself in another world, painting the details, filling in the blanks with your imagination, rather than having it all thrust at you without really participating. Books were different. They allowed you to create your own world. No such luck that morning, though.

The bus finally shuddered to a halt in front of them, they the sheep, with a sigh and hiss of brakes, and they filed dutifully inside, Chris along with them. He ended up about a third of the way down the aisle, pressed firmly against the hard metal frame of a seat edge. The bus was crowded, sweaty, and full of the smell of bodies and something else. The buses always smelled old, musty and damp after a period of heavy rain like they'd had over the last couple of nights. Or had they? Chris couldn't remember. He shook his head, trying to clear the fog. Had it been raining or hadn't it? The bus took off and he quickly threw out a hand for support, cursing under his breath.

An old guy sat in front of where he stood, his neck sprouting grizzled hair, a label sticking out from underneath his cap announcing to the world that his head was large. Beside him sat a middle-aged woman, dyed brown hair showing white at the roots, lying lacquered in fulsome waves. On the other side, another pair was talking loudly, oblivious to those around them. Just for a moment, he drifted into their conversation.

"She's not very intelligent—like mentally—you know what I mean? She's my mother, and I love her and everything, but you have to be tactful with her. That's just the way I am. You know what I mean? It's harder to get through to her these days, the poor dear."

Her companion nodded.

"Will you look at that?" the woman who had spoken said, pointing out the window. "Why someone can't do something to get all the spongers and beggars off the street, I don't know."

Her friend nodded again without saying anything.

Chris sighed and drifted away again. Were there so many beggars on the street? He hadn't really noticed.

Somewhere up the back, a phone rang. He waited for the inevitable and gritted his teeth in anticipation. "Yeah, I'm on a bus. On my way into work."

Why did he care? Why did anyone care? People seemed to lose all consciousness of where they were when they were on the phone.

The bus growled protesting up a hill, outside, buildings and traffic and shops, inside, the commuter crush. He would have tried to watch the passing streets, but the bus was too tightly packed to get a proper view. He had no real option but to turn his thoughts back inside.

Chris really didn't understand how Stase and he had arrived where they were. Where was that anyway? He gripped the top of the seat beside him more tightly, a frown growing on his face, as he thought about that, turning the shape of it over and over. The bus lurched, someone jolted against him, and he looked up at them, still frowning. The man held up his hand in fleeting apology and Chris looked away again with a scowl.

Stase and he had been so good in the beginning. They had swept into one another like passing winds, swirling into each other's existence and into an apartness from the rest of the world where there had been nothing before. They were totally caught up in the both of them, uncaring about the rest of the humanity except how it affected them together; in their tiny windstorm, they swept everything before them. That passing glance, the lightest touch filled with import, every little gesture and nuance had ruled their waking moments. And then there were the hopes and the dreams. Where had all that gone? It was as if it had simply trickled away while they weren't paying attention. They'd loved each other once, hadn't they? Maybe they still did, really, but that certainty was overlaid with a hollow feeling in his guts telling him it wasn't really true.

The bus drew into a stop and he was forced to press himself up harder against the seat edge as an apologetic someone wormed past. He stooped to look out the window, trying to see exactly where they were. A line of people stood at the bus stop staring blankly out into the road while they waited for whatever bus they were catching. His own bus pulled out, and there was barely a flicker from any of them. He saw the same old blank disinterested nothingness day after day after day. He straightened, saw with relief that the seat next to him was vacant and sat gratefully, positioning his computer bag on his lap. Only three stops to go now. Already the start of a headache was creeping up the inside of his skull to nestle firmly behind his eyes. It was promising to turn into a simply wonderful day.

They finally drew into his stop, and he shuffle-stepped off with the last of the remaining passengers. They'd reached the end of the line. How prophetic was that? There was still something out of place, but he couldn't quite put his finger on it. It was just a sort of unease working inside him, an edgy, bottomless feeling as if he were standing on unstable ground, but he didn't know what was causing it. He shook the thought away and wrote it off to lack of sleep.

Here, in the middle of town, noise, dust, motion, everything in sharp contrast to the relatively protected suburban quiet where they existed, Stase and Chris. Chris and Stase. Sub-urban. Was it really below? Beneath the urban sprawl in some sort of ranking. As he decided whether he was going to grab a coffee or not, he glanced up at a billboard. It had just rolled over to a new ad. Once upon a time, they'd been fixed, one single advertisement pasted into place in vast sheets, but now they rolled, four or five in the one hoarding, barely giving you time to take it all in. Or on slit strips that turned, reforming with new images as they repositioned. The one on view now was for an upcoming cinema release. It took Chris a few moments to work out what struck him as out of place, and by the time he did, the poster was rolling out of view to be replaced by a beer ad. What was wrong was that the actress, larger than life in all the sensual imagery of the poster, was dead. She'd been killed in a plane crash some months earlier. But that was just wrong. Her picture was up there as if nothing had happened. His brow creased as he pondered the wrongness. It was relevant somehow. There were things in what he was seeing that meant something. What were they? Field of vision, depth of view, sleight of hand?

He really did need that coffee. He headed for one of the multitude of coffee bars that had sprung up over the last couple of years, breathing deeply of the warm aroma, waiting patiently in line until it came his turn to order. Considering the time, he couldn't afford to sit with his coffee, so he ordered it to go.

The office awaited, pristine in its carpeted blue, white walls and glass, somehow sanitized from the outside world, a capsule of its own reality and in that, a kind of escape. The fluorescent artificiality, stark and unforgiving in its definition, made everything almost hyper-real. Being in no proper mood for conversation, he could have done with his own office, but the open-planned corporate wisdom gave nowhere to hide. He headed for his pod, large cardboard takeaway cup held firmly in one hand.

"Chris. Shit, you look terrible." It was George. George Stoutman. They were working together on the same deal, pitching a process solution to a big corporate. George, with every hair in place, the even tan, the well cut suit, the mani-cured nails, was carefully crafted company enthusiasm.

"Yeah, thanks. Bit of a rough night," he said, trying to sink beneath George's scrutiny.

George continued peering at Chris, his marketing-su-premo face breaking into a slow grin. He looked down, picking some imaginary lint from his jacket. "So, self-in-flicted was it?"

"Yeah, whatever."

"Well, you'll get no sympathy from me, my man."

That was a given. This was George. Chris grunted in response and sat, placed the coffee down to one side, unpacked the laptop and started to set things up.

"George, I'll catch up with you when I've checked mail and stuff, okay?"

"Okay," George said, lifting his hands semi-apologetically and backing off, but still grinning.

Some respite. Chris closed his eyes and leaned back while he waited for the machine to kick into life. Suddenly there was an image of Anastasia lying unmoving on the kitchen floor. What was that? Like some dead movie star. The con-nection came unbidden. Then there was a flash of a couple of clean-cut guys standing smiling in a doorway. Shit, he needed to get this stupid stuff out of his head. He opened his eyes, hunched over his screen, typed in his password and started looking for the presentation files they were working on—lots of pretty pictures and supportive figures to woo the corporate board. Blind them with science, they always used to say. You could do amazing things with graphics these days. He found the files, glanced at them briefly, then called up the news pages to have a quick scan through before getting into work.

The rest of the workday progressed pretty uneventfully. There were meetings, conversations, plans, several coffees and the headache throbbing surreptitiously behind his eyes. Occasionally, in the deader moments, he thought about their relationship, of where it was going; it did little to allay the subtle pounding, and he tried to push the thoughts away. George approached again at the end of the afternoon and stood hovering near his desk.

"You look like you've got something on your mind, Chris." He reached into his pocket and pulled out his handheld, tapping at its screen a couple of times with a designer silver stylus. "You want to go for a drink?" he finally asked.

"No, sorry," Chris said without looking up. "I have to get home."

"You're sure? Look, if there's something bothering you ..."

"Yes, dammit. I'm sure."

"Jesus, Chris, keep it together. I was only asking."

Keep it together. That was a laugh. Keep what together?

George hovered for a moment or two longer; then, seeing that it really was the end of the conversation, he withdrew, slipping his handheld away and giving a couple of glances back in Chris's direction on the way. Chris gave a slight sigh of relief. He could take George when he had to. He was good at what he did and, whether Chris liked the man or not, that earned some respect. He wasn't about to unburden himself to George about his personal life, though, was he? George may just have been genuinely concerned, but Chris doubted it. It was more likely to be some more of that corporate bonding shit he played at. Or, maybe it was another attempt to get closer to him, probe the weaknesses and find ways he could manipulate him in the future. Anyway, Chris wasn't in the mood.

Absolutely sure that he was going to be left alone, Chris shut down the computer and started packing away. Day's end and he was tired, but it was more than simple fatigue. Sure, he'd been up all night. Sure, he'd had a full day of work in a half-defined landscape that stretched his already strained attention, but it was more than that. With a weary sigh, he headed out the door with a don't-speak-to-me aura wrapped tightly about him. They all seemed to get the hint.

As the journey home progressed, the fog descended further. There was no thought, just simple uncomprehending observation. Faceless individuals, intent on getting to wherever they were going, oozed past the bus windows in a sluggish stream. Traffic crawled, hesitated, stopped and took off again, cut through by the noise of a horn or the metallic squeaking of badly maintained brakes. Lines of building, faceless, impassive, funneled the flow down grimy canyons heading out and beyond this nexus of daily industry. It all washed against him, broke, and trickled away. Staring blankly out the window, he saw none of it. In his head, Stase and he were arguing again.

As he finally reached the end of the street, the clouds were making thumbprint bruises across the sky. Back to their place, and he turned the key to open the door on an empty house. That wasn't so unusual. He dumped his bag, tossed the mail on the hall table, and headed into the living room to collapse gratefully onto the couch. The mail could wait till later. With any luck, he could grab an hour or so before Stase got in. He didn't know if she'd even be talking to him, but he'd deal with that when it happened.

Chris woke to the sound of the early evening news. Stase sat there in the armchair, leaning slightly forward, a cup of tea cradled in her palm. He could smell the warm sweet aroma, even from where he sat. She always took honey in her tea. It made it too sickly sweet for his taste. As he struggled to consciousness, he noticed that she still had on her work clothes.

"Aren't you going to get changed?" he mumbled. He had been deeply asleep and he peered at her blearily.

"Yeah, in a minute," she said. "I just want to see the news."

"Hmmm. What do you want to do for food?"

She waved a hand at him to be quiet, and leaned in closer to the screen. He watched her, body angled even further forward as she sipped her tea, attention focused on the moving images in front of her, seemingly oblivious to anything he might offer. He may as well have not been there at all. Maybe he wasn't. Maybe he hadn't actually been there for a long time. Maybe neither of them was. He had to think about that and taste exactly what it meant, but now was not really the time. He needed to be thinking more clearly than that half-asleep state he was in right then.

He rubbed at his neck and shoulder, wincing as he discovered a soreness on the top of his shoulder. It felt like he'd scratched himself somehow. He probed beneath his shirt and frowned when he felt a slight, sore, line in the skin. He didn't remember doing that. But then there were lots of little things you forgot or almost forgot.

CHAPTER FOUR

THE ICE CREAM VAN

He dreamed that night of ice cream vans—square, blocky, white with a window at the side and a cone attached to the roof, a stupid familiar tune floating tinnily from a speaker up front. The man inside the window was clean cut, dark haired, and he wore a white coat. For some reason, he reminded Chris of a doctor. He smiled knowingly at Chris, as if they shared some sort of secret knowledge. He leaned forward through the window and inclined his head conspiratorially.

"We know what you're going through," he said. "We understand. It's only as real as you make it, you know."

Chris woke, clutching at the wisps of dream memory, frowning. Outside, the sun was already high, and milky light filtered through the makeshift curtains they had tacked up shortly after they moved in. They hadn't got around to curtains yet on Stase's list. At the end of the road, the sound of a truck, and glass clinking together with the occasional voice thrown in, incomprehensible, told him that today was trash collection day. It was the weekend. Anastasia yawned and stretched beside him, then opened her eyes. She turned on her side and traced a finger down his cheek, her hair falling in a wave across the pillow and half across her face.

"Morning," she said. "How do you feel?" It was the most affection she had shown him for weeks. Her breath was slightly sour and at the same time a little too sweet across the pillow. It had the flavor of something slightly off.

He took her hand and held it gently away from his face, turning his head to stare at the ceiling. "Mmmm, a bit worse for wear. I was having the weirdest dream."

"What about?"

"An ice cream van of all things. There was this guy in it. Sort of clean cut."

"Huh," she said. "I wonder what brought that on."

"No idea." There was a lengthy silence as they listened to the world shake itself awake outside, several steps ahead of them.

"You know," he said. "I keep having this feeling that something weird happened yesterday."

Her eyes were closed again, her mouth half open. Seeing her lying there like that started to tweak at something in the back of his head. She'd been lying ... where? It had something to do with whatever had happened the day before. He struggled with the memory, but it wouldn't quite come.

"Stase?"

"Hmm?"

"Did you hear what I said?"

She cracked one eyelid, subjecting him to a half-focused look. "What?"

"I keep feeling that there's something strange going on. Did anything weird happen to you yesterday? It's ... like ... it has something to do with the dream I was having. I keep thinking I should be remembering something, but I can't remember what."

"It'll come to you, if you leave it alone," she said, drowsily. Then her eyes were open. "Oh, that reminds me. I forgot to tell you. I've decided to do this meal run thing. It happens on Thursday nights."

"What do you mean?"

"Well, it's like a charity. A bunch of people go around in

this van and give out sandwiches and things to the homeless. Your dream reminded me."

He frowned again. A van? That thought skittered away. This was the first he'd heard of it. "What do you want to do that for?"

"Well, we do well enough. I just want to feel as if I'm doing my bit."

"What is it? Some sort of church thing? You're not starting up that whole religious thing again, are you?"

She sat up and looked down at him. "No, I'm not starting up any religious thing. I just think we could be doing something more than we are."

They'd never agreed on religion. He had his own beliefs, but they had nothing to do with the orthodoxy that was a part of her particular upbringing. It was one of those things they'd agreed not to talk about. Hearing her mention charity always sounded warning bells in the back of Chris's head, and this time was no different. This, from the woman who would refuse to buy a train ticket if she thought she could get away with it, getting missed by the inspector, relishing it as some sort of private pointless victory. He linked his fingers behind his neck and watched her as he tried to work the sleep dryness from his mouth. Maybe it should have made sense, but he didn't really think about it properly till much later. Charity was another one of those things that you could wear like a designer suit or a house or a career. It was one of the things that those who had, did. Certain types of giving he could understand; others, it seemed to him, perpetuated as many problems as they solved.

"So, what do you do? Go around and find people on the street and then what?"

"Like I said, we give them something to eat, something to drink. A cup of tea or coffee. A cup of hot soup. Sometimes it's the only decent meal these people get."

"Don't you think that defeats the purpose? It gives them less of a reason to change their circumstance. If people are always giving them handouts, well ..."

They'd had that particular conversation before.

She sighed. "You can think what you like, but I'm doing it."

He was still skeptical. "Why pick on this? Aren't there better things you could be doing? How did you hear about it?"

"Oh, one of the girls from work. She's been doing it for a while. So, anyway, I'm going this Thursday to see what it's like. Ride around for the night with them."

"Uh-huh," he said, knowing there'd be no point in arguing it. Seemingly satisfied, she lay back down and closed her eyes again.

He watched her for a while, still thinking about the holes in what he was supposed to be remembering. Finally, he sat up.

"I'm going out to get the papers. Are you going to stay lying there?"

"Mmmm-hmmm," she said without opening her eyes.

He got out of bed, went to the bathroom and started to get ready to go out. As he stood under the shower, hot steaming water splashing against his face, his eyes closed, one hand flat against the wall tiles for support, he was still trying to give a name to his unease.

The morning outside was glorious, and as Anastasia dozed on upstairs Chris hesitated in the doorway and squinted against the brightness, staring up at a cloudless sky. Further off, a few streets away, he could hear the trash men still at work. A slight breeze riffled through the leaves up and down the street, carrying with it the taste of newness and freshness, like the first clean blush after a heavy rain. Where had such a beautiful day come from? He'd been expecting clouds. He headed off down the street, his spirits lifted a little by the whole feel of the morning. He walked along Sydney Street.

Something nagged at him there, almost made him stop and chase it, but he shook it away. He passed the bus shelter ... and stopped.

The girl. The young woman from the café. She'd been lying there, hadn't she? He'd stopped and tried to make contact, to see if she was all right. He could see her slender form, the blonde hair, the vacant expression; it had been right there, and then when he'd come back, she was gone. He'd seen her in the café a few days later.

That's what had been tugging at him on Sydney Street— the older fat man, the jogger he'd seen there. Or had he? And then there were the others, the guy in the doorway, the quest, the searching and the finding, and always, always, the white van with the clean-cut guys. That was the ice cream van from the dream. Or maybe he'd just been dreaming it, after all. Dreaming all of it. Something was stepping in the way of his memories, drawing a veil across things over the past few weeks, making it hard to remember. But perhaps, for some reason, his subconscious mind was being vigilant. He didn't understand how he could be forgetting things, especially when it seemed like he'd been so intent on determining what was going on.

He was about to turn around and head back home—still trying to puzzle out what he wasn't quite grasping—when something else happened that sealed it for him.

There was an older man, or maybe he just looked older, who frequented their neighborhood, some sort of down and out. Chris would see him all the time walking the area around the local shops. He was just one of the elements of local color, and he had always seemed harmless enough. He unfailingly wore the same knitted cap and a long, brown tweed coat, whatever the weather. His dark hair hung in ratty strings around his face and a matted beard covered the bottom half of a swarthy hatchet face. His dark, close-set eyes almost disappeared in a deep crease that ran across the bridge of his nose. Occasionally, Chris would see him sitting alone in the local coffee shop, plastic bags piled by his side, sipping at a cup and muttering to himself. His gaze always seemed fixed somewhere in the distance. It was such a rare sight to see him anywhere but around the local shops. Once or twice, Chris, on the bus, had passed him a couple of suburbs up, but always on the main road. Even then, Chris had wondered where someone like him might actually live. He looked up to turn around and retrace his route, when who should come hobbling towards him, but that very man?

The vagrant was muttering to himself, as usual, and waving one hand in seemingly random back and forward motions to one side of his body. His eyes seemed completely unfocused. Chris was about to beat a hasty retreat, expecting to be asked for something, some coins, or a cigarette, when the man called out to him.

"Hey, she was there, wasn't she," he said. The voice was slurred, the words muddy, but they stopped Chris where he was.

Chris debated ignoring him, getting out of there as quickly as he could, but he was already too close.

"Yes, right there." He was talking to Chris, but his wasn't looking at him. He gestured vaguely at the bus shelter.

"Excuse me?" Chris said.

"They took her away. There. Blonde girl. Pretty." He nodded sagely, still watching the road.

"What do you know about it?" Chris asked him, not sure whether he was doing the right thing.

"Know them all," he said. "They came and took her, just like they took me. Seen her again. It took with her, didn't it?"

"Who took her away? What took? I don't understand what you're saying." Chris was about to dismiss the words as mere ramblings of someone not quite there, when the man said something else that made him think again.

"The men. The men in the truck."

"What are you talking about? What—an ambulance?"

He looked at Chris sharply. "You know. You've seen. I've seen you." The gaze was immediately unfocused and he was facing away again. "They took your wife too."

Chris was stunned.

"Sorry," the man suddenly mumbled. "Have to go. Must go."

He shuffled on past. The hand was waving again at his side and the muttering was back. Chris watched his retreating back.

"Wait," he called. "What about my wife? What about her?"

The man waved his hand.

"Wait," Chris called again. "What's your name?"

"Patrick," he mumbled. Chris barely heard it. He watched him hobble off to the end of the road, then quickly disappear around the corner.

All thought of getting the papers had completely gone. He was left with questions tumbling through his head, looking first at the bus shelter, then back to the end of the road where Patrick had last been in view and back again. Chris was pretty sure that had been what he said his name was. It was something to hold on to, at least.

If what Patrick said was true, then something had happened. Something had happened that involved Anastasia. In a bizarre sort of way, it made sense. It would explain the flashes that kept creeping in front of his inner eye. It would explain the semi-panicked feeling of unease that was following him around. But none of it made sense. Why couldn't he remember? If he'd thought about it, he would have followed Patrick then, pinned him down and questioned him, but he was still too unsettled by their brief encounter to think properly. To be honest, the guy scared him too. Never knowingly get involved with a crazy if you can help it.

As he headed for home along empty streets, his head was churning with thoughts, with alternatives for what he could possibly do. He neared the end of his tree-lined street, and there, sitting on the opposite corner sat a large, black bird, watching him, its head slightly tilted to one side. Chris frowned. It was just a bird. He could never tell one from the other, whether it was a crow or a raven. It was big enough to be the latter. Either that or a very large crow. He stopped and watched it back. The bird tilted its head the other way, still with one beady black eye fixed on him. It seemed completely undisturbed by his presence, as if it expected Chris to be there, as if he were the intruder in its peaceful street. The look reminded him of a look he'd had from someone else, recently, assessing, testing.

It hopped along the sidewalk, once, twice, three times, then swiveled its head to look at him again. Chris turned away from it with difficulty. There was something about the bird, something about its presence right then and there that opened up a void-like feeling, cold and dark, inside him. Dark as the color of its feathers. He glanced back at it. He gave himself a humorless smile. Which one was it? Was it Thought or Memory? One of them had come to visit, and he couldn't tell which. The answer wasn't quite with him yet.

CHAPTER FIVE

BLEEDING

For a few moments after Chris turned away from the bird, he thought he was losing his mind. He was imagining all this shit—the encounter at the bus shelter, Stase, the guy with the beard, the strangely aware black bird watching him from across the street. He was losing pieces of his memory and his head was compensating by simply making things up. It was like those sensory isolation tanks. When you start to lose all input, the brain makes things up to fill the void. As he wandered slowly back home, the papers completely unimportant now, he suddenly changed his mind and halfway along their street, headed back to the shops. He wasn't ready to face the need for explanations just yet. If he came back empty handed, Stase would want to know why, hit him with a barrage of questions about what he'd been doing.

"I thought you were going to get the papers."

"Yeah, well, I met this guy called Patrick at the bus shelter and we had a little chat. Then I had a meaningful moment with a crow."

Not likely.

He'd have to find Patrick again, find out exactly what he'd been talking about; that much was clear, but he was hesitant about the idea. He was even starting to doubt that the conversation had taken place in the first place. Had any of it happened, or was his head really conjuring things to fill the gaps in his memory? Though he looked, by the time he reached the corner again, there was no sign of the bird.

He continued walking, grabbing at the memory fragments, trying to weave them into some sort of definable pattern. Other things made connections, drifting thoughts, observations—all of them were part of the one big varicolored weave. The dead actress was one. She was dead, and yet she wasn't. She'd been given some sort of life by the media within which she existed. She was there and yet she wasn't there. The blank faces at the bus shelter. The sterility of the office environment. Flickering images on the television late at night in the darkness. These, all of them, had something to do with the phantom mental sculpture taking shape before him. It was a population, a landscape deserted, yet full at the same time.

The papers were the usual weighty collection of weekend advertisements, magazines, lifestyle columns and sections. He grabbed the two majors and paid, glancing down at the first one's cover. Middle East Atrocity. The words, big and black, nearly shouted from the page. Beneath the banner headline was a full-color photograph of a street strewn with rubble and blood, and bits of body. He scanned the text, knowing what he'd find. Yet another suicide bomber had blown herself to pieces along with parts of the street, some cars and several bystanders. It was right there in his face, and yet there was a distance, a sense of removal. How many times had he seen this already—different pictures, different days, but the same sort of thing? Chris tucked the papers under his arms and headed for home. He had more to worry about than what was happening in the Middle East or Russia. They could shove the stuff in his face, but that didn't mean he had the capacity to feel anything about it. It was just too far away, and besides, he'd seen it all before, we'd all seen it all before.

Maybe it had all started with television. He could remember all those images of starving kids in Africa, flies crawling around their big, brown, forlorn eyes and their mouths. Then there'd been pop stars getting together singing about how they could save the world. The television coverage had gone on for days and weeks. It had been in the papers, on posters, everywhere you looked and in front of it all stood the pop star icons. Crowds of people waved their arms in the air in football stadiums, cutting to images of the starving Africans, cutting to a close up of the band playing on stage. Which became the icon—the pop star or the starving child? Year after year, the images had become more intense, more in your face.

Then there had been the Gulf War, with the images of flashing weaponry and tracer bullets lighting up a night sky that looked vaguely green in the light-enhancing technology they used to sharpen the images. They were nothing more than fireworks in an alien skyscape. The colors weren't right. There was no veracity. How could any of that be real? CNN ran it twenty-four hours a day, day after day. Then there were the Balkans, and the floods in Southern India and the huge mudslides in South America and the mass graves. There was the Middle East, 9/11, the War on Saddam. Atrocity after atrocity buried itself deep into our subconscious and sat there, tangled up with thought and memory and feeling and everything that went with it. After a while, the images just blurred into one another.

He repositioned the papers under his arm and wondered what it was all doing, that profoundly ugly mix. Human tragedy on such a scale was beyond his real capacity to comprehend as something that had any proper part of his existence. So, he walked along the streets to home, the beautiful morning washing over him, pictures of assorted horror casually tucked under his arm, his thoughts returning to the encounter with the man who called himself Patrick and what he was going to do next.

Chris closed the front door behind him and wandered into the kitchen, tossing the papers onto the table. Standing in the middle of the kitchen, he stared up at the ceiling. There was no sign of movement from upstairs. Stase was apparently still in bed, either asleep or dozing. He set about making a cup of coffee and waiting for her to make an appearance. He took a sip of the coffee and sat at the table, slightly grateful for the space that this time of solitude with the coffee and the papers gave him. He did want to talk to Stase, but not yet, not until he had worked through the tangle of thoughts working inside him. If the events of the past few weeks were any indication, he wasn't going to get much of a sympathetic hearing, but things might have changed. The feeling was different, as if nothing had ever been wrong between them. Had he been dreaming that too? All the same, it was better to know what he wanted to talk about before embarking on yet another tension-fraught battlefield of words. He slid one hand forward and jiggled the weekend magazine from between the pages of newsprint, pulled it towards him and started flicking through.

An article about a third of the way through snagged his attention. It talked about perceptual overload. He frowned and paused, then leant closer to the pages. The chill was back inside, working in the depths of his stomach.

The article's main argument was that media, communications, all of the stuff that was thrust at us every day was reducing everyone's capacity to feel. He sat back and thought about that, and then leaned over the magazine and read some more. Something about Nietzsche ... Nietzsche had said, way back at the end of the nineteenth century that they were being bombarded by too many sensations, that it was making their brains numb, dumbing them down. Christ, if he was saying that back then, what did it mean for modern society more than a hundred years on? They didn't even have television. He leaned back again, thinking about the implications. What about television, cinema, mass media, the web? What about the constant news coverage of world events? It was all one massive set of overlapping bombardment, designed to snag our attention and do the thinking for us. It was worse than that, because there was a lack of definition at the edges, one blurring into the other. He'd been noticing it more and more lately, the overlaps. He'd lost count of the number of TV series and movies he'd seen that made offhand references to stuff from other media sources. A brief mention of a popular book, or another series, as if everyone was meant to understand what the reference meant, some half-disguised in-joke based on the assumption that everyone watched everything. It was all part of popular culture, an accepted part, and no one thought twice about it. Maybe that's what was happening to him, happening to everyone—perceptual overload. Was that really it?

Stase stumbled into the kitchen, a white toweling robe wrapped around her, her hair in disarray. She smiled slightly as she leaned in the doorway, scanning the kitchen through bleary eyes.

"I see you made yourself a coffee," she said. "Where's mine?"

It was the most civil she'd been for a long time.

"Sit down, and I'll make you a cup of tea."

She nodded, pulled out a chair and sat, scratching her head, disturbing the already mussed hair still further. "Ah good, you've got the papers."

As he made her tea, he was half thinking about the article he'd been reading. She reached across the table, pulled the magazine towards her and started flicking through the pages. She stopped at an article on living room style, and sat poring over it while he stirred the tea. He wrinkled his nose as the hot sweet steam floated up to waft around his face, then held the cup at arm's length while he placed it down on the table in front of her. She hastily moved the magazine out of the way while he put down the cup. She eagerly reached for the tea, held it in both hands, and lifted it to her face, breathing in deeply. She watched him through a tangle of hair as he retook his place at the table and reached for his coffee.

"So, what's it like outside?" she said, taking another sip.

"Oh, cool, but nice. It's really bright out there."

She reached over and flicked a page of the magazine. "Good. I might do something outside today. At least we can make use of the weather."

She flicked another page.

He sat watching her for a couple of minutes, then decided to broach what had been going through his mind.

"Stase?"

"Hmmm?"

"There's something I want to talk to you about ..."

Again: "Hmmm?"

Another flick of the magazine, and she leaned closer to peer at a picture.

He looked at the table's center, at the headlines sitting there, the graphic photograph in full color. Stase hadn't even glanced in its direction. He waited. Finally she looked up, brushed the hair from in front of her face with one hand and looked at him.

"What is it?"

Chris took a deep breath before starting. "You've seen that guy that hangs around the shops, haven't you? You know, he carries around some bags, wears a long ratty coat, beard, wears this blue wool hat ..."

"Uh-huh." A slight frown. "I think so. What about him?"

"Well, I bumped into him this morning, and he spoke to me. He said some really weird things."

She gave a slight, frowning shake of her head and then a short laugh. "Well, what do you expect? He's not all there. So, what did you do?"

Chris took a moment before answering. "I listened to what he had to say. He said something about you. That was the weird thing. He said something about you, and about the other night."

There was a quick flicker of concern in her expression, and then her face darkened and her jaw set. He had her attention, now. "What did he say? What other night?" she said.

"The night before last."

"What did he say? What does he know about me? Why's he talking to you anyway? Did you do something?"

He sat watching her.

"Chris? I'm serious. What did he say to you?"

He chewed at his bottom lip, took a deep breath through his nose, wondering what he was going to say next. "Before I tell you, do you remember anything weird about that night?"

"Weird ... like what?" She was looking uncomfortable. "We had a fight. What's so weird about that? What, is that fucking guy listening outside our window or something?"

He lifted a hand, wanting her to keep calm. "No, I don't know. I just ... well, I think there's something not right, Stase."

She watched him warily for a few moments; then her expression softened and she leaned forward in her chair and sighed. "I know, you're right, sweetheart. There is something not right. It's the house. It's us. It's always going to be like this in a new place. Living like this, what do you expect? We're both tense. Everything will be better once we start getting the house together and decide what we're going to do. We've both been under pressure at work and here. We've just got to make more of an effort. You wait and see. In a few months, everything is going to be so much better."

She reached across the table and took his hand in hers, fixing him with a concerned look. "I know things have been hard, baby. I know they have. We've just got to try. Both of us."

She held the look for a second or two longer, then withdrew her hand. She sat back and folded her hands in her lap.

"Will you promise me you'll try?" she said, not looking at him, looking back down at the magazine.

"Yes, of course," Chris said, an edge of puzzlement in his voice.

She nodded and flicked another page. "When the house is sorted out, everything will be so much better. You'll see."

That was the end of the conversation. He could tell there was no point pursuing it then, but at least Anastasia was talking to him again.

CHAPTER SIX

A FUCK OFF HOUSE IN THE SUBURBS

Stase had always wanted something with lots of rooms, white walls, something flat-fronted and Neo-Georgian. Actual Georgian would have been better, but their budget didn't extend that far. Chris was happy to go along for the ride, particularly if it kept her satisfied. They were her dreams, and sharing in them brought them closer together. He was never quite sure where those big dreams had come from or whether they would ever end.

In the beginning, that's what he saw them as, simply dreams. Each one was a stepping-stone to something larger, something to stretch them, and her conception of reality and what was acceptable for her life, further. The house became her outer skin, a designer suit that she could parade in public to any who might happen to see and by default, he wore it too. Occasionally, he wondered whether he actually wore it, or was merely a part of it. Whichever it was, he wasn't entirely comfortable with it. When your own self-image becomes a reflection of what you project out to the world and is bound up in what you have and own, then the balance isn't quite right. Chris was careful to keep those thoughts to himself.

When they first saw the place, he had his doubts. It had been vacant for almost a year, the first house in a long line

running down one side of a pretty cul-de-sac. Broad leafy
trees lined the other side, filtering the spring sunlight in a
dappled patchwork along its length. It was a nice street.
There were window boxes and front gardens and lampposts.
Wrought iron fences enclosed the small, well-tended front
gardens. It was a perfect vision of contentment and suburbia.

Stase was all enthusiasm right from the start. The man
who showed them inside had all the sugarcoated demeanor
of someone who thought he was finally going to make a
sale after he'd given up all hope. He'd already seen the look
in Anastasia's eye. There were times when she simply tele-
graphed what she was thinking. He led them, grinning, into
the front hall.

The house was light and airy, a tall staircase running up
from the front hall, lit by an arched feature window at the
top. The smell of old dust and damp filtered through the
first impressions.

"It just needs airing," the agent said, and Anastasia nodded,
her gaze flitting from point to point, already making plans.
Chris saw the look, just as the real estate agent had before
him, and his heart sank. There was little doubt that the house
would be theirs, no matter whether it was a good investment
or whether they could really afford it.

As they were led from room to room, he could tell that
Stase wasn't truly seeing any of it, the stained and torn beige
carpets, the half-finished paint job in glorious mushroom
overlaying an older, stained pink, the cracked ceilings, the
lovely 70's pine paneling thick and orange with varnish,
tacked up over stairs and ceilings, the lurid pink bathroom.
She was already seeing what the place was going to be. She
gave his hand a slight squeeze as they stood together in the
empty living room's center, and that sealed it.

Stase had always said that she just wanted a place where
she could tell the world to fuck off. It wasn't a retreat, a

refuge. It was something she could hold up to the world at large and say, "Look. Look what I've got. Now, you can just fuck off." This new place was a step on that path.

He didn't know then that it would eat her up inside, eat both of them up inside.

The next day, after the initial rush of enthusiasm had faded a little, back at the old place they were still living in, the one they still owned, Stase started her preparations. She bought a stack of magazines. She went through them, page after page, a large pair of scissors in hand, clipping photographs or tearing out entire pages. She put these to one side in a neat pile, had one last flick through whatever publication she was working on, and then moved on to the next. Steadily the pile grew. Each day, the range and variety of magazines grew larger.

"Stase?" he asked her. "Don't you think you're taking this a little too far? We don't even have the place yet."

She looked up at him, scissors poised. "But we will," she said with finality.

"Jesus. Anything could happen yet. It's not guaranteed, you know. He hasn't even accepted the offer yet, and the agent's already told us that there's someone else in the frame."

She slowly placed the scissors down beside her next to the clippings with a clink of metal against glass. "Look, he's just saying that," she said with the hint of a smile. "There's no one else. The place has been empty for how long?"

"Yeah, I know, but—"

"Listen. I know we're going to get the place. I know. If you're so worried about it, why don't you call the agent and see what's happening?"

She looked back down at the magazine she was currently holding and flicked another page, leaning forward to peer at the picture, lifting one hand to brush her hair out of the way.

Chris sighed and watched her for a while, not quite under-standing the depths of this obsession. That driving focus was something he'd not seen from her before, at least not to that extent. And in those few moments, he saw something he didn't really want to see. She looked up again, half-tearing her gaze away from one of the magazine pages.

"Well, what are you waiting for?" she said, glancing briefly back at a picture halfway through the words.

He sighed again. "Okay, okay."

He went to make the call.

Eventually, after several back-and-forths, offers, and negotiations, they did get the house and went through the ritual of packing and moving. Stase had everything under control. There were labels for the boxes, color coded for different rooms. She whipped around the removal men, pointing at this or that, telling them to be careful. Cups of tea and little pastries were already laid out for them, neatly arrayed on round plates. As they arranged the boxes in the various rooms under her watchful, purse-lipped gaze, he wondered if he might not be better off with his own label. Already, in the new house, her pile of magazine clippings was in place on the coffee table in front of the couch, which had been positioned carefully to her instructions. It was left to Chris to tip the moving guys. As the moving men left and packed themselves away in their truck, he could already tell it was going to be a long few weeks.

After they left, Stase stood in the center of the box-filled living room and looked around and around, at the ceilings, the walls, the furniture, all with a critical eye. She took a few minutes doing this, and then grinned and motioned Chris towards her. She took both of his hands in hers and squeezed them.

"It's ours," she said. "Finally. It's really ours."

"What do you want to do? Would you like to open a bottle of wine to celebrate?" he asked.

"No, not yet," she said, her attention wandering back to the room. "Let's start on the kitchen. Then we can do the bedroom. At least then we'll have made a start."

"Yeah," he said. "The bedroom sounds like a good idea. There's more than one way to celebrate."

She became all coy then, dropping her gaze and swinging his hands slightly back and forth. "Oh, Chris, not now," she said. "We've got more important things to do first."

"Yep, you're right," he said, the enthusiasm of the moment gone already. "We should make a start then."

By the time they'd finished unpacking the boxes in the two rooms, collapsing and folding the packing material, arranging the stuff in some sort of way so that they could get in and out of the rooms, they were exhausted. He put some water on to boil—the kettle had been packed right near the top with the coffee making stuff. Stacks of boxes still sat at one end of the room, and he leaned back against one pile, sipping at his coffee while he looked around at the mess, the strong smell of dust and cardboard all about him, and he wondered what the hell they'd done. Stase cradled a cup of tea in her hands, hardly aware of his presence. Her head was still ticking with plans. She glanced over at Chris tiredly, gave a half grin, and turned back to looking at the schemes and visions rolling past the file of magazine clippings in her brain.

They had already made their presence felt in the house. The windows were wide open, the internal shutters of the front room latched back into their recesses, and the smell of cardboard and packing stuff overlaid the must. A slight breeze gave a sharp crispness to the air inside. Not wanting to get into yet another conversation about what they were going to do with the place, he wandered to the back window and looked out into the shadowed garden, the riot of untended vegetation forming bizarre clumps in the darkness. Out there was the smell of earth and growing things, inside was the scent of his growing desperation.

The next morning, he set to ripping out the carpet. Moldy, rotten, it was mottled with black stains beneath and slightly damp. Sweating and dirty, he dragged the offending stuff outside and made a big pile at the side of the house. Inside lay revealed bare, paint spattered boards, long darkened holes where the wood had split and pieces of the wood had gone missing. Bare nail heads stuck up around the edges of the room. He stood in the doorway, wiping his hands on the back of his jeans.

"Jesus, Stase, will you look at the state of this?"

She joined him in the doorway, her hair tied up behind her, wearing an oversized tee and a dust smear across one cheek. She looked and grinned. He wondered whether she was seeing the same room.

"Wow," she said. "Imagine what this is going to look like when it's all polished."

"But look at the condition of those boards."

"They'll be fine," she said. "We can fix them." She patted Chris on one shoulder and disappeared back upstairs to continue her unpacking and arranging, leaving him to stand and stare dubiously at the decay and damage he had revealed. He wondered how long the carpet had been sitting there, nailed in place, hiding what lay beneath. Again, he wandered to the back window and stared out into the garden. He ran his fingers back through his hair, looking out onto the tangle, suddenly feeling overwhelmed at how much there was to do. He stood there for a while, knowing that there was no longer any choice; they were committed.

He'd started on one of the boxes in the living room when Stase appeared in the doorway.

"Chris, what are you doing?"

"What do you think I'm doing?"

"Just leave it." There was clear annoyance on her face.

"What's wrong?"

"We should only unpack what we really need. We're going to be doing things to the house. Just leave all that stuff there. We can worry about the rest of it when the house is done."

He sat back on his heels and looked at her. "But that's crazy. It'll be months before we make a start on it. We can't live like this."

She had her hands on her hips now. "I'm serious. We only unpack what we need. We'd only have to pack it all up again when the builders and decorators are in. There'll be dust everywhere. Just leave it. Why don't you set up the television?"

And that would set the tone of their life in Stase's fuck off house. A few rugs on a cracked and nail-studded floor, a television in the corner and piles of boxes containing the bits and pieces of their existence together—it wasn't much to show, but then they weren't allowed to show it to the outside world. Stase had decided that they weren't going to have visitors until the house was done. They could make excuses, go out to dinner, visit, but they weren't to have anyone around. The house looked fine from the outside, but inside it remained incorporeal and half-formed, except in Anastasia's mind.

CHAPTER SEVEN

A BOLT FROM THE BLUE

The first time at Chris saw Stase was at a college party. She walked into the middle of it and all around her the room made way. He stood, drink in hand, cigarette in the other, and his perception telescoped into a fragmentary instant that denied all else. And he knew then, knew she was the one. She looked across the room, their gazes locked for the briefest of electric contacts, and in that moment he was lost.

Bill Mathews stood beside him. He was talking about some new legislation the government was about to bring in, and Chris was listening with half an ear.

"So, what do you think, Chris?" Bill said, as Chris's awareness reluctantly filtered back.

"Um, sorry," he said. "I guess I was just somewhere else for a minute."

"Right. Come back to earth will you, man? These are issues that will affect our futures—all of them." Bill's voice had that edge of passion that said it was going to be a long night.

"Look, I'm sorry," Chris said with a sigh, trying desperately to catch a glimpse of her across the room. "I was just thinking about something else."

Bill's head turned to follow his gaze. "Hmm, I see. And very nice too. But way out of your league, man."

He knew Bill was right, but Chris ignored the little voice telling him it was so.

The other member of their triumvirate, Andy Gevers, came up between them and put a hand on each of their shoulders.

"Hey, guys. Have you seen what's just walked in? Wow, I'd love to have a piece of that."

Bill grinned. "Typical Andy, eh? Reduce it to the lowest common denominator."

He was right. It was typical Andy.

Bill, Andy and Chris, had shared a house for about two years. For some reason, they managed to tolerate one another. It may have been something to do with being an all-male household, or the fact that, in their own ways, they were all so different. Whatever it was, the arrangement worked. Andy Gevers was in the final stages of an Economics postgrad degree. He was small, dark and full of energy, like a terrier. He never talked much about his background, but from the little he let slip, Chris got the impression that his parents were strict religious types, and he'd had a hard time growing up with them. He seemed to have come out of it all right. He was naturally gregarious and sailed through life on the back of an easy, unforced bravado. How much of that was real, Chris never knew.

Bill was doing Law, but had none-too-secret political aspirations. He was tall, blond, good looking and had the physique of a football player. He had a long flick of hair that rode in a wave above his high, smooth brow. Bill kept himself pretty much to himself. His liaisons were even kept low-key and quiet, normally in the privacy of his own room, not on display for his fellow residents to see. He was rarely home anyway, pouring all his energy into achieving, setting himself on the path to his inevitable ambitions.

And Chris, he was working towards a postgrad degree in English Literature and doing some casual teaching on the side to make ends meet. He had fallen to English Lit more by default than anything else. It felt natural—as if he belonged. His undergraduate degree was a mish-mash of disciplines with nothing holding him for very long. English electives had featured throughout, and it seemed like the inevitable choice. Somehow, the sheltered environment of academic life guarded him from having to make any real choices. So, he coasted along, comfortable and reasonably content. That was, until Anastasia appeared on the scene.

The three of them stood there, together, the party swelling in waves around them, and looked across the room, Andy grinning like an idiot and Bill just shaking his head. Chris stood there, the moment wrapped around him like a cocoon, Andy's hand still resting on his shoulder.

They weren't the only ones she captured. She drew people's gaze in her wake, and plucked at their attention merely with her presence. Dark hair fell to her shoulders. That slightly wide mouth flashing her infectious smile. Clear, green eyes speared her opponent's attention and held it until she'd done. A dapple of freckles traversed the bridge of her slightly aquiline nose, complementing the pale skin. She was slender and long-limbed like a colt and her narrow hands conveyed a vibrant energy when she spoke. She stood across that room and heads turned as if drawn by something far greater.

None of them had seen her before that night, but, oh God, they saw her then. She cut through the smoke and boozy laughter like a knife. Though the party surged around her, it existed only in a half-formed haze and Chris could see nothing else. There are life-changing moments in everything we do.

Bill was the first resident of their house; he'd been there about a year when they met. He interviewed Chris, and then, later, they interviewed Andy together. He came from a family dripping with money, but he wasn't overt about it.

He tried not to let it come between him and others. He was that sort of guy—a man of the people. In some ways however, although he was the first there, he was somehow on the periphery. He had so many things to be involved in, that they rarely saw him. He organized things from the background, unobtrusively. Rent, bills, all were attended to with the minimum of fuss and the place functioned. If it had been left to Chris or Andy, things would have fallen apart in a matter of days, so, wisely, they let Bill get on with it.

The house was one of those large, multi-story affairs with three bedrooms and inconsistent plumbing. Damp and mildew crawled in the high far corners of the walls, but they didn't really notice. They could have had four of them there comfortably, or even five, but once the three of them were established, there didn't seem to be the need.

The party came and went, and within a couple of days, Chris had more or less resigned himself. Life descended, firmly entrenched in its own secure foundation. He had another paper to write and he became immersed, knowing that the deadline was in a few days. He didn't think of her consistently, but now and again images of her face would flash before him. He didn't know what was special about her, but there she was, following Chris around inside his head, haunting the unaware snatches of his thoughts. Eventually, he thought he'd managed to put her from him, and he dismissed it as a one-off, another opportunity missed. He used to play games with himself like that, about what might have been; here he was, playing the same old game and being stalked inside by his own knowledge of the unattainable.

Two weeks passed before he saw her again.

He was sitting in the library, struggling with a particularly difficult text. Then bang, he looked up, and she was there. A line of desks ran up one wall of the library, pale wood, utilitarian, each separated from the other by a chest-high partition. She was about two-thirds of the way along from Chris, leaning on a partition and talking to someone he couldn't see. He chewed on the end of his pen as he watched, his notes forgotten. He observed the arch of her back and the way she moved her hands. He wished he could see who had captured her time; he was suddenly, irrationally, jealous of the faceless object of her attention.

After about ten minutes, she straightened and ran her fingers back through her hair. Then she smiled and turned to leave, glancing back once over her shoulder. He groaned inwardly, staring at her as she left. He hoped that she'd turn, check along the length of desks, but she glided towards the stairwell without another backward glance. He corrected himself; glide wasn't quite right, because she had a forcefulness to her step that he found surprising. It was accentuated by solid, black, square-heeled boots. He kept watching even after she'd gone, and found himself staring at an empty space on the wall. In the briefest moment, she had stolen the rest of his day.

He made a half-hearted effort to regain concentration and get back to the paper, but it did no good and, finally admitting defeat, he shuffled his notes together and headed for the cafeteria. He walked oblivious, head down, and chewed at his bottom lip as he walked his useless notes beneath his arm. The drizzle made a fine mist in the air before him, a screen upon which to project those inner thoughts. People pounded past him, trying to keep out of the wet, their feet slapping on the damp paving, but all he saw was her tight black sweater and that last final flourish when she had pulled her fingers through the ends of her hair.

The cafeteria was sparsely populated when he got there, and Chris moved to the table at the far end, where he huddled over a cup of what passed for coffee in that place. His notes were damp and so was his hair. The smell of half-wet clothing washed around him. He had barely taken his place when Andy wandered in, scanned the faces from the door. He grinned and sauntered over.

"So, what are we doing sitting way over here, all by ourselves?" he asked and pulled up a chair. "In a sulk? In a damp sulk, by the looks of things. You're all wet, my man."

"Couldn't concentrate, I guess," Chris said, busy wiping his notes with his sleeve and running his fingers back through his hair. "Just needed a break."

"Fair enough. So what's happening?"

"Oh, not much. Shouldn't you be in class, or the library?" he said.

"Yeah, yeah. Got bored. Nothing world-shattering going on. So, lighten my life. Tell me something interesting."

"I've seen her again," Chris told him.

"Who? Who have you seen? Which her?"

"You know, the one from that party a couple of weeks ago."

Andy thought for a moment. "Oh her."

"Yep, her."

"So ... what happened?"

"Well, nothing. Nothing happened." Chris shrugged. "I just saw her."

"Uh-huh." Andy smiled and tilted his head in acknowledgment as someone he recognized walked in.

"So?" Andy said, turning back to face him.

"So, I think I'm in love."

"Yeah, right," he said. "You've seen this woman, what, twice? And now you're in love. In lust more like it."

"Call it what you want, but there's something about her."

"The only thing about her is that she's hot, and you're not getting enough. Too much of the old five-fingered exercise, my man. That's your problem. It unbalances the perception of reality. What you need is some healthy bar time, pick up a little number. That'll sort you out." Andy grinned at him.

"Right. What would you know?" said Chris.

He stirred his coffee and Andy watched the room.

They used to play a game with each other, ranking the yearly intake. This one had a great face; another: the face wasn't so good but oh, what a body. And so it went. Andy was always eager to play, Bill hardly ever.

As Chris sat there in the cafeteria with Andy, it all seemed a touch shallow. Plastic tabletops and metal chairs ranked across the room, only a few full. This time he didn't have the heart to play. Outside the drizzle went on. Andy tried to spark his enthusiasm, and as class ended and the cafeteria started to fill, Andy nudged him.

"Good God, will you look at that one."

"Hmm, not bad," Chris said without enthusiasm, his heart not really in it.

"Oh, come on! She's more than not bad."

"Yes, well, I suppose she's all right," he said, half-agreeing, mainly to shut Andy up.

Somehow, this woman from the party had struck to the very core of him. Andy was right; all Chris had done was seen her. He hadn't even talked to her. There had been that electric contact when their eyes had met, but he had no idea whether that was a mere construction that existed nowhere else than the inside of his head. Andy went on and on, and Chris's gaze strained at the doorway, hoping against hope that she would appear. Not that he knew what he'd do if she did. There was no way he'd go up and introduce himself, or start talking to her. That was more Andy's style.

That was where they differed. Although he tried to cultivate an air of the debonair on the surface, deep inside he was somewhat shy and unsure of himself. Cool uncaring was his way of coping with the insecurities. After his father had died—they'd been close and Chris had thought the world of him—he had became wary of forming bonds. He'd learned that they invariably let you down in the end.

"So, what are you going to do about this girl?" said Andy. He'd realized at last that Chris wasn't interested in playing.

"I don't know. What do you suggest I do? We don't even know if she's a student here."

"Listen, if she was in the library, it's a fair bet she's around for a reason. Ask about. See if anyone knows her."

"Sure, and who would I ask?"

"Hey, whose party was it? Claire's wasn't it? Claire McDonald. Why don't you ask her?"

"I hardly know the girl. Sure I'm just going to walk up to her and ask her about this mystery woman."

"Well I could ask her. She's been in a couple of my classes, and she hangs around with some of the guys I drink with."

Andy's circle was pretty wide. Someone he knew was bound to know, or at least know someone who did. For a moment Chris had hope.

"Can you do that for me?" he asked.

"Sure, why not? It might take a couple of days to come up with anything though."

Chris shrugged and stared back down into his now cold coffee, looking at the white scum that had formed on the surface. He poked at it with his finger and wiped it on the table. Andy was watching him with a curious look on his face.

"Man, you've got it bad," he said.

Chris said nothing.

"I'll see what I can do for you, my friend," he said. "You can trust Andy to look after you."

Andy got up and left him in that solitary corner, shaking his head while he walked away. As he departed, Chris lifted the disposable cup to his lips and sipped thoughtfully at the remaining almost-cold coffee.

CHAPTER EIGHT

CONQUEST

It was three days before Andy came up with anything, but true to his word, he'd found out what he could.

"So ... interesting," he said, cornering Chris in the kitchen at home. Chris was standing in his robe and pajamas making breakfast. Bill had long gone. He was an early riser and was usually well away by the time they stumbled to their own particular versions of consciousness.

"What?" Chris looked down at the half-burnt toast on his plate. It surely couldn't be that.

"This woman. The woman."

"What, have you found something out?"

"I certainly have, dear boy. Doesn't Andy always come up with the goods?"

Chris put down his plate, then sat, looking across at him expectantly. Andy could see his eagerness and he played it for all it was worth.

"So tell me ... is she involved?" Chris asked.

"Involved? Oh, I'm sure she's very involved. Strikes me as the type, doesn't she?"

"Come on. You know what I mean."

"Oh, I see." He grinned and Chris barely restrained the urge to throw a piece of toast at him. Andy dragged out one of the chairs opposite, spun it around and sat, leant over the back and reached for a piece of Chris's toast. Chris slapped his hand away.

"Come on, tell me," he said. Mornings were not the best time for Andy to play games with him. "I'm really not in the mood, guy."

"Right," Andy said, leaning forward with his elbows on the chair back and his fingers steepled in front of his face. He knew better than to push it too far. "Yeah, she's a student. Anastasia. Anastasia Robins. I couldn't get much on her background at all. No idea what the family does, but rumor has it that she comes from money. She's come down from the big smoke, living locally in town somewhere. Sharing an apartment with another girl. She doesn't hang around on weekends. And ... what else? Oh yeah, she's majoring in Biochem."

"Great. Just great," Chris said, his hopes of anything already dwindling.

"Well, you wanted to know."

"Yes, but what hope have I got? We're not even in a related department. If she's doing Biochem, she's hardly likely to take English as an optional elective. She doesn't stay around on weekends, and what are the odds that she's not going to mix with riffraff like yours truly?" Chris pushed his plate across the table and buried his head in his hands.

"Well, just forget about her and get on with your life. She's only a girl."

"Christ! But what a girl," he looked up again. "Why do I always go for the ones I can't touch? Can you answer me that?"

"Good old masochistic Chris Baron," Andy said. "You just like beating up on yourself. I tell you, you ought to be like me. Just forget about it and have a good time. She's probably so far up her own backside that you wouldn't get anywhere anyway."

"Well, thanks for the encouragement."

"What are friends for?" Andy finished off the last of Chris's toast, pushed his chair back, stood and grinned down at him. "Anyway, I've told you what you wanted to know. So, pull yourself together, man. It's a new day out there. I'm off. Women to conquer, classes to skip, hearts to break."

Only after he'd gone did Chris realize that Andy had managed to finish all of his breakfast. He wasn't really hungry anymore, so he stood and got himself ready to leave. He didn't have any classes until later in the afternoon, but he wanted to get some research done in the library. Not that he was in any mood to find the concentration he needed.

First stop was the cafeteria—the haven before the storm of his intellectual struggle.

She was there.

He stood at the door and the whole world rushed past his ears. She was sitting at a long table with a group bedecked in white lab coats. It took him a moment to see that she was wearing one too. Someone pushed past him and he wavered, powerless to move. The sight of her had pinned him to the doorway like a dead butterfly. With a swallow, he pulled himself together. Briefly she glanced over in his direction and his heart stopped. Then she looked away and he could breathe again. He fumbled to readjust the notes and books held under his arm, then stirred himself from the door and walked inside.

There was a table running parallel to her group. A couple of other tables ran between the two, but they were empty. Chris took up position facing where she sat. A hulking white lab coat blocked his view, and he shifted marginally to get a better angle.

It was the same as at the party. A corridor of silence closed in on his head and there, at the end of that long tunnel, sat Anastasia. He chewed on his thumb and watched. Others came and went, forming vague shadows in the edges of his vision, but they meant nothing. Every time she spoke, she had the attention of the entire group she was with. He was torn then. Should he get up and get himself a cup of coffee and stop sitting there staring like an idiot? What if she looked across and caught him?

The lab coat in the way stood and wandered over to the serving area. Suddenly, unexpectedly, Chris was afforded an uninterrupted view. She looked across and he quickly dropped his gaze. He pulled out a book from his pile and opened at random. When he looked up again, she was talking to the girl beside her. She laughed, tossed back her head, and ran her fingers back through her hair. That gesture again. The same one she had made in the library.

The owner of the lab coat returned and sat squarely in his way. He groaned to himself and gritted his teeth. He wasn't going to shift position again.

"Chris? Hello ... Earth to Chris Baron."

He looked up and Andy was standing there at the end of the table grinning across at him. He lifted his eyebrows in acknowledgment.

"So where were you?" he asked.

Chris tilted his chin towards the other table.

Andy glanced over and his grin became even broader. "Oh, I see," he said. He walked over and pulled out the chair beside Chris. He sprawled down on it and clasped his fingers behind his neck. With his legs stretched out and crossed beneath the table, he looked as if he owned the place.

"God, she's not bad, is she?"

"I told you."

"A bit skinny for my taste."

At that moment, members of her group started looking at their watches and scraping their things together. A couple stood. He recognized one of them at the table's end. He was in one of his classes. He knew him vaguely. His name was John Samson or something. As with most of the hard science majors, he probably took his class as an easy elective. Perhaps he had hope after all.

Anastasia was still talking to someone, pushing her files and folders together as she stood. As a group, they were heading off to class, all boring geeks together, except Anastasia, of course. She glanced up, saw Chris looking. She held that glance for an instant too long, and a brief speculative look flashed across her face, then she looked away. Then, as a group, they left the cafeteria.

"Contact," said Andy.

"Oh God," Chris said and slapped his forehead with his fingers, once, twice, three times.

"Well, what are you going to do about it?"

"Oh God," he said again, shaking his head. "Nothing. Nothing."

"What do you mean, nothing? I saw it."

Chris shook his head. "Well I can't just walk up to her and introduce myself. She'll think I'm an idiot."

"You're an idiot if you don't, my boy. Come on, what's wrong with you?"

"Well, she's gone now anyway. So that's that. You don't really expect me to walk up in the middle of that lot do you?"

Andy snorted. "I would."

"Yes, I know you would. No class, Gevers. No class."

"Who needs class when you've got style and panache like me?"

"Yeah, right."

"I don't know, Chris. Sometimes you disappoint me. I have such high expectations for you. Make her yours. Make her quiver beneath your dominant touch."

Chris just shook his head again.

"You want a coffee?" Andy asked and got to his feet.

"No, thanks. Surprise, surprise, but I've got some work to do," said Chris. He scraped his things together and left Andy to get his coffee while he headed for the library. He read the same page for the next two hours, over and over again.

He saw her regularly over the next few days, now that he was looking. The cafeteria became his hunting ground as he sat in ambush, hoping for a glimpse. She clearly noticed him more than once, but feigned to look as if she hadn't. He caught her looking over in his direction from time to time. Chris was beginning to wonder if she might draw attention to his presence and his constant watching, a nudge and a gesture in his direction to one of her friends, but she didn't. She continued blithely sitting following the group discussions, and occasionally looking over at him. He didn't know what she was playing at, and yet, as much as he thought about it, he couldn't muster the courage to breach the barrier he had constructed around himself.

Sometimes he wished he had Andy's guts. It didn't seem right with the way he'd been brought up—what was proper, what was right. After his father had died, his grandfather, an old-school bank manager, had been a significant presence. It was funny how politeness translated to reserve in his upbringing. So he sat and watched, longing for something to happen and yet afraid that it might. On occasion, he would pass her on the way to his class or the library. He'd be walking, composing notes in his head and look up and suddenly she'd be there. His insides would drop away and leave him feeling cold and empty, flustered, all thought gone from him. And then she'd be gone.

There had to be an end to it. He started to think of ways he could contrive to be near her, to work up to a point where he could engineer an introduction. Slowly, over the next couple of weeks, Chris kept watching. He monitored when she'd be in the cafeteria, and where she went when she left. He noted the times that he passed her on the way to the library, and he watched whom she sat with and tried to work out if he recognized any of them. Time and again, it came back to the same thing. : there was no real common link. But despite all that, his obsession continued.

One day, he was sitting in the cafeteria watching, Andy beside him. Anastasia stood, left the group she was with and strode across the intervening space to their table. She leaned down and planted her palms firmly on the tabletop directly across from Chris. He looked down at those slim, pale hands and then, slowly, slowly up to her face. She was wearing a black tee shirt that looped at the neck, giving him an uninterrupted view of her chest as his eyes rose slowly to her face. She fixed him with that clear green gaze, making sure she had him, just as he'd seen her do to a hundred others, and then she spoke.

"All right," she said. "So, who the hell are you?"

That was it. He was lost.

He stammered out a reply, not really paying any attention to what he was saying, but it didn't matter. It was too late for it to matter. Far too late.

She nodded and strode away, leaving him there to bang his head slowly on the table, muttering, "Idiot," while Andy , grinning like a fool, sat next to him.

CHAPTER NINE

BUBBLES

After the conversation with Stase at the kitchen table that morning, Chris decided he wasn't going to talk to her about his suspicions any more—not until he had some sort of concrete proof that he wasn't imagining everything. And he set about making plans about how he was going to get that proof. The first step was to find the old homeless guy who called himself Patrick.

Despite his memory of what Patrick had said, the doubt was still there working away in Chris's mind. He wondered how one could ever be sure that he was not losing his mind, that he was not simply conjuring things as a circumstantial convenience. That was the question. : what happens when you can't even believe the stories you tell yourself, the stories that the world and everything that shapes it concoct to make you believe? Everyone shared that particular gift to some degree, coloring their personal truths with their own version of reality, but it was a matter of magnitude. He wondered whether it was possible truly to recognize faults in your own mind—belief becoming a construct of personal experience and need. Well, now things had happened that made him determined to find out.

There was still work and the house and the day to day. He could have easily just gone back to the everyday routine and slipped into that easy non-thinking existence without pause, but the doubt wouldn't let him. From what Chris believed he could reliably remember—but he didn't know how much of that was even barely reliable now—he'd only really seen the man calling himself Patrick in the daytime. It's funny how you notice people every day and yet don't notice them at all. When you needed to put them into place and context, it was harder than it might at first seem. Chris needed to see Patrick soon and if he had to see him in the daytime, that meant work wasn't an option. He had some vacation days accrued and he decided he was going to use them. He'd go in on the Monday, arrange it as soon as he could and take the time he needed. He had to come up with some plausible explanation to tell Stase, but he could think of something, especially the way things had been going in their relationship. And on top of everything, even though they were talking again, he still had an uneasy feeling about what was happening in the strangely movable life between them.

Dutifully, he turned up at work on the Monday morning as he'd planned. Things were pretty slow in the office, so it was no problem to take a few days. When he came home that evening and told Stase, she was clearly not impressed.

"Why now?" she said, a faint frown etched between her brows.

"I just think I need some space to get my thoughts together. Just a few days, that's all."

This seemed to mollify her a little, but she wasn't completely happy and she wasted no time making her feelings felt. "It's important that we spend time together. Don't you understand that, Chris? I don't think it's very considerate of you to take this time without talking to me about it first. We should spend our break time together. You know I can't afford to take any time off at the moment."

Chris walked up behind her and put his hands on her shoulders. "I would have talked to you about it, but it was a sort of spur-of-the-moment thing. I don't need the distraction of work at the moment. Things are slow enough that I won't be missed and I thought I'd take the opportunity. I really need some time to think and sort things out in my own mind. You must understand that."

She turned from what she was doing and put her hands on his waist. Only it wasn't her hands; it was a pair of thick yellow rubber gloves. The bright orange smell of freshly chopped carrots washed around them. He hated the smell of carrots.

"Okay. It's probably a good idea, but I'm still not happy about it," she said. "I think we both need to think about what we need to do—for each other. Maybe you can spend some time thinking about what we're going to do with this place. Clean up the garden a bit. Whatever we end up doing, at least we can do something about the mess out there."

"Sure I can do that. But I'm not sure I under—"

She put a hand up, her fingers covering his lips. "We have to make a few decisions, Chris, about what we're going to do. What we're going to do with the house. Where we want to be. Important stuff. Okay?"

He nodded. She turned back to continue chopping vegetables. In Stase's mind, her point had been made.

The house and everything that went with it, everything that had happened, were still dominating her thoughts. The fact that all of her plans were on hold for the time being in a concrete sense seemed to be the only thing on her mind. It was all she wanted to talk about, and for the moment, there was nothing to talk about.

For now, that suited Chris and played right into what he felt he needed to do. Discussions about the house itself could wait. Of course, there were choices, things they had to decide, and he knew that his thoughts on the matter were at odds with hers, but they'd been like that anyway, almost from the start. Events had not worked out as expected with Anastasia's filigreed dream, and the tarnish had crept like a shadow across her expectations, stubbornly refusing to shift despite her constant rubbing. He was all for compromise, but he wasn't quite sure you could really compromise a vision that had been so carefully and painstakingly fed to obesity.

Chris left her there in the kitchen and wandered out to the tangle growing wild in the backyard, ostensibly to think about where he would start. The garden was a small, enclosed suburban space. A large eucalypt stood at the far end, dominating everything. Small decorative shrubs squatted against either side wall, running towards the back. In between lay a sea of weeds and hummocks, thorny vines, broad flat leaved plants darker than the rest. Vines had grown through and over the shrubs. He'd wanted to get started on imposing some sort of order on that tangle as soon as they moved in, because he knew it would take days, weeks, even months to make any significant headway. The yard, then entire garden, had been left to run wild for years. Stase had argued against him, saying that as they were going to make modifications to the house, build the extension, there was no point doing anything out there. There'd be workmen, tools, excavations and the garden would just end up being a mess again anyway.

Chris sighed as he stood there, knowing how much there was to do. They could have paid someone to clean it up, but really, it was probably good therapy just to do it themselves. Besides, waiting to do it until the house was finished just wasn't an option now.

Houses sat on either side, neatly tended gardens and hedges, pride and diligence and care. The house to the right had carefully trained climbing roses trailing over one wall, and a thick night-scented jasmine vine trailing along the dividing fence. A small hedged archway sat near to the back gate. He glanced up at the top window, the one that overlooked their own tangled mess and wondered what the next person to live in the house would do. The woman who had lived there had sold up and moved after their brief conflict. It was a strange thing to do, considering how much effort she'd put into maintaining the sanctity of her surrounds. He thought Stase had had a lot to do with that decision.

On the other side lived Stella, an old widow. Her garden showed all the peculiarities of her generation's approach to what made good gardens—beds of flowering plants, a neat little concrete path, a small goldfish pond at the back and roses, roses, roses. She'd lived in that house for about forty years, working her way through two husbands in the process. When she'd initially moved in with her first husband, Stan, the area was very different. She had talked about it with Chris a number of times after they'd first moved in. Time and economics had changed the face of her neighborhood. Meanwhile, she had continued to exist in her little bubble, pushing a shopping trolley to the supermarket and getting picked up by her daughter the florist, who ferried her to the hairdresser for her regular dose of blue.

He glanced up at the window on the other side again. There was no one there. Hollow, echoing inside, the neat little house was a shadow of itself. Did houses contain memories? He had often thought that they did. He looked back at their home, watching Stase through the back window as she fussed about in the kitchen. Stella had told them about the previous couple who'd lived in their house before the long period when it had lain vacant. Lived there properly, that was. After their separation and divorce, the owner had rented the house for a few years, not really caring about what went on inside. His wife had been an avid gardener, and most of what remained in the back was her personal touch. In the front, the bed of strong, sweet but damp smelling nasturtiums crawling with snails had been the husband's legacy until Chris got rid of it and replanted it with hedging. From time to time, small green succulent shoots still pushed their way through and he had a constant battle to pluck them out.

Tomorrow he'd feign to start on clearing some of the mess, and then he'd wander into the town and try to track down Patrick at the shopping center. There was so much disorder in the backyard that it would be hard, at least for a couple of days, to tell how much he'd done. How he was going to explain walking up to Patrick and talking to the guy was another thing. People studiously avoided the man, and yet he managed always to have enough to pay for coffee in the small sandwich place in the center's middle. That would be his starting point. The tables gave a reasonable view of both main wings of the complex and he could watch the comings and goings. It was also positioned slightly towards the main glass doors leading to the street, so it would afford Chris clear sight of the people passing outside as well. He had his plan. He linked his fingers behind his neck and looked one more time around the garden. Then he turned and went back inside.

"Have you thought about where you're going to start?" asked Stase.

"Yeah, I think I know how I need to approach it," he said.

Chris chose his table carefully, selecting one which gave him a reasonably uninterrupted view of the main doors. His back was to the wall and he was close enough to the rear to see all the other tables in the place. There was a mothers' coffee morning off to one side, a huddle of women surrounded by baby carriages and strollers, coffee and pastries spread between them. They'd pushed three or four tables together and leaned forward, talking with each other, occasionally leaning back in mutual laughter, a strange multi-colored organism bound cell to cell by their circumstance and their progeny. The junction of the two shopping corridors was wide and echoing. A bench sat across the other side of the bright shiny space and an old man sat, huddled at one end of it, rocking gently back and forth. Chris pressed the plunger down on his coffee and poured a cup, breathing in deeply of the rich scent of the freshly ground brew. This place was upmarket enough to have proper cafetières, but some of its clientele most definitely was not. He had seen Patrick sitting here more than once. That incongruity struck him for a moment.

He watched the people struggling past with their bags and trolleys seeking some sign of what he was looking for. Old ladies, couples, kids, it was an entirely different universe to the daily hustle and grind of the city's workday. But there was no sign of Patrick.

He observed as he waited, sipping slowly at his coffee. Before long, a little tableau played itself out in front of him. An old man, quite old, headed towards the tables. He was thin. Twig thin. All skin and bones. His limbs seemed almost to creak and stretch with every halting step. A woman stood on either side of him, supporting his elbow, helping him to walk. The one on the left was round of feature and hip, her hair piled in artistic coils atop her moon-shaped face. She'd dyed blonde streaks into the black hair—black that was probably dyed as well—and a brown plastic clip held the strands draped at the back of her head. Here and there, a random trail hung trailing at the sides. She was dressed in black with a long brown cardigan that swirled around her hips.

At his other elbow, another woman, a little older than the first. The swaying of her floral print dress rocked up and down and from side to side as she walked. Her flesh swelled upon her neck and back and hip, pillowing her in multi-colored flowers. She wore strong glasses, the sort of thick plastic lenses that looked as if they'd been steamed up by a shower, tinted vaguely yellow, and the frames were pale pink. She peered at the old man between them, through the foggy lenses, as they shuffle-stepped along to make sure he was all right.

They sat him down, faced the old man's chair to watch the crowds of shoppers, and then took up places on either side. They conversed across him as if he wasn't there. The old man lifted a trembling finger to prod at his left eye. Something was annoying him. A bit of grit or dust. Perhaps an insect.

Brown Cardigan leaned across and peered into his face, then tutted. She pulled a white handkerchief with a border of yellow and pink flowers from her sleeve, moistened it with her mouth and dabbed at the offending eye.

"Is that better, dear?" she asked. In the wide open space, their voices came to Chris clearly.

The old man nodded slowly. It was all he could seem to manage.

The woman nodded, her lips pursed, tucked the hand-kerchief away in her sleeve, and then turned to resume her conversation with Floral Print. The old man stared out at the passing shoppers, barely seeming to see them.

A pot of tea, two cups and a small glass coffee plunger appeared in the center of the black metal table, shortly followed by two cream cakes. No cake for the man. The round ball at the top of the plunger's handle sat directly in line with the old man's right eye, just in front. He slowly worked his jaw.

Floral Print reached for the teapot and carefully poured herself a cup. Eventually Brown Cardigan finished what she'd been saying and pulled the coffee plunger to her, taking her plump hand and pressing it down, slowly squeezing the goodness from the grounds. A young woman was watching them from a nearby table. Out in front, people continued walking past, their footsteps and voices echoing from the polished floor and glass-fronted shops. The voices swelled and faded, blurring.

The pair had forgotten to pour the old man's tea.

Floral Print pulled out a nail file and started to work at the edges of her pointed nails as she talked.

"Mmmmph," said the man, forcing the sound from his throat. "Mmmmph."

"Now, Robert dear, what is it?" said Floral Print, peering through her thick yellowing lenses. A pause, a quizzical look, and then: "Oh dear, we've forgotten your tea, now haven't we?"

Floral Print put the nail file away and fussed about pouring a cup. She dribbled milk into the cup from a small white jug and then spooned sugar—one, two, three.

"Nice and sweet. We need to keep your energy up, now don't we, dear?"

She watched him intently as he raised the cup to his lips, his hand trembling slightly with its weight. He slurped noisily then carefully lowered the cup.

"There now. That's better, isn't it?" She turned back to brown cardigan to continue her conversation.

While he summoned the energy for another sip, the old man watched the space in front of their table. A wide circle of darker tiles marked the floor's center. The central tile covered an access box for switches or controls or something, and when anyone walked across it, it made a hollow drum sound. A small round-faced boy with pink cheeks was there now. As he jumped, he looked at the old man and chortled.

Jump, jump, jump.

The old man closed his eyes.

The child's mother retrieved her noisy progeny and dragged it away, gripping it by the arm the same way the two women had gripped the old man's arm. Slowly, slowly, the old man opened his eyes and took another sip of tea.

"Right, Robert," said Floral Print. "We've had a nice walk and a cup of tea. Time to go back home now."

He'd only had two sips.

The two women pushed their chairs back and maneuvered at either side of him. They helped him push his chair back. As they steered him out between the tables, he watched his feet.

Chris watched them disappear towards the outer doors and slowly shook his head. Would it come to that? Would he come to that? He didn't even want to consider it. He wondered how much control people really had over their own existences. The old man had simply reminded him of the helplessness, about how reliant everyone was on someone else. He looked almost as if he'd been battered into numbness. Chris had the same sort of reliance on Stase—different, but quite similar: . she led him where she wanted to go.

He sat there for most of the latter part of the morning, and then reluctantly made his way back home after browsing in a bookstore for a while. He spent an hour digging up unknown growth from the lawn's center and piling it nearby in obvious heaps. He wanted it to look as if he'd been working. The physical activity was good, because at the same time he was probing his memories, testing for the weaknesses that he knew had to be there. He was increasingly certain that the only way he could fill those blank spaces was to find the man he sought.

That afternoon, he wandered the local streets, seeking, observing, watching, but to no avail.

CHAPTER TEN

THE TRAMP

The next day he went through what was to become a ritual. Chris would do a bit of work in the tangled mess that was the garden, and then would head down to the shopping center. He varied his time of departure, walked up and down the local streets, even caught a bus on a couple of occasions, straining at the window, hopeful of spotting the disheveled, bearded figure with his blue knit hat, ratty sweater and long gray-brown coat.

Late on the third day, he was standing outside the music store, looking at the latest video and CD releases in the window, really just passing the time and almost ready to give up hope, when something made him glance up. Further down the street on the other side came a familiar figure, slightly hunched, watching the pavement in front of him, two large plastic shopping bags clutched in either hand, one blue, one green. It was a busy afternoon, and Chris really didn't want to race across and confront him in the street. There were too many people around. He still didn't know what he was going to ask, but this was the first step; he'd found him. He stepped sideways into the shop doorway and watched. The man called Patrick was heading for the shopping center.

Someone came from inside the store and pushed past Chris. He realized he was standing right in the doorway. With a quick apology, he stepped fully into the store and, pretending to have his attention focused on a CD rack nearby, watched Patrick out the window. It was funny that he still thought of it as a record store when they no longer sold records, hadn't done for years.

The shopping center's main doors were recessed underneath a faux marble archway with a couple of pillars. Patrick pulled up under the shelter, turned a couple of times, like a dog trying to find his place to rest, then moved over to one side and placed the bags down by his feet. Chris drew in his breath, waiting for the opportunity. Patrick fumbled around in his pockets for a moment, shaking his head, then reached down and retrieved one of the plastic shopping bags. Chris grimaced. It looked like Patrick was going to be on the move again.

People walked past and around Patrick, as if he wasn't even there. Did they see him? We block so much of what we see, why not a person? Chris was ready to be on the move again too, but then Patrick placed the bag back down and reached into his pockets once more. He seemed only to half notice those that walked around him. He dug out a crumpled cigarette and a box of matches, lit the cigarette and stood looking across the street as he smoked. All the time, he was talking. Every now and again, he waved his hand as if dismissing something. Chris wondered as he stood there watching whether Patrick was talking to anyone in particular or just himself.

Patrick was only halfway through his cigarette when he stubbed it out against the side of one of the square marble pillars and spirited it back into his pocket. This time, he was definitely about to move again. He reached down, picked up both bags and headed out from under the archway, or he was about to, then, as if changing his mind in mid flow, he turned and headed for the double doors. He shouldered his way through them and disappeared inside.

Chris was out of the record store in a heartbeat, looking up and down the street for a break in the traffic and
dashing across the road, holding up one hand to stave off
an oncoming car. He slipped inside the double doors and
stood panting. Patrick was meandering slowly up the center
of the polished wing, looking totally incongruous among the
afternoon shoppers. Pretending to browse shop windows,
Chris followed at what he believed was a discrete distance.
Patrick stopped. Chris stopped too. Patrick stood there for
several seconds, swaying slightly in the middle of the passing
wave, a rock against the tide, or more like a branch. The
next instant, he was walking—no, rather, hobbling—rapidly,
heading towards the small cafeteria where Chris had been
waiting for him for what seemed like weeks. Patrick found
himself a table towards the middle, planted the shopping
bags on either side, and sat.

The staff evidently knew him, and as Patrick fumbled in
his pocket and placed a greasy crumpled bill on the table,
without saying a word, a steaming cafetière appeared in front
of him with a large cup. No milk. The waitress took the
money gingerly between thumb and forefinger, holding it
some way from her body, and headed back to the till. She
reappeared a few moments later and spilled some change
onto the table. Patrick seemed barely to notice the trans-
action. He was gently rocking back and forth, muttering
to himself. He pressed down the plunger and then slowly
poured himself a coffee. All throughout, he had one hand
propped just in front of his face, one elbow on the table, as
if he held a phantom cigarette. Chris headed into the café
and took up a table nearby. He ordered a coffee, barely glancing up at the waitress, and waited for it to arrive, watching
Patrick all the while. Patrick seemed not to have noticed
Chris's presence, though it was hard to tell what he did
notice. If the conversation he'd had with him that day on

the street was any indication, it was a lot more than was immediately apparent.

Chris took a couple of sips of coffee, still hot, before he plucked up enough courage.

"Patrick," he said in a loud stage whisper across to his table. No reaction.

He tried again.

This time he got something. Patrick waved one hand to the side as if waving away an annoyance. Chris grunted to himself. There was nothing for it. He stood and walked over to his table, standing right in front of him across the other side of the table.

"Patrick, I have to talk to you," he said.

Again, the gesture with the hand.

"Patrick?"

Patrick lifted his face briefly. His dark cloudy eyes focused on Chris's face for an instant, narrowing; then, he looked away.

Chris sighed, pulled out a chair and sat. The noise of the chair moving across the polished floor seemed unnaturally loud. "Listen," he said. "This might sound crazy — but you know something, don't you?"

The waitress was standing behind the counter watching them. He'd kept his voice deliberately low. He didn't know what he was dealing with, or if there was any threat in even talking about it. Patrick's reaction at their last meeting had told him that there was need for caution. Patrick leaned down to one side and shuffled around inside one of the shopping bags. He came up empty, then reached for his cup and lifted it, completely ignoring Chris. His gaze was fixed towards the entrance to the shopping center.

Chris leaned forward. "Listen. You spoke to me before. You said something about Sta ... about my wife. I need to know what you meant, what you were talking about."

Slowly, slowly, Patrick's head swung about to face him.

Again, he narrowed his eyes. There was understanding in those dark shadowed depths. The lank hair falling on either side only increased the impression of darkness. He flexed and unflexed his brown, soiled fingers. This close, Chris could smell the man, old, unwashed human wafting mustily across the table to him. Patrick worked his mouth as if readying himself to say something, but reached for his coffee cup instead.

Chris watched as he took another noisy slurp and placed his cup back down, rattling against the brightly painted yellow and white saucer.

"Can't smoke here," Patrick said, flexing his fingers again. He frowned, making the deep line across his eyes even deeper. "Can't smoke. Could before. Could do lots of things before."

He stared at him. What did that have to do with anything?

"It is Patrick, isn't it?" Chris said, growing uncertain now.

"Patrick," he said. "Patrick. Was Patrick once. Is Patrick. Not Patrick." A quick flickering glance and he looked away again. It was as if he were afraid to meet Chris's eyes.

"I'm Chris."

Patrick gave a little nod.

"Look, Patrick, you said something to me the other day at the bus shelter. Do you remember? You said something about my wife, about someone taking her away. Do you remember that?" Patrick waved his hand several times in succession fluttering his fingers in the air. Chris suddenly remembered. This was the very table where the old man had sat with the two women. He glanced up over towards the counter. The waitress was still watching. He grimaced.

"Dammit, Patrick, I need you to tell me," he hissed.

Patrick's gaze shot to Chris's face at his outburst, but again he looked away. Chris put his hand flat on the table and leaned further in towards him.

"I need you to tell me what it is. What do you want? Money? Is that it? I have money."

Patrick wiped his hand on his greasy blue sweater.

"Don't need money. Got money."

Chris hadn't thought about it before, but it was strange that someone like Patrick would come and sit in this little café and sip at designer coffee from designer cups.

"Well what do you want?"

Patrick shook his head.

"What is it about my wife?"

"Pretty girl," Patrick said thoughtfully.

"What did you see?"

Patrick nodded to himself. "See. Always see. Took her, didn't they? Took her to the place."

"What place? Who? What are you saying?"

"The men. Came and took her. Just like Patrick. She's okay now. Worked for her. Not for Patrick."

Chris frowned, not really understanding what Patrick was getting at.

"You too." He pointed at Chris, then wiped his hand on his front again. He ran his tongue across stained teeth, his attention slipping away again.

"Go to church," he muttered.

Chris sat back. "I'm sorry, Patrick. I don't understand what you're saying. No, I don't go to church. I'm not religious. Is that what this is about?"

Patrick shook his head and grimaced. He pushed back his chair and stood, staring across at the shops on the other side, through the passing people, seeing only something he could see.

As he leaned down to retrieve his shopping bags, Chris grabbed at his coat.

"You have to tell me."

Though soiled, the coat was surprisingly soft beneath his grasp. Patrick shook off his hand.

"Go now."

Chris made another grab for him, gripping a good handful this time. Patrick pulled against him, struggling to get away, but still not saying anything, just making small wordless grunting sounds in his throat.

The waitress was over in an instant. "Is he bothering you?" she asked Chris.

Chris let go of the handful of Patrick's sleeve and Patrick staggered away, bearing his twin plastic shopping bags with him. Chris hadn't even thought to try to see what was inside them to try to get some more clues about the man.

"No, no, it's fine," he said to her, watching Patrick disappear towards the exit.

She looked from Chris, then out after Patrick's retreating back, then back again. "You're sure," she said dubiously. "Did he do something? He comes here a lot, drinks his coffee. He seems pretty harmless, so we let him be. He's never made any trouble."

"No, no. Nothing," Chris said. "I'm sorry. Everything's fine."

She retreated to the counter, still watching him. With a wordless mutter to himself, Chris stood and returned to his own table to retake his seat. He lifted his coffee cup thoughtfully and sipped at the lukewarm brew. He'd achieved virtually nothing. He had a couple of scraps of information. According to Patrick, someone had taken Stase away, just like he'd been taken away at some point. The whole business about church was confusing though. Maybe he was just mad after all. Some reference to repentance and salvation. He remembered the old guy in the city, dressed in a double-breasted suit and carrying a bible, who used to harangue passers-by with shouted religious monologues. He'd been a banker or something, and had just simply lost it as he got older. No, but that didn't make any sense at all. Patrick didn't seem like a ranting religious lunatic, not at all, so what did he mean about church?

Well, apparently Chris had wasted roughly three days and was none the wiser for his efforts. All he had were a few more intriguing clues—intriguing and frustrating at the same time.

The thing that worried Chris most was what Patrick had said about something happening to him, to Chris personally. At least that's what he thought he had said. If something had been done to him, surely he'd have some memory of what took place? He wasn't the crazy one. It wasn't good enough. He had to find some other means of working out what had been going on.

As he walked out of the shopping center and headed for home, he passed Patrick huddled in a corner in the entrance-way, cigarette clutched between dirty fingers, staring out into the middle distance and muttering to himself in incomprehensible phrases. Chris almost hesitated, but then thought better of it. There was not even a flicker from Patrick as he passed. It was as if Chris didn't even exist, as if their recent conversation had never even taken place.

CHAPTER ELEVEN

SKELETONS

Before they moved, Stase's plans had blossomed like a garden of expectations in her head, culled from magazines, newspapers, the television and anywhere she could find her inspiration. You know what they say—if you're going to steal, steal from the best. For some reason, right around that time, house programs, renovation, buying, decorating were all the rage on TV and they seemed to multiply with every passing day. There were celebrity gardeners and celebrity decorators and celebrity home make-over experts. Then came the shows wandering through the houses of the well-off, peering into grand rooms with grand furniture and fittings. It was almost as if the whole of the media industry was suddenly targeted to fulfill Anastasia's personal desires. Maybe it was just that Chris had started to notice it.

After that first flurry of moving, when they were finally starting to get settled in the new house, those plans grew and started taking over everything Stase did. Chris lost count of the number of times he walked into the bare-boarded lounge, sighed and turned around to leave and find something else to do. There was no talking to her when her shows were on. Well there was, but it was all "what do you think of that" and "isn't that wonderful," barely pausing to hear whether he had an opinion or not and then substituting it with her own.

They had a local builder whom they'd used on their old place to do small things, and as they hadn't moved far away, Stase invited him around to discuss plans, or her conception of plans. Michael, short and wiry, with a tightly bunched head of curly hair, slightly thinning at the crown and temples, was always eager to explore the Anastasia's ideas. Chris had always assumed it gave him a creative outlet on top of his kitchens and garden sheds that were the stock of his normal trade. Michael also apparently fancied himself as a creative genius and charged them an arm and a leg for the privilege of being able to play. Money was no object as far as Anastasia's plans were concerned. Once, Chris came back to find them standing in the back garden of their old place talking about pergolas and decking and garden landscaping. He could hardly believe it; it was such a small house.

He talked to her later about it and she told him earnestly about how much value those renovations would add to the place, regardless of the thousands they would cost. Chris put his foot down. Six weeks later, he was away on business. He returned to find a transformation—pergola, decking, paving stones, the lot. Anastasia had gone ahead and arranged for the work to be done while he was gone. There wasn't much he could do apart from be furious. Stuck in the impotence of a fait-accompli. He got over it, like he got over many things. She was right, of course; it added thousands to the value of the house when they ended up selling it, but that wasn't the point. It was yet another grudging concession he made to her perfect dream. Another thing to be shoved away, buried deep in the minefield that becomes the history of any relationship.

Michael came over and they huddled together on the couch, poring over sketches and clippings, page after page strewn across the coffee table. Chris sat back in the armchair, sipping at his coffee, watching. After about an hour, Michael sat back and nodded approvingly.

"You've got some great ideas here," he said.

Anastasia put her hand on his forearm. "Do you really think so?"

"Yes, of course. You've got a great eye, Stase. Of course you're going to need planning permission."

She sat back then. "What do you mean?"

"Well, for extensions this size, you'll definitely need approval."

She started shuffling through the papers in front of her. "But that's not going to be a problem, right?"

Michael took a moment before answering. "Well, some of the things you're planning are pretty ambitious. There are all sorts of considerations. You have to make sure of maintaining the local character. And then you have to worry about the neighbors, make sure there aren't any objections. Of course I can help you."

Stase stood and started pacing. "They can't object can they? What do we need to do?"

Michael tracked her as she walked. "Well, there's a bunch of forms to fill in, and then there are the sketches. I've got a friend. He kind of doubles as an architect."

Stase looked thoughtful. "So we need an architect?"

"Oh yes. The detailed drawings always help with planning approval. Do you want me to talk to my friend?"

Stase stopped her pacing and returned to the couch. "Chris and I need to talk about it first."

"All right," said Michael. "But you just let me know."

Chris could see that Michael was convinced he was in for the job and the dollar signs were already clicking behind his eyes.

As soon as Stase had ushered Michael out the door and thanked him for coming around, she had that look on her face that told Chris she had more than plans.

"Right," she said. "We need an architect."

"But Michael said that—"

"No," she said, lifting a hand. "If there's any possibility that we can't get approval for this, then we have to do it properly."

Chris felt another sigh growing within him. "Okay, tell me what you mean."

"I mean we get the best architect. We have plans drawn up, proper plans, and we do the whole approval thing properly. We can't blow this."

He frowned at her and shook his head. "This isn't some grand mansion, Stase. We're not building a palace."

"But if we do this work, the house is just going to be worth so much more. This is a good place, but it can be better. It's not the place I want, but if we do the work properly, we can live here for a couple of years, then trade up." She held her hand out flat and hit the empty air several times in succession as if patting something into place.

Chris sighed. He knew it was no point trying to talk her out of it. She believed she could do it, so why not let her try. There was a level of comfort to be had from her contentment and focus. Once upon a time, Chris had been the project; now it was the house.

The next day, Stase started making calls, and for the following two weeks, they interviewed a procession of architects. One by one, she ushered them into the place and listened to them as they discussed their visions. As they trooped past down the hallway, he could see the expressions of doubt on some of their faces. Why were they being called in to a job this size? Some of these firms worked on huge public buildings and residential complexes. They narrowed it down to three possible contenders and Chris wasn't convinced about any of them. All he really knew about them was their price tag.

"What is it about these guys?" he asked her.

"It's simple," she said, looking at him as if he was slightly slow. "These are reputable firms and if we're going to do this thing, we're going to do it the right way. You heard what Michael said about the planning authority."

"And what's this going to cost?"

"That's not important. It will add so much value to the house that we'll get it all back in the long run."

The following day, she called Michael again. "We want you to be involved," she told him. "Mainly for the internal decoration, but I want to hear what you think about the architects. Will you come over and look at some sketches?"

So there it was again. Another evening of drawings and plans and visions. As usual, Chris sat in the chair and watched.

Michael rubbed his jaw and looked doubtful. "You have to be careful about these people," he told her, slightly put out that he apparently wasn't going to get the lion's share of the work. "Have they talked about using site managers?"

"Well, yes," said Stase.

He sat back. "You may as well just throw your money away."

"What do you mean?"

"Well, if the architect employs a site manager, he gets in the way of the builders and you end up having more trouble than it's worth. They'll never agree on anything."

Stase frowned. "I don't get it."

"Look," said Michael. "The architect is there to make as much money out of you as he can. The more he can do to up the costs of a particular job, the bigger cut he gets. They work on percentage of the total job cost, and that's on top. It's in their interest to make sure the job costs more."

"But we can put a ceiling on it."

"Sure, but there's always unforeseen circumstances, parts of the job that have to be redone."

She wasn't convinced. "As you said yourself, the important thing is to get the building approval, and these people are among the best. They don't have a reputation for nothing.

We can use that reputation and then once we've got what we want, then we decide what we want to do."

Michael nodded slowly. "It would be much easier to knock up some sketches and just put those in with your planning request. You'll save yourself a lot of hassle and expense."

Chris was all for following Michael's advice and said so. Stase turned and gave him a look like thunder.

"No," she said. "We'll do this properly."

Chris bit his lip and shut up.

It didn't take her long to swing the conversation back to the plans themselves, and she spent the next couple of hours picking Michael's brains. Chris listened to the ideas patiently, looked around the living room and felt the sinking feeling wash over him again. Everything was starting to get out of proportion. The feeling had been coming back more and more over the past couple of weeks. The plans were becoming grander and grander, extensions, remodeling—she even started talking about cathedral ceilings, and this was all in a fairly modest house in the suburbs. She was trying to turn it into a distorted reflection of what she eventually wanted, her ideal house. No matter what they had in front of them, all she could see was her dream future overlaying it. Chris knew that what she was talking about was grander than it should have ever been, but any objections he voiced were swept away in an obsessive rush of committed words. They were going to do this and he knew then, that he was fighting a losing battle.

CHAPTER TWELVE

THE VIGIL

Together, Chris and Anastasia puzzled over the forms and wrote up the descriptions required for planning permission. They assembled a package of the architectural drawings and various sketches, checked it over one last time, then sat back, reasonably content that they had done a good job. They put in the relevant forms and detailed drawings to the local planning authority the next day and settled in to wait. As the days passed, Anastasia grew more and more excited at the prospect of the work they were about to begin. The local authority sent someone out to check the house, look at the plans and determine whether they met the guidelines. He was only there for about a quarter of an hour and left with the assurance that he could see what they were trying to do and that he saw no problems with getting the approval. Of course, the plans would be lodged for public viewing and letters would be sent out to the neighbors, but as far as he was concerned, it was all a formality. He didn't like to say so, but it was pretty much a done deal.

Three weeks later, the first objection letter came in.

A week after that, it was followed by another.

Stase was furious.

She rounded on Chris in the kitchen, which had somehow become their place for any discussions of note. They knew already which neighbor had prompted the first objection.

Her name was there in black and white on the letter and it told them which house she lived in.

"Who does she think she is?" Anastasia said.

The neighbor was a single woman, living on her own as far as they could tell. She was probably in her late thirties. Chris didn't quite understand her objection himself, but as he stood there being buffeted by Stase's ire, he could find some sympathy. Her letter had claimed that the size of their intended extension would block her light and impact her quality of life. There was something to it, but he thought the woman was over-reacting. It was just as likely that she was really concerned about the months of building work that would be taking place just outside her side windows. All the houses on their street were close together, so there would be no avoiding it. There would be no avoiding it for Chris either, as Stase had already told him that she planned to continue living on site during the work so she could keep an eye on things to her satisfaction.

"Dammit," Stase told him. "If she screws up our planning permission, she's going to be sorry. She's behind the other letter too. She must have talked to them. They're all getting together, having little chats together." Her lip curled. "Damn them. Who do they think they are?"

She consulted the architects. She consulted Michael. There was nothing they could do but sit back and wait for the decision to come through.

Two weeks later, the letter came. Their building approval had been denied.

He came home to find Anastasia on the couch, the crumpled letter clutched in one hand, her body racked by sobs.

She looked up at Chris with an expression of disbelief and despair, her tear-tracked face pale.

"How can they do this to us?" she said. "I don't believe it."

He looked out the back window into the dark tangled garden, and all he could feel was relief. Up till now, the house had dominated everything, magazines everywhere, the plans constantly folded and unfolded on the table, the strategy sessions. And their isolation; the fact that Stase wouldn't let them have anyone over. There just didn't seem time for anything else. Maybe, just maybe, they'd start to get their life back. He moved to the couch, sat down beside her and put his arm gently around her shoulders.

"We knew this was a possibility, Stase."

"Yeah, but it's not fair. It's just not fair. Stupid, interfering bitch." She shook the letter in her hand. "I didn't really read what it said, but there's something in here about an appeal process."

"Okay," he said, gently rubbing her back. "We'll look at that later. How long have you been sitting here? Can I get you anything?"

She shook her head. "Bitch," she muttered. "Bitch."

"Okay, listen. It's okay. We'll work it out."

Again, she shook her head.

They sat there for about twenty minutes, saying nothing. He knew that nothing he could say would make it any better.

"Stase," he said, finally. "I'm going to get out of these clothes and work out something about food. You going to be okay?"

She nodded.

He did just that—went upstairs, changed out of his work clothes and headed back into the kitchen to prepare something for the evening meal. Something simple, like pasta, he thought. There was no point fussing under the circumstances. He dug out a couple of wine glasses and a bottle of halfway-decent red and set them up ready to take into the lounge. He was standing by the sink, grating some cheese, when he glanced out the kitchen window. There, in the darkness, in the middle of the back garden, stood Anastasia. While he was upstairs, she had gone out the back. She was staring up at the neighbor's window, just watching. He shook his head and thought nothing of it. When he happened to look out again a few minutes later, the pasta well underway, she was still out there. She hadn't moved.

Okay, he thought to himself, she was upset. She blamed the neighbor for what had happened, and that was okay too. He just had to let her work through it.

He finished the preparations for the evening meal and went out to the backdoor to call her back inside.

She turned slowly and walked back towards the house, shooting the occasional glance up at the next-door window as she came. She slipped past Chris without looking at him and headed into the living room with a fixed expression on her face.

"Bitch," he heard her mutter under her breath as she passed.

Moments later, the sound of the television came blaring out of the room. Chris gave a sigh and started carrying in the meal, putting everything down carefully on the table as Stase stared with a fixed expression and set jaw at the moving images in front of her. They ate in mutual silence, the television the only contribution to noise in the room. A commercial break came then, pushing the volume and thudding against the empty space surrounding them.

A few days later, Anastasia took up smoking again. She'd smoked, briefly, when Chris had first met her, but it was a social activity, not something she did in earnest. Well, now she took it up with a vengeance.

As soon as she got home from work, she would change out of her work things, into an old, gray tracksuit and head out to the backyard to smoke. She stood in the middle of the yard drawing aggressively at her cigarette while she watched the windows of the house next door. She made no pretence about hiding what she was doing. She was there in plain view in the midst of the tangled vegetation that they hadn't really got around to clearing yet, blatantly staring up at the windows. Chris would watch her from the kitchen window, or from the lounge, frowning as she blew smoke between her bared teeth, scowling at the neighbor's fence. As the days passed and they finally got the paperwork done for the appeal, she got a pinched look about her face, becoming even more pale and drawn than usual. Where her look before had been aesthetic, attractive, now she was starting to look unhealthy.

One evening, she came back inside from her vigil, a distracted look on her face. "Where can we find out about her?" she said.

Chris frowned at that. What was she planning now? "I'm not sure what you mean," he said.

"The bitch has got to pay."

"Oh, come on, Stase. What are you saying?"

"Well, there has to be records about her somewhere. I don't know, electoral register, ownership details. What kind of car does she drive? We don't know enough about her. If we're going through an appeal process, I want to make sure that she can't do anything else. Do you know what she drives?"

"You're being ridiculous now." Chris put down his mug and leaned back against the kitchen cabinets. "What on earth do you think you can do?"

Stase didn't meet his eyes. She reached for some papers on the kitchen table and started straightening them. "Maybe we should hire a detective."

Chris blinked. "What?"

"Well, there's got to be something about her, doesn't there? All we know is that she lives alone. I've tried to see inside her place, but I couldn't see enough to tell anything really. You've seen her haven't you?"

"Well, yeah, a couple of times. We exchanged some words over the back fence when we first moved in. I've seen her hanging out washing every now and again. I don't know. What are you asking?"

Stase put her hands flat on the table and looked across at him. "Listen, there's no way that bitch is going to get in the way of our plans. She has to know that I'm not going to let her. If we can't do what we want to the house, then there's no point having it."

Chris sighed. "I think you're taking this a bit far, Stase. Maybe we can do some of what you were planning with the extensions, maybe a scaled-down version and get approval for that. Either that or we sell the house and move somewhere else where we won't have the issue. Sit down and let's talk about it. I'll make you a cup of tea."

Stase sat, but she was gazing out the window at the back-yard. Chris shook his head and put the kettle on, waited for it to boil and poured her a mug of tea. He made himself a coffee and carried both mugs over to the table then sat.

"Look at the way we're living, Stase," he said. "Look at this place. It's a decent house. If we put some effort into fixing it up properly, we could be comfortable here. Do we need all this trouble, really? Not to mention the expense that goes with it."

She looked down into her mug and shook her head. "No, it's not good enough. It's not fair."

"What do you mean it's not fair? We made some plans; they got bounced. It's not the end of the world."

She glanced up through narrowed eyes. "No, that's not good enough."

"Well what do you suggest we do?"

"We go ahead with the appeal, and we show the bitch that she can't beat us. We get the best."

"The best what, Anastasia?"

She turned her mug around and around on the table, not lifting it. "Shit, I don't know. Whatever we have to do. I'm not going to give up." She looked up again and there was absolute conviction in her expression. "We are going to do this."

"Fine," said Chris. "I just think you're going over the top."

Her voice became very quiet. "You think what you want. If you're not going to support me ..."

He sighed. "Of course I'm supporting you. Okay, listen, you find out what we have to do, talk to whomever you have to. I don't know, the architects, Michael, and we'll do what we have to, but there's no point going off half cocked, not knowing what we're doing, is there?"

She bit her lip and nodded slowly.

"Okay," he said, reaching out a hand to squeeze the top of her arm. "I'm going in to watch the news. You coming?"

She shook her head slightly, chewing at the inside of her cheek.

"Okay." He stood and headed into the lounge, carrying his coffee with him. He barely watched the small snippets of footage and talking heads, flipping one to the other in an endless succession of sound and image bites, as he waited for Stase to appear. There seemed to be a new trend with the newsreaders. They were no longer sitting behind desks. It was more personal, he guessed. Right there in your living room, having a chat about world events. Before there'd been the barrier of their desk, the headshot, but now ... they were there, standing like some sort of attractive old friend come to visit. The news came and went, and still there was no sign of her. He flicked off the television, about to carry his mug back to the kitchen and look for her when a red glow from outside the window snagged his attention.

Stase was out there again, standing in the middle of the yard in the darkness, smoking. The red light had been the flare of her cigarette end. She was facing the neighbor's house again, slightly angled towards their own back windows, and as she drew in on her cigarette, the orange aura illuminated her pale face in the darkness. Her eyes were merely dark hollows in the night's own darkness.

CHAPTER THIRTEEN

CREATING A FOLLOWING

Despite wanting to think otherwise, Chris knew his conversation with Patrick had drawn a blank; the resultant frustration was working deep inside him. The brief and unhelpful encounter had left him with more questions than he'd started with. As with many circumstances in his life and choices over the years, Chris had simply expected the solution to come to him. It didn't always work like that, but sometimes things worked out the right way if you waited for them to fall into place. That, in turn, built an expectation that they would. It was like Stase and the precious house. They hadn't gotten the planning permission. They couldn't do the things they wanted to. Things didn't work out just because you wanted them to, or because you put in a modicum of effort to push them in the right direction. Even channeling your entire focus and energy sometimes wasn't enough to make things turn out the way you imagined they might be. Life itself conspired to make things happen and sometimes those things were like nothing you ever wanted.

Chris shook his head. He had to find another way to work out what had caused the memory-free spaces patterning his thoughts with dappled blankness. He also had to try to understand what really had occurred with Stase and him as well. He now had no doubt that something had certainly happened and whatever that was, it had happened to both of them.

The next day he saw Stase off to work as usual and wandered out to the backyard. Standing there amidst the smell of barely damp earth and rotting vegetation, he decided he needn't even bother with his carefully constructed garden pretence. He simply locked up and wandered down to the bus stop to catch a bus into town. Going back to the observational ritual he'd established a couple of weeks before seemed the only sensible course of action—finding those clues that pointed to the something that had taken place beyond his remembering.

It was late enough in the day to miss most of the rush hour, so he had no trouble finding a seat. A mother with her kids; an old lady in a floral headscarf; a shifty looking kid in a hooded sweatshirt, the hood pulled up all the way, who Chris gave a couple of extra suspicious glances; and an old man with horn-rimmed spectacles and a leather briefcase were the only other passengers. The bus shuddered and lurched beneath him. It was old, and every time they stopped at lights or at a bottleneck in the traffic an irregular vibration ran through the metal seats, making Chris' vision of the outside scene shudder annoyingly. How could you search for people who weren't moving when everything was imparted with an unnatural vibrating life of its own? Chris almost decided to get off and change buses, but eventually chose to stay put and deal with it. His real watching would take place in town anyway, right there in the center of population. Most of the cafés he frequented had those broad glass fronts with seats or benches running along the inside of the front window. He could sit in one of those, more than one of those, watching, observing and nursing a coffee or two for hours at a time and nobody would even bother him, except perhaps for a couple of questioning looks from the staff who cleared the tables, but they weren't really going to say anything. It was part of their stock in trade.

He got off the bus in the center of town and stood at the stop, scratching the back of his head, looking this way and that while he decided which way to go. He could start at the place where he had seen the girl and her companion, right in the thick of things. That was about where he'd seen the guy in the doorway too, but that might have just been a fluke. Synchronicity working overtime. There was the guy in the doorway and the girls in the coffee place, but his recollections were still foggy. He wasn't really sure how much of it was dream and how much was real.

Office workers strode around him, on the way to appointments or meetings, undertaking errands, or simply late for work. A delivery guy wheeled a trolley stacked high with green cardboard boxes. A couple of young girls, heads close together, hung around outside a shop window and giggled at something. Chris watched them all, assessed, inwardly shook his head and let his observation wander on. He scanned faces as they passed him, looking for any clues, any sign that would indicate they were something else, something different, knowing at the same time that he would have no real way of telling. What were the signs he was looking for, anyway? Farther down the street, a large billboard moved with digitized images of happy smiling faces, leaning in and smiling large colorful grins, pushing yet another product by displaying an imagined lifestyle. He barely glanced at it.

He didn't actually care where he was going now. He headed for one of the ubiquitous coffee chains and, after ordering, found a seat by the window while he thought through what he was looking for and what he could remember. He recalled the bus shelter, the girl lying there. Patrick had confirmed that much at least. There was something about an older fat man. For a while, he watched shapeless faces passing outside the window, and as those nameless, unrecognizable individuals wandered past his field of vision, it started to rain. Fat, bulbous drops descended from the heavens, shattering into a myriad of lesser drops on the almost black pavement outside, lending it a look like tarnished stainless steel.

Outside, the people quickened their pace, ducked into doorways, lowered their faces and hunched their shoulders. Chris watched the drops, coming more steadily now, bleeding into each other and merging into one damp indistinguishable skein of wetness, now slicking the darkening ground with color and light from the windows of the building opposite. Blurred reflection made wavy lines across the ground, a smeared neon simulacrum of the commercial reality opposite, the reversed and wavy words bleeding into incomprehensible streaks.

Chris tore his gaze from the subtle reminder of his life's own dissipation, casually painted on the roadway in front of him. Nothing was solid. Everything blurred. He glanced around the café, then back out onto the street. Somewhere out there lay an answer; he just had to find it.

Chris concentrated, trying as hard as he could to remember what he really understood. Somewhere, inside, he was aware of the solution, he knew what had been happening; he just had to find the trigger that would make it come to him. The problem was, there was no certainty in his memories. It was no good just forgetting about it and hoping it would come to him later. Whatever had in fact happened, it had tampered with the way he remembered things, the way he thought. That, itself, was a distinctly uncomfortable realization. Who had the power to screw with a person's memories?

Looking across the street, he saw doorways leading to buildings and offices and shops. Simple mundane places, but significant now. He had seen someone inside a doorway—he remembered that too—someone who was there and yet not there, a reflection of themselves. It wasn't one of the doorways across the street; it was another doorway. His forehead creased with concentration. It had been at the coffee house near work. And there he had seen ... the girl from the bus shelter. Patrick had said that they'd taken her away. But Chris had seen her in the café. She'd been talking to a friend. He didn't even know whether he could trust what Patrick had told him. That stuff about church had drilled a seed of doubt into the back of his head.

The rain had started to ease, so he took a last sip at his coffee and thought about heading outside. He wanted to wander the streets for a while thinking, and then he could head for that coffee shop, his coffee shop near work and try to piece together the few fragment of memory that remained. If he was there, with the familiar cues to prompt his memory, he might make a better job of recalling things than he was doing now. He shoved his hands into his pockets and headed out onto the street, leaving the fragrant warmth of the café's interior for the suddenly gray and cool damp of the air outside.

As he walked, traffic growled past and people strode past him, occasionally having to step out of his way. Chris's preoccupation made him almost oblivious to the little things that what went on around him. He watched the pavement, looked into doorways and through shop windows. Everything was just as he remembered it should be, but he almost expected it not to be, as if the way he was seeing things had changed. If he had some real clue about what he was looking for, all this might make sense. The clouds above had passed, leaving a blue sky and sun bounced off plate glass windows and shiny building surfaces making shattered stars of reflected light. Within about half an hour, everything had dried.

He came across an old wooden bench on the pavement, set into cement blocks outside a small park. The park was some solace from the city's bustle and grind, an urban haven that he knew became packed with office workers during the lunch hour when the weather was good enough. He'd walked past it enough during the day when running errands from work. At night, it became the refuge of drunks and street people. He stopped and sat on the bench, crossing his legs and watching the people coming up the street towards him. After a while, he leaned back, draping his arms over the back of the bench and feeling the sun's warmth playing across his face. He glanced back into the park, which was empty at the moment. Back in one corner was a crumpled brown paper bag, an empty green bottle poking out of one end. A couple of other benches sat nearby and a small cement plinth with a metal plaque set into it graced the center. The metal was tarnished and faded. He was familiar with the park, but he couldn't remember having ever read the plaque. He stared at it for a while, thinking about memory, about the mark people made on the world. The plaque was probably there to commemorate whoever had made the bequest or whatever it was that had enabled the establishment of the park in the first place. Or maybe the park had just been set up to commemorate someone or other, now nameless and faceless in the city's midst. He wondered if anyone actually bothered to read the thing, or even if they'd be able to make out the lettering any more. Whoever the benevolent patron might be, even their legacy was obscured by time and the elements. Did they even realize that they'd been forgotten, nobody even paying attention or caring? Chris had never bothered.

He shook his head and he was just about to look away when a large black bird fluttered down and perched right on top of the plinth. It tilted its head to one side, looking at him. Chris sucked his breath through his teeth. The bird hopped once or twice, fluttered, steadying itself and then tilted its head the other way, fixing him with a one-eyed gaze.

Slowly, Chris got to his feet, and took a step backwards, nearly colliding with someone who was walking past.

The passing pedestrian cursed at him and Chris muttered an apology, never taking his eyes away from the bird. It was still watching him.

What was it with birds? What was it with black birds? He took another step back, forcing himself to look away. He could feel the damned thing watching him. He started walking away, heading towards the part of town where his particular coffee shop lay. Several yards up the street, he looked back over his shoulder. The bird was still there watching him. It hopped once to reposition itself, keeping its black gaze fixed in his direction. He stopped and turned to face it.

"What?" he said.

The bird tilted its head one way, then the other, and then squawked at him, a harsh, rasping sound, clear against the background rumble of traffic.

Chris swallowed, turned and quickened his pace.

It took him around ten minutes to reach the coffee shop and by the time he did, his heart was hammering. He knew it was irrational, but the incident with the bird had unsettled him and the cold hollow of the encounter rested inside him, working away at his chest. He pulled open the coffee shop's glass door gratefully, seeking solace from the unreasoning fear in the familiar smells, sounds and tables. He glanced out the window before heading to the counter. Although he knew logically that it was unlikely that the bird was going to appear out there, he wanted to make sure, he needed to make sure. He wasn't certain what he would do if the thing actually showed up, but the brief look granted him a reassuring sense of relief.

It was nearing lunch hour, and the place was about two-thirds full. Thankfully, there was still a seat near the window. He headed for the display cabinet, picked out one of the plastic-wrapped designer sandwiches and handed it to the person behind the counter as he ordered his coffee. She would toast it and bring it to his place once it was done. He kept glancing out at the street while he waited for her to fix his coffee and then he juggled the cup and saucer carefully back to the seat by the window. Just in time, because a whole string of people came through the door just as he pulled out the high stool and sat.

Taking a tentative sip, he half-listened to the conversations going on inside. He angled himself on the stool so he could both watch the street and have the ability to look at the other customers without having to look back over one shoulder. A mirror along the café's inner wall let his slight angle be just enough. He could watch things in the mirror without being too obvious about it. Meanwhile, he plucked at the faded recollections wandering through his head. Yes, he had definitely seen the girl here. He had ... gone up to her, tried to talk to her ... She'd been with a friend. They'd looked at him strangely and then left, talking about him. Actually, Chris didn't blame them. It was unlikely that his reaction would have been any different.

The fragments were starting to inch together, pulling themselves into a tissue-thin fabric.

The bird was still worrying him though, despite knowing that it was probably just coincidence coupled with his own fragile paranoia.

His sandwich arrived, a ciabatta toasted with salami, black olive pesto and mozzarella. There was a time when you'd be hard pressed to get a toasted ham and cheese with any sort of decent cheese on it. Instead, you'd just get processed stuff and on any bread other than white, that left dark brown toasting marks in stripes against a paler background, always slightly stale. Merging of cultures happened in all sorts of little ways if there was the chance of a profit driving it. He picked at a piece of the paper napkin that had adhered to the melted cheese.

He had the half sandwich partway to his mouth when the girl from the bus shelter near home entered. Chris stopped in mid action, his mouth held stupidly open and watched her as she headed to the counter with her friend. It was the same friend, he was sure.

Shit. He hadn't expected to see her, either one of them.

He placed the sandwich slowly back down into the plate and watched her in the mirror. She hadn't noticed him, even if she'd remember him, which he doubted. They got their coffees and some pastries to go with them and headed for a table near the corner, one of the ones with big comfortable leather chairs. Had he not wanted to watch what was going on outside, he would already have moved to one of those very chairs as soon as it came free. The girl sat with her back to him, her friend half obscured by her shoulder. Rather than turning all the way around, Chris continued looking at their reflection in the mirror. He was absolutely sure that it was the same pair of girls. There was nothing to tell him that there was anything special about her, anything unusual, and if it hadn't been for the incident at the bus shelter ...

Her friend looked around the room and caught him watching. A brief frown and she leaned in close to her companion to say something. Chris swiveled quickly back to face the outside and picked up his rapidly cooling sandwich. He didn't want any sort of incident, not this time. Christ, he was turning into a stalker. There'd been so much in the press about stalkers over the last few months, celebrity stalkers, others. You could get arrested for that stuff.

There was a time, earlier in his relationship with Stase, that he'd been just that. He'd followed her desperately— there was no other word for it. He had stood in the rain, rivulets of water trickling into his eyes waiting for her to emerge from a classroom. He had lain in wait in places he knew she was going to be. He didn't really like remembering that obsessive part of his personality. He picked at a bit of the sandwich, popped it in his mouth and chewed thoughtfully. Whatever had happened to his obsession for Stase? When had fascination turned into apathy and numb acceptance?

A quick glance in the mirror revealed that the pair was no longer watching him. That was fine. He wasn't going to follow her or her friend, but her presence had helped confirm the shard of memory which sliced at his intellectual discomfiture. He finished his sandwich and coffee slowly, waiting for the girls to leave.

After they had gone, he waited for a while, then pushed his stool back and headed back outside. A look in each direction confirmed that they were nowhere to be seen. Chris walked quickly up the street, looking for the doorway where he had seen the other man. He knew it was around here somewhere, he just wasn't quite sure where. It was the shop front over the other side of the road from it that gave it away. He remembered the grainy marble ledge he'd rested against as he'd watched the doorway. Chris walked along beside it, running his fingertips across the surface, and then he walked back again, looking at it all the while. Large iron studs had been set in a regular pattern all along the top surface, clearly to discourage people from sitting on it. He had sat over there, about a third of the way along, his backside resting just on the lip, avoiding the dull metal points. He took up the same position, looking across at the three broad stone steps leading up to double glass doors, slightly in shadow at this time of day.

He sat there for about quarter of an hour, not really sure what he was trying to achieve. The image lurking in his memory was firming in his mind, but the same thing was hardly going to happen again. He wasn't going to see another hollow man resting in the doorway waiting for ...

Waiting for ...

The van. A white van. That was what Patrick had been talking about. The image was cloudy, but he remembered a white van. Two clean-cut guys and a white van. And there had been a man there, hadn't there? He frowned. He thought he had seen the same guy a couple of days later, looking slightly lost. There was the feeling of shock and surprise. It had stopped Chris in his tracks.

One by one, more puzzle pieces were slotting into place.

Patrick had said they'd taken Stase away. He had a vague recollection of the white van and something about the kitchen too. Patrick had said that they'd done something to him. To him. To Patrick, but to Chris too. And to Stase.

Piecing things together in his head was not enough. He could still be imagining it. He had to find proper evidence.

Chris pushed himself from the wall and picked a direction at random. He knew what he was looking for now. He started walking, keeping his eyes peeled for evidence of another one of the nameless. He walked and he walked. He looked in doorways, under overpasses, in small alleys. Faces floated past him and he looked at every one. He varied his route, taking small side streets and across the courtyards of large building. Still there was nothing. Late, late in the afternoon, he was ready to give up. He had to get back in time for Anastasia's return home, though he was sure he could think up some excuse for being out without revealing the true details of what he was doing.

Feeling downcast, he headed for the nearest bus stop that would take him home. It was about three blocks away from his current position. He'd get home, spend the evening with Stase and then return in the morning and start the search again, although his hopes of finding anything else were starting to trickle away.

His mind was elsewhere, fixed on the evening and the need to get home when he saw her. Sitting at a bus shelter, not lying, sitting. She was staring across the road. She had a shopping bag at her feet and some papers had fallen out of it, lying scattered about her feet. It was this that attracted Chris's attention. No one else seemed to be paying any attention to her. She sat in the corner, staring blankly across the road. He stopped in mid stride. A bus pulled into the stop, obscuring her from Chris's view, a big smiling set of white teeth on a toothpaste advertisement squarely in the way. A couple of seconds later, it pulled out again. The woman was still there. It was one of them, he was sure. And yet, how come he was seeing her and no one else seemed to be noticing? He couldn't waste time on thinking about that now ...

He dashed across the street, avoiding traffic, walked quickly up to the bus shelter and stood right in front of her. Tightly permed, dyed deep red hair, a bone-colored coat, a brown skirt and a floral print blouse, he put her somewhere in her fifties. Still her expression hadn't changed. The skin on her face was loose, papery, but still tinged with the color of life. Her hands were folded neatly in her lap. A car raced past behind him and the wake of its passage stirred a couple of the papers at her feet, but still she didn't move.

"Excuse me," said Chris.

Nothing. Not a flicker.

He bent down, started scraping the papers together. They looked like invoices from the little he could ascertain from the brief glance he gave them. He righted the bag and shoved the papers inside. From the woman, there was no reaction. He crouched there, looking up into her face. No, she wasn't breathing either, or didn't seem to be.

"Excuse me," he said again.

He glanced to left and right, wanting to make sure he wasn't attracting too much attention, but people walked past, apparently oblivious. There was no one else at the bus stop, but then, the bus had just left a few moments before. Chris chewed at his lip, assessing, deciding what he was going to do next. Again, looking left and right, he slipped around the side of the bus shelter and headed for the doorway of a nearby building. He positioned himself just inside, his face barely poking around the corner, watching.

Chris waited. For a long time, nothing seemed to happen. The woman sat there. People walked past. Chris waited.

He was about to give up, when, at the next corner, a plain white van turned and headed towards them. The bottom dropped out of Chris' stomach. His breath quickening, he bit his lip. He had to see. Trying to keep out of sight as much as he could, he leaned against the corner of the wall. The van came nearer. It reached the bus shelter, slowed and pulled to a stop. He glanced up and down the street, but everyone else seemed wrapped in their own little worlds.

The van's near door swung open and then a pair of black shoes was followed to the street by neatly pressed dark trousers and a white coat. A short, clean haircut completed the picture. Around the other side of the van, another door slammed. Another man, looking remarkably like the first, appeared around the front of the vehicle and joined his companion. After a brief consultation, they both stepped under the bus shelter. The first one leant down, retrieved the woman's shopping bag and headed to the back of the van. Chris presumed he was opening the back; a moment later, the sound of a door handle turning and the doors swinging open confirmed it for him. The man reappeared without the bag.

Both men moved to either side of the woman and eased her to her feet, then slowly walked her to the back of the van. A couple of seconds later, there was the sound of slamming doors. The first man moved back to the front of the van, opened the passenger door and climbed back in. The sound of a closing door from the other side told Chris that the man's companion, the driver, had also climbed back in. The next instant, the motor started and the van pulled out from the bus stop and started heading down the road.

Chris got a good look at the man in the passenger's side as they passed his location. There was an incredible blandness about his features beneath the neatly tended blond hair. There seemed to be no distinguishing features at all.

He had to decide what he was going to do and quickly. He stepped out onto the pavement, watching the van as it picked up speed. He could hardly chase it. Chris cursed. He should have been better prepared, much better.

He looked back the other way and spotted a cab. With a triumphant "Yes!" he waved at it frantically. The cab pulled in and Chris wrenched the door open, slid into the back and pulled the door shut behind him.

"Quickly," he said. "I'm in a hurry." He leaned forward across the seat, pointing at the rapidly disappearing vehicle ahead. "Follow that van. Don't let it out of your sight."

The cab driver, a dark face beneath a flat cap turned and looked at him. "What are you talking about?"

"The van, there. The white one. Quick, before it gets away."

The driver turned to follow Chris's pointing finger, then shook his head. "I don't know what you're talking about."

"Quickly, dammit," said Chris. "The van, there. The white one. You can't let it get away." He craned desperately after it.

The driver shook his head again. "I can't follow something that ain't there, can I? You dreaming or something?"

The van had gone. Chris slumped back into the seat. No, it wasn't there. At least it wasn't there any more. He glanced back out at the bus shelter, then buried his face in his hands.

"Are you all right?" asked the driver.

"Yeah, sorry," said Chris, looking up with a sigh. "Just take me home, I think."

He gave the driver his address and leaned back with his head against the seat, staring up at the cab's gray-green ceiling, seeking solace in the plain, featureless stretch of fabric and avoiding the slight shake of the head and the suspicious glances from the cabbie in the rearview mirror. He didn't want to look at anything outside. Not right now. Now, he had to find another way.

CHAPTER FOURTEEN

DANCING AT A DISTANCE

At first, the whole thing was about conquest, about ego, about lust. Being with Anastasia, having her want him, felt good, because for so long he had believed she was unattainable. The mere prospect that she might truly desire him back was like a fantasy just beyond his fingertips. The guys, Andy and Bill, had helped convince him of that, so he spent those first few months in a wondering disbelief. He kept on wanting to check that he wasn't actually dreaming it all; any moment, he expected her to turn around and have that last terrible conversation with him that would tell him he had been right all along. Sometimes he even tested the words, trying to imagine what she would say to him when the day came and she finally left. The thing was, she didn't. Gradually, the disbelief, the suspicion of some grand joke, turned to expectation. Chris started to believe that they really were in a relationship together, though in some ways, he still couldn't quite accept that fate had delivered him such good fortune.

He ignored the growing snide comments that came back at home in the shared house. "Oh, off to see the little woman again are we?" they'd say and smile knowingly, conspiratorial in their feigned pity of the poor manipulated fellow male. "Man, she so has you under the thumb."

"Yeah, yeah," he'd say, making a good attempt at ignoring their jibes.

Hesitantly, tentatively, Anastasia and Chris tested the boundaries around themselves. When you first start seeing someone, there are all sorts of accommodations that have to be made. The energy is different. There are friends, the social circle, everyday existence and the things you do that you're used to coping with as an individual rather than as a couple. As you move closer together, the energy changes. You're not even sure in the first instance, whether there's going to be a relationship or whether the whole thing will just end in tears or even spend a very brief insubstantial existence in little more than tears. We don't, any of us, have a predictive capability when it comes to other people, no matter how much we like to think that we do. One of the things we try to manage as we make those adjustments is to protect that inner core of what we are—the place where real vulnerabilities lie. Chris knew that, and he knew that he and Anastasia were no different.

Of course there were discussions late into the night and shared revelations, but Chris held things back from her. He wasn't quite ready to let go of his own life yet.

One by one, slowly but surely, Chris divested himself of his other involvements. At the same time, he was wondering how many others Stase herself was or had been involved with. She was an attractive woman, after all. She was very close about the details of the people she associated with and wouldn't be drawn. In response, Chris drew the protective barriers around himself too. It was funny how he could be jealous of those things that may or may not have occurred in the past, people he didn't know, feelings he didn't quite know had existed or not, acts that could have, or perhaps hadn't taken place. His imagination worked overtime, filling in the gaps of those parts of her past and present that she refused to supply. Chris, like Andy, had a bit of a reputation as a lady's man, and he was sure that some sort of reputation had preceded him. Anastasia had told him that she had found out all she could about him before making that first approach. She had gone into it with her eyes open, or so she claimed.

The problem was that Chris had things that he kept from the world, or at least from those outside his immediate circle of Andy and Bill. He wasn't ready to let those go yet either. On the odd occasion, he'd been tempted in that rush of initial proof that you really cared about someone to spill more of the reality than was prudent. Safety dictated that he shouldn't reveal too much of it. He couldn't help feeling a twinge of guilt, though. It was as if he was lying to her, in a way.

Anastasia still returned to the city on the weekends, and she remained close-lipped about what went on there during their time apart. She'd return late Sunday night or Monday morning.

"So, how was the weekend?" he'd ask.

"Yeah, fine."

"So, what did you get up to?"

She'd shrug. "Oh you know. The normal boring stuff. Family stuff."

And that would be that. Chris wasn't in a position yet where he felt he could push it, so that little nagging kernel of distrust sat and worked in the back of his head, glossed over because he didn't really want to think about it. How different it would become as their relationship progressed.

In the beginning, rules are unclear, if there are rules at all, and while Anastasia disappeared back to the city, Chris occupied himself in other ways. Because it was primarily an industrial town with a university attached, the population was both mixed and floating at the same time. Many of the students returned home to other places on the weekends and during break time. Others, fewer, became local, moved to the area and conducted life as local residents. The social circle became smaller during the times when much of the student body was away.

There were Andy and Bill, of course, and Chris still went drinking with them or out to see bands, but there was another circle that Chris had moved in before Stase had appeared on the scene. The university bar was renowned for big sessions on a Friday night, but mainly among the locals. They'd either stay there in a group or drift off to another place as a ragged collection of companions. Chris liked the Friday-night sessions and looked forward to them, hanging on to the vestiges of his former life and bits and pieces of the social circle that he used to move within. It gave him a way to pretend that things hadn't really changed that much. Besides, it was like a safety net, a place that he could simply fall back into if things with Anastasia all went horribly wrong, and that particular uncertainty still lived within him.

One of the bar circle was a student called Beatrice, Trish to her friends. Trish was short and blond, not a great looker but she was lithe and fit. She came from German parentage and she had that look of German girls, all cheekbones and nose and narrow jaw. Chris had always had a slight thing about Trish. A couple of times he'd been to her vast sprawling place. It looked over the beach and she shared it with four other students. They were a part of the university fringe, purveyors of large loud parties and dazed smoking sessions where everybody faded into incomprehensible vegetative lumps on the wide, Indian-print covered couches. In the summer months, the house, set on a slight hill overlooking the water benefited from the salt-tang of sea breezes flowing gently through the wide, open window along with the sound of waves crashing across the beach below. He'd seen and recognized the signals from her a few times, but the burgeoning fascination with Anastasia had steered him away.

One Friday night, Chris was at the bar, not with any particular group, but Trish's crowd was there as well. Someone suggested they all retire back to the house. Stase had left for the city a day early—a wedding or something—and Chris was feeling slightly lonely and abandoned. He had nothing else to do, so after the few drinks and a long, slow, evening, the offer seemed attractive. He wasn't with Trish at the bar. He was with another small group that decided to tag along, and he ended up getting a ride back to the house with one of the other residents. About a dozen of them made it back to the house, and Chris ended up at the kitchen table with Trish, the lights low, the smell of the ocean and night roses filling the room. He could have avoided the consequences, but there seemed little reason to do so. There was no pressure, just boozy, pleasantly numb inevitability and Chris and she ended up in her room on the single mattress on the floor. It was an act of passion and want, primal in its energy; it was great, sweaty, and consuming. She moved against him with natural ease, and there was not an instant of self-consciousness between them. He had no thought of the consequences, only of the moment.

The next morning, Chris woke feeling slightly sheepish as soon as he worked out where he was, but it was different. There seemed to be no pressure or expectation from Trish, but then that was the first time. They got up, had coffee together as if what they had done was the most natural thing in the world, and perhaps it had been. Society has a tendency to burden the simplest things with meaning and import that just isn't there.

When Stase arrived back on the Sunday night, he didn't tell her. He thought there was little point. He was already committed to her, and what had happened with Trish was just a passing aberration, a one-off. There was a twinge of guilt that walked in his footsteps for the next few days, but he tried to ignore it. He ran into Trish a couple of times during that week and she smiled and said hi, but that was about it. Chris put the whole incident away from him and away from his relationship with Stase.

Two weeks later, he ended up back at Trish's place again. He spent nearly the entire weekend.

Chris didn't actually think of it as being related to his involvement with Stase. They were separate time streams, separate realities, neither one impacting on the other. How could they? He told himself that he could keep those spaces removed from each other, islands in the overall flow of his life and as it had nothing to do with Stase he didn't actually have to mention anything about it. He didn't even recognize the inconsistency of that self-created justification.

He spent hours talking with Trish, even about things that he and Stase had done together. Trish seemed fine with that, not really caring if their interaction was a separate thing at all, listening and commenting occasionally in those still quiet times between the spaces where they were making love—but Trish wasn't exactly big on conversation.

CHAPTER FIFTEEN

REVELATION

The bombshell came about three weeks later. Stase told Chris that she didn't want to see him any more. She broke the news at her place. The other girl she shared with, Barbara, slightly overweight with dirty blond hair, was strategically placed in the next room, just out of earshot, but close enough to step in if things got ugly. There were no tears. Just this simple deadpan expression as she told Chris, in a voice completely devoid of emotion, that it was time for him to go. Andy was waiting for Chris in the car parked outside on the street—they'd come to pick her up to go out to a movie—and he got out of the car as Chris emerged from the apartment block, walking slowly, barely able to believe what he'd just heard.

"You okay, my man?" Andy asked, putting his arm around Chris's shoulders.

At that moment the heavens opened and they dashed for the car, all thoughts of conversation gone for the moment. As Chris pulled out onto the road, he still didn't feel like talking.

The rain beat down upon the car windows, forming streams and little rivulets that obscured Chris' view despite the wipers. The steady chunk, chunk beat on above the rain noise. Andy and he had gotten wet running for the car and the interior was all steamy with their dampness. Andy seemed to sense the mood and respected Chris' need for silence for the first few minutes as they drove back down the highway.

Chris peered ahead through the deluge, concentrating on the road ahead, barely aware of Andy's presence in the seat beside him. Trucks roared past and threw up trails of dirty spume to make his vision even worse. It's funny, he could remember the details so well, but he couldn't remember where they were going. All thought of the movie had just disappeared. There was an empty wrapper on the floor by Andy's feet, all crumpled into a ball in the corner, red and yellow. Trails of mud striped the dark gray flooring beneath. One of the wipers was slightly worn, and it caught against the windshield, squeaking slightly as it dragged.

Chris was thinking about Anastasia, about the expression, or rather lack of expression on her face, when Andy spoke.

"You've got to get yourself together, Chris," he said.

Chris dragged himself back to awareness.

"Huh?"

"You've got to stop thinking about her. Get on with your life. Everything's falling apart for you. I've been watching it happen and you just can't let it get to you. You're losing your friends, Chris. You don't do any of the stuff you used to. You're just letting your life slide past you. I'm worried about you, man. Forget about her. She's only a girl."

"No, Andy, Stase is a little more than that."

A truck roared past and splashed water in a torrent across the glass.

"Well just forget about her, will you? She's not going to come back to you, you know."

"And how the fuck can you know that?"

"Well, she's not."

"And I suppose you know. I suppose you know fucking everything. Well, let me tell you something. You don't know anything, Andy." He slammed the steering wheel with his open palm.

"I do know. I promise you that's the end of it," he said in a calm voice. "She was no good for you, Chris. Everything was fine before she came along. You've changed, and not in good ways."

Another semi-trailer growled past, its wheels whirring beside his window. Its lights trailed orange snakes through the water on the glass.

For a few moments he didn't make the connection, didn't wonder why he was so certain. Then a suspicion started to grow.

"Andy, what do you know that I don't?"

"Just that she won't be coming back to you," he said.

"And how can you be sure?"

"She just won't."

The silence stretched between them, and Chris tilted his head in query.

"Because I made sure she wouldn't," Andy said quietly, a slight smirk on his face.

Chris slammed his foot on the brakes. The car slid crazily to the side of the road, spraying a fountain of mud as it careened across the shoulder. A car horn behind them blared and kept blaring as it shot past, the note drifting downwards as it sped on to the distance. He didn't care that he could have almost killed them. Slowly he turned to face him.

Andy looked back at him impassively.

There they were, the motor stopped, stalled, the wipers going chunk, chunk, chunk across the windshield and the rain drumming on the roof. A car went past, then another, then a truck.

"What do you mean, you made sure she wouldn't," Chris said, slowly.

"Just what I said. I made sure that she won't be around to screw up your life any more." His expression hadn't changed.

"Look, Andy, if this is some kind of joke ..."

"No joke. She won't be back to get in the way, my man."
He smiled openly. "I did it for you, Chris. The girl was
really fucking you up. I hated seeing what she was doing to
you. Whatever happened to the Chris Baron we all know
and love, eh? You deserve better than that. You've got to be
able to see that."

Chris's guts were feeling cold and he spoke very quietly
and very calmly. "I'm not sure I understand. What exactly
did you do, Andy?"

"I had a quiet word with her, that's all. Told her a few home
truths. That's it. The end. I told her about the other ones,
about the things you've been up to when she's not around."

Chris could feel the hysteria rising deep inside him, but a
struggled to keep it there. If this was one of Andy's sick jokes,
he was really going to pay for it. He raised his eyebrows as
he swiveled to face him.

"I think you'd better explain," he said.

"I don't know how many ways you want me to say it. The
girl's history." Andy shrugged. "I just told her some things,
that's all. I told her about the Professor's wife, about that
little German number. She took it all pretty well, considering.
I have to give her points for that."

Chris stared at him. He couldn't possibly be serious.
His heart hammered in his ears and he reached across and
grabbed a fistful of Andy's coat. He was no longer hearing
the wipers or the rain and the road. Andy's words kept
ringing in his ears. This was more than a mere joke. He
knew it was now.

"Andy ..."

"Haven't I always told you that you could trust me to look
after you?" He extricated himself from Chris's grip and sat
back looking smug. "You needed looking after. You've always
needed looking after."

The horror of what Andy was saying started to wash over him, but it was replaced with disbelief.

"You had better tell me in precise detail what it is you think you've fucking done." He was shaking his head. Perhaps this was some weird fantasy. "All that stuff was ages ago. It's over. It's been over for ages."

"Listen, Chris," Andy said. His voice was so matter-of-fact. "There's no thinking about it. You're free. Free at last, free at last. I had a dream." He grinned.

Chris sat back and stared at him. He had to think. Another truck horn blared as it roared past them. And still the wipers went chunk, chunk, chunk.

"Get out," he told him. He reached across Andy and shoved the door open. "Just get out." When Andy didn't move, he shoved him.

"Calm down, man," Andy said, looking puzzled.

"No! Just get out of this fucking car. Now!" Still Andy didn't move.

Chris wrenched his door open and stepped out into the pouring rain and mud, oblivious to the traffic on the road behind him. Slipping and sliding, he rushed around to Andy's side of the car and reached in and grabbed his arm. He dragged him out.

"Chris? What the fuck do you think you're doing?"

Andy staggered to his feet, rain and mud dripping from his clothes. He held his hands out by his sides. Chris could barely see with the water sheeting into his eyes. He reached back and he hit Andy. Andy fell back against the side of the car then pushed himself upright. Chris hit him again.

"Fuck off. I don't want to see you again. I've had enough of your shit, Andy." He was shaking. He pushed his shoulder and Andy fell, sprawling back into the mud. Then Chris stepped past him and slammed the passenger door.

"Chris!"

He stalked back around the front of the car, leaving Andy where he lay, and got back in. He slammed the door and wiped his face. His fingers fumbled with the keys, trying to start the car again, but he was shaking so much that he couldn't turn them. He couldn't think.

Then Andy's face was up against the glass of the passenger window, pressed against the streaked pane and distorted with the wet. A trickle of blood ran down from his lip where he'd hit him. It mixed with the rain and slipped in a fog across the glass. Andy banged on the glass with the flat of his hand.

"Chris! What the hell are you doing?" He banged on the glass again.

Chris tried to turn the key, but the car refused to start. Andy wouldn't go away. He stood there covered in mud with the blood trickling from his lips banging against the glass. It was too much for Chris then. He slammed his hands against the steering wheel and rested his forehead on it, trying to shut out the sounds. Andy had to be joking. He just had to be.

Finally, Chris managed to get the engine to turn over and cough into life. He hit the accelerator, ignoring the spinning wheels, heading up the muddy verge for a way, too distracted to pull out on the road, too distracted really to drive.

"Fuck!" Chris yelled, and slammed his foot on the brakes again. The car slid to a stop and he sat there, staring through the steamed up window. Finally, he leaned across and pushed the passenger side door open, hearing the rain spattering into the wet earth and gravel. Cars hissed along the road. A truck roared past.

Andy's running feet slapped along the wet ground, coming closer.

"Get in," Chris said, still looking straight ahead.

"Listen, Chris, I ..."

"Don't say a fucking word. Just get in."

"Chris—"

He lifted a hand, not looking at him. "Not a fucking word."

Andy pulled the door closed, the smell of rain and mud filling the confined space. Chris used his sleeve to clean the inside of the windshield, and peering through the deluge, wound down his window, watching for a break to pull out onto the road.

He negotiated an entry into the traffic, wound up his window and gripped the steering wheel, concentrating on driving. Beside him, Andy cleared his throat. Chris ignored him. Andy was smart enough not to try to start a conversation, to talk about anything.

They drove for a while in silence and then Chris pulled off the main road and down a street that would take them back to their place.

The small road led over a bridge that crossed the highway. He was halfway across the bridge when he noticed something strange about the car. The steering suddenly felt sloppy beneath his grip. He frowned, trying to work out what it was. He turned off the bridge and was halfway down the hill, when, with a huge crash and the sound of scraping metal the car tilted to one side.

"What the—?" Chris slammed on the brakes. From the car's other side, something rolled down the street in front of them. It was a wheel. The damned wheel had come off. He'd had the car in for a service a couple of days before. They mustn't have tightened the nuts properly when they'd finished dealing with the brakes. He sat staring, his mouth hanging stupidly open, at the wheel disappearing down the hill, wobbling slightly as it went.

Slowly, he turned his head to look at Andy. Andy was sitting there with an idiot grin on his face.

"What?" Chris said. "What?"

Andy's grin grew wider. "The wheels have really come off this time," he said.

Despite himself, Chris laughed. There wasn't a lot more he could do.

CHAPTER SIXTEEN

SHARED SPACE

They got over the whole thing, got over the rift that Andy had put between them. Chris never did get over the rift Stase had put between Andy and him though. Perceptibly, the space between Chris and Andy grew.

It took a few weeks before Stase and Chris even spoke to each other again. They spent awkward hours glancing at each other across empty rooms. The rooms weren't quite empty, but to them they were. Nobody else existed between those heavy glances, full of mutual understanding and pointed, unspoken meaning. Their eyes would meet, and then, instead of looking quickly away, they'd hold the gaze for just a couple of seconds too long.

He kept seeing her in places, her sporty little green car parked in places where he didn't quite expect to see it. He'd be driving along, listening to something on the car radio, and there it would be. He'd slow, turning to look at it as he cruised past, then speed up again, looking in the rearview mirror. Who was she visiting?

He asked her about it later, but she told him some story about having lent her car to someone. He saw it there a few times as he passed. Maybe he just wanted to believe the story. It was better to hold on to that than the other possibilities. So he sought his own special displacement. Part of that was denial. Part of it was removing himself from everything that reminded him of the formative relationship that had been. He couldn't trust Andy any more, and living in the same house with him had become uncomfortable as well as a constant reminder. There was enough discomfort for him outside the house without coming home to it as well. Chris announced to the other residents that he was moving out

When he told them, Andy looked at him accusingly, as if he should feel guilty about what had come to pass. Chris knew he shouldn't, but he felt the guilt despite knowing that he was making the right choice. What his mind kept telling him was that Andy was bad news. Stase had said it more than once in their brief time together. She'd even called him a jinx. In the past couple of years, everything that had seemed to go really wrong had occurred when Andy was with him. There was the tire incident, the time he'd been beaten up late at night outside some club or other that Andy had convinced him they should go to together; then there was the whole thing with Stase. They'd been strong friends, Andy and he, but Chris had some decisions to make. As they discussed the logistics of what they needed to do, Chris couldn't meet Andy's eyes. It was as if Stase were there, watching him do what he knew he had to.

For the next couple of weeks, Chris looked for somewhere he could live alone. He couldn't face the prospect of sharing space. He wanted somewhere that was truly his own. He saw a few places, but there was always something wrong with them, something he couldn't quite put his finger on. Toward the end of the two week period, he was becoming nervous. He knew the guys would understand, but he didn't want to have to ask. Besides, he'd already made the decision. When he was just about to give up hope, two days before he was due to move out, he found it.

The apartment sat at the end of a block of four. They stretched in a single line; stairs ran along one side. It was simple: two bedrooms, a lounge, a kitchen, bathroom and broad windows looking out over treetops and the steel plant out in the distance. There was enough space for one person and it was in the right price range. He signed the papers that afternoon. The apartment had the luxury of a garage below, enough space to store some of the few possessions he'd accumulated and really didn't fit with the space inside. It also had space enough for his car. A shared laundry sat on the other side of the building, backing on to the garages. It was everything he needed.

Both Bill and Andy helped him move the next day. Awkwardly, he shook hands with both of them, thanked them, and waved them on their way. He headed inside, closed the front door and stood in the center of the living room, feeling the space, feeling the reality of being alone for the first time. Chris looked around and smiled. This was his space. He could do anything he wanted in it, within reason.

That night, he cooked a simple meal and sat looking out across the suburban lights, into the alien glow of the steel factories beyond. A rail track serving the mill wound around its circumference, and the irregular ore train crawled along its length. It was a quiet street and at night, the plant's noise and the locomotive steam drifted across the rooftops. He sat there in darkness lit by distant industrial lights wondering what he was going to do next with his life. An occasional flare lit the plumes of gases from within, casting an orange glow across the skyscape.

In the spaces between, he kept seeing signs of Anastasia and strangely coincidental incidents kept dogging him—at least he thought they were coincidental. The whole thing with her car. Other things. One night, he was at Trish's place when he noticed a photograph stuck to the fridge with a magnet. It was a guy he knew vaguely from around campus. The photograph, slightly blurred, showed him with a towel draped around his neck; he was sitting in front of a mirror. There were other people in the photo, and Chris leaned in to look closer. It seemed to be some sort of collective hair-cutting effort. He was about to ask Trish what it was all about when, as he looked at the details, Chris felt himself go cold. There, reflected in the mirror was Anastasia. He recognized the skirt first, a green satiny number she was fond of wearing. And although she was only half in shot, the line of her back, her arm, half her head, they were all too familiar. He swallowed and shut his mouth. She was doing it again ... appearing in places she wasn't supposed to be. It was as if she had found some way to be where he was going to be and managed to plant evidence that she'd been there.

Two weeks later, Stase and he passed their first few words together in a long time. A social function at one of the colleges brought them from their separate paths into a common sparring ground. He saw her across the room and it was just like that first time, but something new had been added to the mix. The empty chill where the bottom of his stomach should have been was something fresh. He angled his way through the crowd.

"Hi," he said tentatively.

"Hello." She glanced at him then turned her gaze to the other people in the room.

"So, are you here alone?"

She spoke without looking at him. "No, I came with a couple of the girls."

Silence beat between them for several seconds.

"So," he said. "How have you been?"

"Fine. Yeah, fine."

"I've seen you around," he said.

"Well, that wouldn't be too hard," she responded, taking a sip of her drink. She placed the glass down on a table behind her.

She wasn't making it easy.

"Listen, Stase ..."

"Hmmm?"

"Can we talk?"

She turned to look at him, a flat expression on her face. "Isn't that what we're doing?"

"No, I mean talk. Properly ..."

"Put your drink down," she said.

"What?"

"Chris, put your drink down, will you?"

A little confused, he complied.

She gave the room a quick glance, and then grabbed his sleeve. "Come on. Let's get out of here."

She led him quickly from the room, down some stairs and out into the chill night air in the middle of the parking lot.

"Over this way," she said. She'd let go of his sleeve by now. He followed meekly. They wound their way through parked cars over to the other side of the parking lot beneath some trees. There sat the little sporty green number. She dug out her keys and opened the door. "Get in," she said.

He stood for a moment, debating; then, intrigued, he complied, opening the door, sliding in beside her and closing the door behind him. He was staring at her pale features in the darkness. The car windows were fogged white around them.

"So talk," she said.

"I've missed you," he said slowly. "I've missed you terribly. I haven't been able to stop thinking about you."

Her green eyes were black in the darkness, wide and watching. She passed the tip of her tongue over her bottom lip, her mouth left slightly open. Even half-seen in darkness, she was beautiful, had some special aura about her that was holding him, fascinated. She gently closed her lips, waiting.

"Look, I'm sorry. I'm sorry for all that shit with Andy. You never let me explain."

"You don't have to explain," she said quietly.

"But I do. Listen, I've moved out, got a place on my own."

She looked down at her hand. "It's about time. You spend too much time hanging around with losers like that."

"Andy's all right."

She met his gaze again. "He's a loser," she said, daring him to contradict her.

"Anyway, that's not the point. I'm on my own now. I need to see you."

She turned the key in the ignition, turning on the heating, watching the windshield as the demister kicked into play. "Let's go for a drive."

"Okay ..."

She fired up the engine, pulled out of the parking space and headed out of the grounds and onto the street. They'd barely left the front gates when she slipped her hand across the space between them and rested it lightly on the top of his thigh. Neither of them had said a word since leaving.

He was conscious of how brittle the moment was.

"Where are we going?" he finally asked, seeing streetlights fogged with small coronas of white flicking past them outside the window.

"Well, aren't you going to show me your new place?" she asked, her attention firmly fixed on the road ahead, not even looking at him.

In that sparsely furnished apartment, lit by an industrial glow, on a mattress flat on the floor, they made love. He didn't question what they were doing there in that place that was supposed to be his own, because there, for those few hours, he had everything he wanted in the world. Afterwards, with the metallic production voices grumbling and moaning in the distance, they lay in the semi-dark. He traced her features with his fingertip, running across the curve of her cheek, along her long, pale throat, across alabaster shoulder and small, perfectly-formed breasts. A train clattered and hissed along the tracks in the distance.

"Stase, listen to me," he said quietly.

She was watching him, something working behind her eyes. She put a finger to his lips.

"Shhhhhhh," she said.

He turned his attention back to the pale skin at her hip and waist, then back up to the gentle curve of her throat. People talked about swan's necks, about how women had graceful swan's necks. Looking at the smooth unblemished curve of her throat, he could understand why.

They slept for a while, and he woke sometime in the night, turned and found her there. He could barely believe it, and an involuntary smile came to his lips. He leaned over, gently brushed some hair out of her face and propped up on one elbow, he watched her sleep.

The next morning, she lay there staring at the ceiling, working her mouth, her hair in disarray. He slipped from beneath the covers, padded into the kitchen and brought her back a cup of coffee, squatted on the floor next to the mattress and sipped at his own. She hadn't started drinking tea yet. When she'd finished her coffee, she rubbed her eyes, ran her fingers through her hair and smiled at him, pulling them through with that last, characteristic flick. Her knees were pulled up in front of her beneath the sheet.

"Listen, Chris," she said. "I think I should move in here."

Considering what had happened over the last few weeks, that came as a bit of a surprise. He managed, barely, to suppress his reaction.

"Really?"

She hugged her knees. "Yes. I've been thinking about it

while you were in the kitchen. It would be perfect."

Gently, he placed his coffee mug down on the floor and pulling up the sheet, slipped into the bed beside her. He traced her arm with one finger, barely brushing the fine hairs.

"But you've got your own place."

"Yes, I know. But that doesn't matter. Nobody has to know. We can live here together during the week."

"What about your parents?"

"Hmmm," she said. "They don't have to know."

"How can they not know?"

"Let me worry about that."

He didn't say anything, then. It looked like she'd already made up her mind and he wasn't going to argue with her. Somehow, the previous night, they'd sealed something in the act of making love. He didn't quite understand how, but that was the way it was.

She moved in during the week, keeping on her own place, but only returning to pick up the occasional article of clothing or something else that she needed. One by one, her possessions accumulated in his small space. The other girl at her apartment, Barbara, was sworn to secrecy. Stase had told her to give the one word answer: "Out."

The ground rules had changed. In the beginning there had been no rules. Now there were conditions.

He, he was starting to get hints about what drove Anastasia, what shaped the choices she made.

One day, they were walking back into the apartment. They had been down to the beach to watch the waves. They used to do that a lot—just drive places and then sit, watching. He was heading up the stairs into the apartment, when a baby lizard ran halfway across the third step up and stopped. He paused to look down at it and beckoned her closer.

"Look at this," he said, smiling.

The next instant, her foot came down hard, right on top of it.

His mouth dropped open in horror. He stood and stared at her. "What have you done?"

She returned his look blankly. "What? What's your problem?"

"I can't believe you did that."

She laughed. "Oh come on." She strode up the rest of the stairs and headed down the landing to their apartment, leaving him standing there, staring after her.

He argued with her about it later, without resolution. He didn't speak to her for the rest of the evening and most of the following day.

Something had changed, then and there. He was in love, though; his passion blurred the edges of that memory, insistent that he had to put it away from them. It took a couple of weeks for it to disappear fully, but then it was just another thing suppressed in the back of his consciousness, left to sit and rub up against the other memories you aren't prepared to deal with in your day-to-day life, the memories that you even deny are there. They are there, sharp and spiny, but the barbs are softened behind curtains of mental construction draped carefully by the world at large.

CHAPTER SEVENTEEN

WHEELS WITHIN WHEELS

Chris knew that if he was to have any chance of tracking down where the white van—or the vans; he didn't even know if there was more than one—was taking people, then he had to have transport of his own. Living pretty much in the city, he and Stase had never thought there was a real necessity to own a car. They were close enough into the center of town and public transport was reliably good enough to service all their needs for most of the time. If they needed a car to go somewhere on the weekend, or on vacation, they could always hire one. That was Chris's argument anyway. Besides, there was insurance and parking and the extra expense that owning a vehicle implied. As all their resources had been going into the house, architects, everything else, a car also just seemed like an unnecessary expense at the time. As far as Chris had been concerned, there were other considerations anyway. He knew, deep within, that if they were going to buy something, it couldn't just be anything. It would have to be a certain make, a certain model, something that Stase could be seen in. It was just like the little green sporty number that her parents had bought for her when she was at university. Bought to order. When she'd finally graduated, it no longer suited the image—not old enough to be classic, and too old to be presentable—so she got rid of it.

Of course, he couldn't tell her why he suddenly needed a car. He chose his moment, looking for an appropriate excuse. It was nearing July, and Stase would want an annual vacation, somewhere new, somewhere nice, as she always did; something they could talk about to their friends and her colleagues at work. Usually, they booked something overseas in a luxury hotel for the big annual vacation, but this time, Chris thought he could use it as an excuse to get what he needed.

He waited for an opportunity when they were both settled in front of the television.

"Stase, I think we should go somewhere new this year, try something different. What do you think?"

She looked at him, got a thoughtful expression on her face. "Like what?"

"Well, I think we should go for a touring holiday, drive through the country. Maybe stay at a few nice hotels here and there. It would make a change from what we normally do. Give us a chance to spend some real time together instead of rushing through airports and taxis and hotels and stuff."

She pulled her robe tightly around her. "So, you're suggesting we hire a car or something?"

"No, I thought it was about time we did something else. I think we should buy one. It increases our options. You've said yourself we need to spend more time together. We can go for drives, do stuff like that. Things we used to do. Besides, if we're going to be getting things for the house, this house, or any other house, eventually, it makes it easier, doesn't it? We can drive to places, pick things out, and bring them back if we need to."

She sat forward, eagerness written all over her face. "Really? You're serious?"

He nodded.

She jumped up from the couch and came and knelt in front of him. She reached out and gripped his forearms. "Really, baby? You mean it?"

"Yes. Of course I do."

"Ohhhh." She gave a little shiver. "I've missed driving so much. Oh great. Yes!" She looked up into his face. "Oh baby, you've made me so happy."

"Well, we need to look into it."

She stood and started pacing. "I can do that. I can get hold of some magazines, look at the listings, ask around at work." The words came out all in a rush.

Chris watched her guardedly. "If that's what you want to do ..."

"Yes, yes. Of course. I've got some ideas already." She sat on the couch again, her face glowing as she looked into the middle distance.

It looked like Stase had found something else she could get her teeth into.

Magically, more magazines appeared on the kitchen table and on the coffee table in the lounge. They were auto mart listings, car magazines. Stase did her usual, leaning over them, flicking from page to page and sticking little pieces of paper or paperclips between the pages. She'd look up and make comments like: "I think we should buy something about a year old, if we're going to get something newer. Cars lose their value so quickly that we could probably pick up something decent for a good price. We're probably better off going for a private sale rather than a dealer. It's going to be less expensive that way."

Chris would nod in an accommodating fashion. "So, have you any idea what you might want?"

"Oh yes," she said. "I haven't decided what sort yet, but I want a Merc. A red Merc."

Chris looked at her doubtfully. "Why a Merc?"
"Oh, they just look so good. It's got to be red. I just haven't decided whether we should get a new one or an old one."

"What do you mean an old one?"

She smiled. "An old sports one. You know the sort. A vintage Merc. They're gorgeous."

Chris remembered. Stase had worked with a woman once a few years ago who owned an old white convertible Merc. She'd been in love with that car then—actually she'd been in love with the woman, or at least the image she'd portrayed— and it seemed she was still in love with that particular image, but in her own way. It had to be red.

"Are you sure," he said slowly. "I mean it's not really practical. We've got nowhere to park it for a start. Do you really want to leave a vintage Merc out on the street? What about the insurance? We'd end up paying a fortune for something like that."

"Hmm, maybe you're right, but can we at least look at a couple?"

He agreed, but only to placate her enthusiasm. He believed that he could make the appropriate arguments when the time came. He didn't really want anything as obvious as a bright, shiny red sports car, nor a vintage one at that. What he wanted was a practical car in which he'd not be too obtrusive, but one that would satisfy Stase's need to look good in public. It was going to be a fine line.

The whole process took about two weeks, but they finally compromised and ended up with a top-of-the-range Audi, not brand new, but still top of its line. It was barely acceptable in Stase's eyes, but it was perfect as far as Chris was concerned. They had a bit put away from Stase's last bonus, earmarked for the house, but there wasn't any specific need for it right then, not after the rejection of their planning appeal.

Her reaction to the car was funny. Because it wasn't exactly what Stase had wanted, she didn't drive it. She refused to drive it. She still wanted to go driving, but it was not with her at the wheel. If she wanted to go anywhere, she'd insist that Chris did the driving himself. Though he found it a little strange, that suited him too, because it meant that he'd have the opportunity to get out, alone in the car, with only small excuses needed.

He asked her about it, but all she'd say was that it was really his car, that it had never really been her car. He found that strange too.

Chris tried to find plausible reasons to get out in the car, simple things like filling it up, or claiming he'd forgotten something and needed to do a run to the shops. It was all deliberately designed to get Stase used to him being away in the car. The weekend after they got it, he took them both for a long drive in the country. Twice he saw white vans that reminded him of the one he'd seen in the city and followed them for a while, but they ended up being delivery vans or builders. Stase didn't seem to notice, wrapped in her own perception of the outside world, the CD player blaring with her current music obsession. She paid scant attention to what was going on outside. She only seemed to listen to music in the car—it was part of the whole package—and seemed to be quite content just to be in the car, moving along, regardless of where they were headed. One of her favorites was the theme music from a gangster series that had been recently run on TV. He liked the stuff too. They had a good soundtrack, but there were limits. She played it over and over again and it became their driving music.

There was something working inside Chris's head about all of it, about her reaction to the car, about her reaction to the outside, but he couldn't quite pin down what it was that was disturbing him.

When they got home, he made a suggestion. Things between them seemed okay at the moment. The car had done something to smooth the apparent tension that lay there dividing their lives from each other.

As they climbed the front stairs, he asked her. "Why don't you take the car out tomorrow for a drive?"

As he pushed the key into the lock and opened the door, she shook her head. "No."

"Why not? You told me how much you miss driving."

"But it's not the same. I told you. It's really your car. It's just not the same."

He filed that away. It was almost as if she'd lost confidence. He didn't dwell on it though; he had his own plans about what he was going to do with the car and now he was nearly in a position to be able to follow them.

CHAPTER EIGHTEEN

ALLIANCE

There was a couple, originally from Stase's work-based social circle, with whom Chris and Anastasia maintained a fairly friendly relationship. There were dinners and cinema excursions, and the occasional theatre outing. In many ways Jason and Claudia were not that different from Anastasia and Chris. They kept pretty much to themselves and had a narrow circle of friends. Jason worked for one of the major brokerage firms at a fairly senior level, Vice-President or something, and Stase met Claudia through work. Claudia was Austrian, a heavier-set girl with long blonde hair. She was opinionated and brusque, always speaking her mind and not really giving a thought about what the consequences might be. She was apparently damned good at what she did at work, so even though she was seen as a bit of a star by management, she wasn't particularly popular among her colleagues. Stase, on the other hand, was unpopular for other reasons. She threatened the other women in her workplace. Her attitude, her hunger, her image as a focused, hard-nosed bitch totally dedicated to success did nothing to win friends and influence people among her female colleagues. She used to laugh that the males at her work simply lived in fear. Chris was convinced that in a way, women were a lot more competitive than men, and that was just another example of it. The history of women's roles in the workplace probably had a lot to do with it. Over the years, they'd had to compete a lot harder and though Chris understood it, he didn't really relate to it.

It may have been that Claudia and Stase recognized something in each other, but they naturally fell in together. Claudia eventually moved on to another firm, chasing opportunity, but they remained friends despite the fact that Claudia had the apparent gall to tell Stase exactly what she thought about some of the things she did.

Jason came from a background of money, and was just the sort of person that Stase liked to cultivate. She did well enough, her background was of a level, but always she seemed to want more. It was just like the house. An icon she could hold out to the world. As much for that reason as any other, Claudia and Jason became the perfect addition to Stase's social circle.

When Chris first met them, it was out to an introductory dinner at an upscale restaurant that was starting to build a reputation for itself in the city. The food was superb and indulgent and the wine flowed freely. Jason and Chris hit it off straight away. He was a stocky guy with a broad, jolly face and a wickedly wry sense of humor that Chris appreciated immediately. All through the dinner, they were passing little pointed one-liners between themselves while the girls were talking about this or that person they both knew but who meant nothing to either of the boys. Most of the traded one-liners seemed to go right over the heads of the women, or else they simply weren't interested in what the pair of them had to say.

Jason, having made a lot of money through bonuses and shrewd investments to go with the money he'd inherited from his family, had bought a couple of blocks of apartments and simply decided to retire. He hadn't even passed his thirties. Meanwhile, Claudia continued to bring in a good income.

This was the sort of existence Stase aspired to, but despite everything, Jason seemed totally unaffected by it. Perhaps it was a luxury of being in that position in the first place. He no longer had to try to maintain a particular lifestyle, so there was no reason to make a big deal of it. Claudia and Jason lived in a reasonably modest house in the suburbs, compared to their means. Claudia went off to work, and Jason stayed at home, researching things that interested him. From time to time, he'd disappear for weeks at a time on some trek or other, like the Galapagos or Mongolia or Easter Island, things that had taken his fancy. It was as if he just wanted to see and experience everything he could in life, just because he could.

One afternoon, when they had had a few drinks, Chris asked him what he was hoping to do with all that stuff. Jason had just looked at him from beneath the thick eyebrows and chuckled.

"Oh I don't know. Maybe something one day. Maybe I'll write a book one day. Who knows? I just like doing it. Why's it important?"

Chris looked thoughtfully into his drink, thinking about the question. Finally, he looked up.

"I don't know. I guess ... well, with all that stuff. No, I don't know. I guess I've always thought that we need to make a difference some way. I know that might sound idealistic or naïve, but we have to be here for some reason, right?"

Jason looked across at him, considering. "I'm not sure. I don't know whether I believe that. I mean why should there be any purpose? As far as I'm concerned, we're just here and while we're here, we may as well make the most of it."

"Hmmm. We're getting a little deep, aren't we?" said Chris.

Jason chuckled again. "Here, let me get you another refill."

That had been the end of that particular conversation; for some reason, it had stuck with Chris, lingered with him sometimes when he was in a reflective mood, thinking about life and where he was going with it. Was there any point to it all? He wondered if everything that was happening to him was in some way related.

Chris was still concerned though about his own perception of what had happened over the past few weeks. He'd seen the films and read some stuff about schizophrenia; he was a little worried that he might be becoming delusional. If it hadn't have been for the brief conversations with Patrick—even though he wasn't entirely sure about that either—and the snatches of memory that kept floating up in his head, he would have doubted even more. The repeat performance with the businessman from the doorway and the girl from the bus-shelter added weight to his belief that he wasn't in fact going mad. He tested the thought, probing it from as many directions as possible. No, he didn't believe he was mad or that he was imagining things. The older woman at the bus stop in town was more evidence. Still, he needed some sort of confirmation and he knew he wasn't going to get it from Stase. The tenuous link between them was too fragile to test with that particular set of theories. He wasn't going to get it from going out and finding more of the apparently afflicted either. He could be just as possibly imagining that as well.

He debated the prospect, but it didn't take long. After due consideration, he decided that Jason was open enough to listen to what he said and not judge him too harshly. He headed for the phone and gave him a call.

"Jason, hey. You busy?"

"Ah, my man. Not particularly. What's up?"

Chris thought for a moment before answering. "Hmm, listen, I've got a couple of things I want to talk about. You free for a coffee?"

"Um, sure. What's it about?"

"I'd rather talk to you about in person."

Jason chuckled. "All very mysterious. All right. I'm in the middle of something at the moment—you know, the renovations—but I'll be okay in about an hour. Yeah. It's been a while since we've really had a chance to talk. You know the coffee shop down the hill from my place? How's that?"

"Yeah, good."

Chris slowly put down the phone. He was committed now. He found it strangely ironic that Jason was doing renovations. Chris had the car now, so instead of having to rely on public transport, there'd be no problem getting there. Stase was out meeting a couple of her friends, so there was no explaining to do either.

He left himself enough time and then drove to the place, parking in a side street. The coffee shop was a local outfit, not one of the chains, with a dark blue painted exterior and broad windows looking out onto a pedestrianized section of the local shopping area. Inside were simple dark wooden tables and chairs covered with plain patterned tablecloths. Jason was already there, sitting at a table by the window sipping at a large mug of coffee, wearing the big chunky sweater that he seemed to prefer. He'd placed his silver-gray helmet on the seat beside him. Chris had a quick look around, but couldn't see the scooter anywhere. He nodded to Jason as he passed the window and opened the door. A bell rang as he stepped in through the door, a quaint and slightly anachronous touch. A girl, black tee and white apron, appeared from the back at the sound of the bell and stood smiling behind the counter. Chris gave her a brief smile in return and a quick nod before crossing to Jason's table to say hello before making his order.

"How you doing?" he said.

Jason put down his coffee cup. "Yeah, good."

"You all right there?" Chris said, pointing at Jason's cup. Jason nodded.

"Okay, just let me get a coffee," said Chris. While he headed over and ordered, Jason turned back to watch the outside. Chris ferried his coffee back and sat opposite.

"So ..." said Jason.

"Yeah, well," said Chris, not really knowing where to start. Jason looked at him quizzically, waiting.

Chris scratched at the back of his head and grimaced before beginning. "Um, thanks for coming," he said. He was having difficulty meeting Jason's eyes, on the verge of having second thoughts about telling him anything, but he'd come this far, so he thought he might as well take the bull by the horns.

"Listen, Jason, I want to talk to you about some stuff. Do me a favor and hear me out, and then you can ask what you want. I've had some really weird shit going on and I needed to talk to someone about it, just to make sure that I wasn't losing it."

"Okaaay," said Jason. "What is this? Something with Stase?"

"No, not really. Yeah, well, sort of. I don't know. It has to do with Stase and it has to do with me, with both of us, but it's more than that."

Jason lifted his eyebrows and took a sip of his coffee. Chris took his spoon and thoughtfully stirred his own. He took a steadying breath and then he began. Briefly, he recounted the incident with the girl at the bus shelter, the encounter with Patrick, the businessman on the street, the woman at the bus stop. He told him about the van and the night that he and Stase had argued. He told him about the middle-aged woman and the cab and trying to follow the van. He recounted his fears about his memories and the fog that seemed to slip over everything when he started really thinking about the things that had happened. And finally, he told him about the black bird. Jason listened to it all impassively, occasionally lifting his coffee and sipping while he listened, watching him over the rim of his mug.

Chris's rush of words trickled to a stop. "And that's about it," he said.

Jason sat back and blinked a couple of times.

"Okay," said Chris. "You can tell me I'm fucking crazy, but that's really not what I want to hear right now."

Jason shook his head slowly, and then grinned. "Now, would I do that?"

Chris sighed with relief. "I thought you were going to get some sort of weird look on your face and make some excuse to get the hell out of here as fast as possible."

Jason chuckled again. "Hadn't you better drink your coffee? It's getting cold."

"Yeah, yeah," said Chris. He lifted his cup, watching Jason for some sort of reaction.

"Hang on," said his friend. "I need to get another coffee. Maybe I should get one for you too."

Chris nodded. Jason stood and headed over to the counter, looking a little like a bear in his big sweater. He carried back the two coffees and sat down, shaking a little sugar packet, tearing the corner and pouring half of it into his cup before picking up his spoon and stirring.

"So," he said finally. "Of course I should tell you you've lost your mind, but I'm a little more open-minded than that. You know me, Chris; I like to investigate things, like to find stuff out. Now, whatever you've got going on, I'm intrigued." He lifted his hands. "Even if I accept only half of what you've told me, I truly am interested." He placed his hands flat on the table. "Jesus, even if you're projecting something from some weird shit going on in your head, that's got to be worth taking a look at." He grinned. "I already know you're a sick man."

Chris smiled in spite of himself. Jason was right; he always liked getting absorbed in twisting paths of his little investigations. "Okay, I've got an idea about what we need to do, but I want to keep it quiet from the girls," Chris said.

"Sure. So, tell me what you've got. Hit me."

"Well, next week I'm going to take another day off. Most of what I've seen has occurred in the city. Of course it could be happening in other places, probably is, but I think starting where I know this stuff is happening will be best. I need you to come with me. I'll drive over, pick you up, and then we can head in to town. It might mean driving around for most of the day, but you never know. If it doesn't work, we'll spend another day."

"Yeah," said Jason. "I'm up for it. And trust me, Claudia won't know a thing."

Chris felt like a huge weight had just been lifted from his shoulders. He gave a little half smile and lifted his coffee.

CHAPTER NINETEEN

LIFE HAS A WAY OF STICKING IN YOUR THROAT

The planning thing came and went, seeming to pass into a place where Stase was able to put it away from her. They'd been denied. Okay, there was the appeal to deal with—and they were going to appeal—but their life seemed as though it had returned to something reminiscent of what it was before. Chris was a little confused by that. There should have been lingering tension between them, but it almost seemed to have gone away, trickled away to insignificance. They still had arguments about the whole thing, but in comparison to the previous ones these were mild, healthy and impassioned discussions of what the next steps were and what they needed to do. For some reason, the cold, stark chill that had huddled between them had been warmed by her need to push forward. If she could deliver the perfect house, everything would be all right, and as a result, everything between them would be all right.

In the meantime, the neighbor who had put in the original objection became the enemy. Stase, with her back-yard vigils had focused her aggression on the house next door. Everything between Chris and Stase was not exactly rosy—there wasn't the passion that their relationship had once had and she was still a little distant in that regard. They barely made love any more, and when they did it was as though it was automatic, programmed, something they were supposed to do—but the naked hostility had dwindled or at least refocused.

She was still concentrating on the house, on putting in the appeal and winning whatever the cost, but where Chris had previously in some way been the enemy because he didn't quite understand her driven needs, now he was ally, confidante, someone she could rely on for support to achieve her ultimate goals.

The magazines, the renovation programs, the evening conversations with Michael the builder, all continued, but there was a new positive undercurrent to everything she was doing. That was, if he made the effort of will to ignore the continuing sessions late at night in the backyard, with her staring up at those blank windows of the house next door.

Stase had a weekly appointment at one of those trendy natural therapy day spas, a small luxury in the austerity of their hollow shell existence. She'd head off, get a facial, a massage and whatever else went on in the secret female sanctum that Chris had no real desire to understand or investigate. One day she came back, and instead of the newly relaxed demeanor she normally sported on her return, she looked troubled.

She was quiet for most of the evening and then later, just before they retired, she showered, changed and appeared in the white toweling robe she often wore.

"Chris, can you come over here for a minute?"

"Sure," he said and moved to join her.

"Will you look at my neck?" She tilted her head back, arching her neck so he could see.

Chris shook his head. "What am I supposed to see?"

She stroked the skin at the base of her neck. "Here. Do you see something unusual?"

He leaned in closer. "Um, I don't know. What am I supposed to be looking at?"

"You don't see anything?"

Chris shook his head. The light wasn't great and he wasn't sure what he was meant to be seeing. Stase walked over to the mirror and tilted her head one way then the other, probing at her throat with the ends of her fingers. She beckoned him over. "See, here."

"Tell me what I'm looking for."

"Does that look swollen to you?"

"Hmm, I suppose. A little. Why?"

"Oh, it was just something the girl said while I was getting my massage. It doesn't matter."

She said nothing more about it until two days later. Chris came back that night to see her looking even more drawn than she had over the past few weeks.

"I want you to sit down," she said, as soon as he came through the door.

"What is it, Stase?"

"I went to the doctor's today. He thinks I may have cancer. He's given me a referral to a specialist. I have to have some tests."

Cancer? But how was that possible? Stase was young. Young people didn't get cancer.

"What do you mean? I don't understand," he said.

She laughed. "I always knew I'd get cancer. Two of my uncles died from it. I had three aunts die from it. My mother had cancer. What are the odds, hey?" She laughed again. It was a short, hollow laugh.

Chris stood and walked over to the couch, his mind reeling. He went down on his knees and took her hand. "You're serious, aren't you?"

She looked down at him and her eyes welled with tears. She nodded slowly.

He moved up to join her on the couch. "It's not certain though, is it? I mean, you have to have tests. You don't know anything yet."

"I know," she said quietly.

"Jesus, Stase," he said. "Jesus."

If she was totally convinced that she had the dread disease, he felt that there was no real possibility that she wouldn't. People can convince themselves to get sick. Sometimes, that's like a kind of enforced life redundancy. He remembered his grandfather, who, after retiring from his country-town accounting practice, had developed cancer within eighteen months. He just had nothing left to do, and within two years, he had died. Stase's statement that she always knew was troubling. Perhaps she had always known.

"Shouldn't you tell your parents?"

Her gaze flashed briefly, then she shook her head. "I can't do that. My mother would freak."

Chris nodded. "Okay. When are you seeing the specialist?" he said.

"I have to go in on Tuesday. The doctor said we shouldn't waste time. It's the leading cancer hospital around and the guy I have to see is one of the best oncologists there is, or so he says. Of course he could have just been saying that to make me feel better."

"I doubt that," he said and stroked the back of her hand. "Jesus, Stase."

She was threatening to cry, but she never quite did. Chris chewed at his lip, not really sure what he was supposed to say. He could make as many reassuring noises as he could come up with, but that was going to do little to alleviate the problem or the way she must be feeling. They'd just have to wait.

✦ ✦ ✦

The next week came and went. Stase went in for her appointment with the oncologist and Chris tagged along. The doctor looked, had tests done, confirmed the suspicion and booked her in for exploratory surgery at the start of the following week. They took a biopsy and the results came back.

Chris and Stase went back in to see him to get the results. The doctor was late and they spent forty-five minutes in the waiting room, nervous and on edge. There were roughly fifteen other people in the waiting room, women, men, children, old and young. Chris looked around at the faces, the different people, feeling awkward and out of place. He couldn't meet any of their eyes. This was cancer. This was the stuff you didn't talk about. He watched them surreptitiously, wondering what it was that singled you out to be one of the file of people who came here. They said cancer was the modern disease, but how did they know? Was cancer always there, just under different guises? He'd remembered seeing old woodcut engravings of people with goiters, so at least that form had been around for a while. The image had been so bizarre that it had stuck with him. He'd done his own research, despite the fact that Stase had not wanted to know. As far as he could see, there was nothing to distinguish any of the people sitting around the ranks of chairs, flipping through magazines, occasionally heading to the coffee machine. There were no visible signs that he could tell showing that the disease worked within any of these people. That was the thing about cancer, wasn't it? It worked away inside, silent, unseen.

After the minutes stretched on to almost an hour after their appointment time, they were called into the inner sanctum. The doctor was very solemn when they went back in to see him. Chris wasn't filled with confidence. The doctor had grizzled unkempt hair and a strangely vague look in his eyes. It was as if the things he had to deal with every day had placed a distance between him and the rest of the world.

"The tests have come back," he told Stase. He didn't look at Chris. "I can confirm that you have cancer of the thyroid. Now, generally that strikes women in your age group, and it is treatable, and normally the prognosis is positive."

"But what does that mean?" said Stase.

The doctor fixed her with a steady gaze, the apparent vagueness suddenly gone. "We're going to have to operate to remove the growth. It's lucky that we caught it as early as we did. If we don't operate, the cancer will spread and take over your whole body. You're lucky. You're young and we caught it in time. Of course, the operation will necessitate removal of the cancerous area of the thyroid, and until we operate, we won't know how much of the gland is affected. It may be half, it may be all."

"And what happens then?"

"Well, assuming the operation is successful and we don't have to go in again, you will have to have regular tests, and depending upon how much of the gland we have to remove, you'll be required to take medication to balance your system from then on."

Stase frowned. "What do you mean, medication?" She hated pills of any sort and had problems swallowing them at the best of times. She would physically gag as she tried to force the pills down, with or without the requisite glass of water.

The doctor held her gaze. "The thyroid is responsible for producing a chemical secretion that helps to balance the way your body functions. Without the medication, your body would be out of balance. Eventually it would harm you greatly. Depending what happens with our operation, as I say, we may have to try for a little while to balance the dosage until we get it just right, but we won't know any of that until we've done the surgery."

Stase's hand fluttered to her neck. "Will you be performing the operation?"

"No. That will be up to the surgeon. He's one of the best. He specializes in this sort of procedure."

"And do I get to meet him?" she asked.

"You'll meet him on the day of the operation."

Chris and she were very quiet on the way home. There wasn't a lot to say. Their healthcare covered the procedure and the appointment had already been made. Stase would go in to have her throat cut open in eight days time. In the meantime, there was little else to do but worry.

That evening, Chris cooked them a simple meal. They ate in silence.

Afterwards, as he cleared away the dishes, he tried to bolster her. "The guy seemed fairly positive. It was almost as if this was routine for them. Do you want me to look up some information for you on the web?"

Stase shook her head. "No, I'd rather not know."

"It'll be okay, Stase," he said, pausing in the doorway.

"You don't understand," she said, eyes shining damply again. "It's my throat. I love my throat. It's one of my best features." She was quiet for a moment. "I guess I'll just have to get some scarves and chokers." She gave that short hollow laugh again. "Start a new fashion trend. This is real cancer chic."

Chris bit his lip and headed for the kitchen, carrying the plates through the darkened hallway. As he stacked them away in the dishwasher, he shook his head. How would he be reacting in the same situation, if he was the one who had cancer? He really didn't know. He couldn't even imagine it.

At the appointed time, he helped her pack a few clothes, toiletries and things, and headed for the hospital. Stase had not eaten the previous evening on doctor's orders and she was tired and irritable. She hadn't slept well. They stopped on the way in and bought a stack of magazines.

The hospital room was quiet, private; together, they put her things away. Stase changed and climbed into the bed. A nurse came in and told them that Mr. Walters would be in soon to see them. Stase dragged a magazine from the stack by the bed and started flicking through it, while Chris sat mute beside her, holding her hand. He hated hospitals, didn't really like doctors, and he felt uncomfortable sitting there in silence with the disinfectant smells washing over him. Even though he felt ill at ease, he knew he had to be there. This wasn't about him. It was about them, together, about Chris supporting her.

The surgeon, Mr. Walters, breezed into the room about twenty minutes later. He was a big, good-looking man, with square face and curly light-brown hair. He wore a pale blue shirt under his white coat. He walked quickly up to the side of the bed.

"Well, hello. This is our patient is it? Anastasia Baron, am I right?" He looked around, spied a chair and pulled it over to the side of the bed before sitting on its edge.

Stase nodded.

"Okay, good," he said, his face all smiles. "Well, I'm going to be doing your operation, Anastasia. I'm Dr. Walters. You can call me Nigel. And is it Anastasia? Or is there something else you'd like me to call you?"

Stase swallowed. "You can call me Stase."

"Stase it is then." He flashed her another smile. "Now, Stase, I don't want you to be nervous. I've done thousands of these procedures. It's really not a big deal. In over 90% of the operations, the whole procedure is a success."

Stase nodded slowly.

He leaned forward, resting his elbows on his knees and

clasping his hands in front of him. He looked briefly over at Chris, gave him a brief smile and then turned back to Stase. "So, is there anything you want to know?"

She lifted her hand to her throat, touching it gently with the tips of her fingers. "What about my throat?" she said. "Is it going to be bad? Is it going to be a big scar?"

He smiled again. "Now, Stase, surgical technique has improved over the years. Of course there'll be a scar, but ..." Stase moved her hand out of the way, and he reached over and traced a line on her neck with one finger. "We will try and keep the incision in a place that follows one of the natural lines on your neck. That way it will be hidden. As the scar fades, it will just fall naturally into that line. You'll hardly know it's there eventually." He sat back down.

Stase didn't look convinced. She touched her throat tentatively. "You're sure?"

He laughed. "Yes, of course I'm sure. We don't live in the Dark Ages any longer." He turned to Chris.

"And you ...?"

"Chris."

"So, Chris, do you have any questions?"

Chris shook his head.

"Okay, then," said Dr. Walters. "I'll see you in a couple of hours, Stase," he said standing. He reached over and squeezed her hand.

And then he was gone.

Chris waited around for about another hour, while Stase flicked through magazines and occasionally reached up to touch her throat. When it was finally time for Chris to leave, he felt awkward, uncomfortable. He reached over and took her hand.

"You'll be fine, Stase," he said.

She just looked straight back at him, expressionless.

✢ ✢ ✢

He came back the next morning, a bunch of flowers carried before him, almost like a sacred totem to wards of the medical smells and the reality of what was happening, what this place was all about. He walked up the shiny, clinical corridors, listening to the hospital noises echoing around him. The floor was dark gray, buffed to an unnatural shine. The tall walls were white, but it was off-white, tinged with a gray that matched the floor. The whole place was washed with an aura of depression. It was a place full of the sick, the dying, the dead, and it did nothing to hide that reality from those who walked within its walls.

A man came up the corridor pushing a drip stand beside him, bundled in a big, dark-red woolen gown. Chris walked past him, avoiding making eye contact.

He made it up to Stase's room and nervously poked his head around the door. She was lying in bed, a pink nightgown open at the front, her hair in disarray. Thick, cream bandages concealed her throat, a darkened red stain at one side. He frowned and swallowed. Twin clear tubes ran from beneath the bandage to a stand with a pair of bottles on the floor next to the bed. Only the tubes weren't quite clear, a thin trail of dark blood ran down the inside of one of the tubes, down to one of the bottles, which was about a third full of dark liquid. He swallowed again. On the other side of the bed, another tube ran from the back of her hand up to a drip.

"Hey, baby," he said quietly as he stepped hesitantly into the room.

Her eyes slowly opened and she looked over at him and gave a weak smile. "Hey," she said and frowned, giving a short half cough and a frown.

"I brought you these," he said unnecessarily. In that stark clinical environment, with the tubes and the bottles and everything else, he didn't know what else to say.

She looked over at him, gave him a weak half smile, but there was something else in her eyes, something cold and distant, almost accusing.

CHAPTER TWENTY

GOING THE DISTANCE

They had no real idea whether the operation had been a success or not. Dr. Walters, Nigel, had said he was pretty confident that they'd gotten the whole thing. When he broke it down, what that really meant was they'd removed Stase's thyroid completely. She'd have to take thyroxin tablets for the rest of her life, but that was a small price to pay considering the alternative. They, the oncologist and the surgeon, still weren't sure that the alternative was not going to happen. Stase and Chris didn't really want to think about that.

For the next week or so, Chris treated Stase with kid gloves, all thoughts of anything else gone from his present focus. The entire world had narrowed into one tiny reality. Despite the claim that they'd gotten it all, the treatment was not over. Stase had to go in a week later for a comprehensive nuking. They were going to put her in a lead-lined room and dose her body with radiation to make sure they had the last of the cancer excised from her body. Chris had always been slightly bemused by the fact that they used radiation to cure cancer, radiation which gave people cancer in the first place, but he had no illusions about the fact that he didn't really know enough. He was no medical expert.

The treatment was scheduled to take place at another hospital several miles away, and Stase was going to be in there for a week. During that time, she would be off her medication and not allowed to have direct contact with anyone. His visits would be limited. He accompanied her down to yet another hospital, yet another set of corridors with drab walls, shiny floors and antiseptic smells, people wandering the corridors with thick robes, shuffling along wheeling drip stands beside them. Stase's room was in a side corridor, set away from the rest of the hospital. He saw her in, looking out through the window onto a featureless parking lot and the flat gray roof of another floor. All sorts of machinery were set into the room's ceiling; the nurse explained that it was monitoring equipment, meant to test the radiation levels. The room's walls were a pale blue-gray and the door was thick, split in two with a top section and a lower thicker part. The bottom was apparently lead-lined, designed so that people could sit and talk to Stase with no risk while she was still invisibly glowing.

"Hrmmm. Good idea that," said Chris. "There are certain things you like to protect."

Stase gave him a nervous half-smile, not really appreciating the humor right at that moment.

He left her in the care of the nurses assigned to that wing and headed back for home, feeling useless. All there was to think about was what was happening with Stase. The doctors had said they couldn't be sure she was out of the woods yet, wouldn't be for weeks and all they could do was wait and hope. He was allowed to visit her only after two days had passed, after the radiation levels had dropped to a point where she could be around people at a distance.

He found the corridor, walked up to the doorway. The bottom half of the door was closed and there was a simple metal chair sitting just outside it. He dropped a pile of magazines on the flat ledge on top of the bottom door and sat in the chair.

"Hi, Stase," he said. "I've brought you these. How are you doing?"

She sat up on the edge of the bed and looked at him with a brief frown, as if she didn't quite know who he was. "Yeah," she said. "Yeah, thanks."

"So, how are you doing?"

She shook her head, stood, padded over to the window and looked out. "I'm bored. God, I'm bored."

"Well maybe the magazines will help."

She turned from the window. "Magazines? What magazines?"

"These," he said, pointing at the stack. "I brought them for you."

"Oh yeah," she said. "Thanks." She turned to look back outside into the nothing of the parking lot.

He wanted desperately to go in there, to walk up to her and hold her shoulders and look into her eyes, but he was stuck out there on the other side of a lead barrier. He wasn't allowed to get anywhere near her.

She turned and looked at him vaguely. "How long have you been here?" she said.

Chris frowned. "I've just gotten here Stase. I've been here about five minutes."

"There was something ..." she said. "Something I wanted to ..." She lifted one hand to her bandaged throat. "How are the plans? Has the architect come?"

"Stase, we're not thinking about that now, baby. There are more important things to worry about."

"Hmmm? Oh yeah?"

"Have they got you on painkillers?" he asked her.

She shook her head. "No, not allowed any medication. No pills. Just the stuff when I first came here."

A nurse came down the corridor. "You need to be going soon," she told him, looking at her watch. "Her radiation count is still pretty high."

Chris nodded. "Is that right? Is she not on any medication?"

"Only the radiation treatment," the nurse said.

"Okay," he said. "Stase?"

She turned to look over at him. Again, her expression seemed glazed.

"I have to go now. I'll see you the day after tomorrow, okay?"

"Hmmm? Sure." She turned back to the window.

Chris pushed back the chair, stood and headed back down the corridor under the nurse's watchful gaze. Seeing Stase like that had troubled him. The doctors had told them that they may need to regulate her dosage, but if what he'd seen was any indication of the consequences of getting it wrong ... what if she simply forgot to take it?

No, he had to assume that the medical people knew what they were doing. And in the meantime, he had to wait for the radiation levels to subside enough so that she could go out in public safely. There was a complete leaflet warning about public transport, about getting close to people and the risks involved. The nurse had handed it to him as he'd departed and he'd been reading it on the way out of the hospital. He shoved it deep inside his inner pocket with a sigh.

If anything, Chris's next visit to the radiation ward was worse. Stase seemed even more distracted and vague than she had on his previous visit. He tucked the thought away, concerned, but not wanting to inflict any of his concern upon her. She had enough to deal with. The end of her irradiation came, and he filled her prescription at the hospital pharmacy before taking her home in the back of a cab in a long silent ride while Stase watched the world outside, saying nothing. Thoughts of her radiation levels kept scuttling through his head. When he got her home, he set her up on the couch in the lounge with blankets, magazines and the television, stuff to keep her occupied, though she didn't seem to be very interested in anything.

Over the next few days, her mood gradually improved and she seemed to regain some interest in what was going on around her. He could understand a little; it must be a strange thing to believe you might die, because there, in her head, that's where she'd been. It wasn't surprising that she was withdrawn. Chris himself had tasted the possibility, run it over and over in his head, wondering what the hell he was going to do if they didn't fix her, if she went through a slow decline and he was forced to care for her through that transition until she finally went away for good. He didn't know how he'd cope, or even if he would have coped.

About a week after she came home, she seemed ready to face the world again. She was taking her medication and seemed to have lost her previous vagueness. The stitches were out, but it was strange seeing her with that dark circular slash at the base of her throat, white at the edges and slightly frayed on one end. She had rooted around in drawers, pulling out a collection of scarves and trying them one by one, only half-satisfied with what she'd found. Despite the assurances from the surgeon, the marks of his work were plainly visible. A couple of days later, she returned to work, business suit and scarf in place. Chris saw her off, his concern trailing after her as she headed down the street. Later that night, she broached the subject of the house again for the first time.

"Chris," she said as they sat in front of the flickering television, eating from plates held in their laps. "Where are we with the appeal?"

"Well, we have the forms. Things just sort of got in the way."

"Hmmm. Well we can't afford to hang around any longer. We have to get the whole process moving again."

"Last thing we spoke about," said Chris, a little off balance with the sudden change of pace, "was that we needed to get supportive evidence. I don't think the process we went through before was right. Maybe we should have talked to the neighbors some more."

It seemed to Chris that Stase had decided that she had been through whatever she'd been through and it was time to get back to normal life, if it could be called normal. It might have just been displacement activity on her part. He suspected that was really the way things stood. If she could get her teeth into something properly, it would take her away from the memory of the disease that walked around with her like that tender, half-healed badge on her throat.

"I don't agree," she said. "Why should we talk to them? No way I'm going to give that bitch the satisfaction."

"Don't you think you should take it a little easy for a while, Stase?"

"What's the point of that?" Her response was short, clipped. "We've wasted too much time already."

"Okay, if that's what you want ..."

She set her plate down on the coffee table and gave him a hard look. "Yes, it is what I want."

Chris realized he'd been put on notice. The game was afoot again and they were going to play it to Stase's rules.

"Okay," he said, lifting a placating hand. "We'll look at it on Saturday and make some plans."

She picked up her plate again and started eating, watching the television. End of conversation. The TV noise was the only thing to fill the gap.

Chris watched her for a while. Suddenly he felt as if he was to blame for everything that had happened, as if Stase resented the set of circumstances that life had dealt her and Chris himself was the root cause of all of them. She looked up and caught him watching, but simply turned back to watch the television with a little shake of her head.

✦ ✦ ✦

On Saturday morning, they pulled out the plans, the paperwork from the planning authority, and the copies of the letters and spread them out on the kitchen table. Chris inwardly suppressed the sigh that he felt rising within him. It was back to the same old thing, back to the folly and the grandiose schemes. He was starting to wish that the whole thing would simply go away. Stase, poring over the neatly arranged document, moving from one to the other, cross-referencing, sitting back and nodding, was focused, but quite often her scrutiny was punctuated with a frown.

"I don't remember that," she'd say.

"What?" Chris would say, leaning in, wanting to be helpful, but she waved him away, apparently determined to solve it herself.

That was not the only evidence Chris saw pointing to something not quite right with her memory. Daily, he noted little things, things that she forgot, conversations she couldn't remember having. It was starting to become a concern. The whole planning thing was something that was keeping her occupied, her dedicated obsession the same as it had ever been, but Chris was starting to suspect that there was something else going on. There were echoes of the way she'd reacted when she'd been down in the hospital's radiation ward, but he thought that enough time had passed for all that to no longer be an issue. He decided he had no option but to confront her about it. He waited till late on Sunday to broach the subject.

They'd just come in from the backyard, still overgrown, still a mess, not yet bearing the holes and piles of weeds where Chris was to make a start on the garden, where Stase had cast a few suspicious glances in the direction of the neighbor's house, but not with quite the same intensity that she'd shown before.

They were standing in the back hallway, Stase closing the backdoor when he touched her shoulder.

"Stase, are you feeling all right?" he asked.

"What do you mean?" Her brow was creased.

"Well ..." How could he put it? "I'm a bit worried about you. You seem to be forgetting things. I've noticed lately, you sometimes don't seem to remember things that happened only a short time before."

Her mouth took on a sour downturn. "What are you saying, Chris?"

He took a breath and bit his lip. "I think maybe you should check your medication. I'm not convinced that they've got the dosage right."

She flew at him, pushing right up close, putting her face right up next to his. "And since when have you been a doctor? What the fuck would you know, Chris? Hey? What the fuck would you know?"

He stepped back from her sudden pale-faced ire. "I'm just saying, Stase. I'm worried about you. Don't you remember what it was like down at the hospital when you weren't taking anything at all? Don't you remember that? You barely knew who I was or what you were doing. If the stuff can affect you that much, don't you think you should look at it?"

"You think I don't know what this is?" she said, turning away.

He leaned back against the wall with a sigh. "What is it, Stase?"

She whirled. "You're trying to undermine me. That's what it is. Trying to make me think I don't know what I'm doing. There's nothing wrong with me. I know precisely what I'm doing, and if you think you can control me by making me question what I'm doing, then you've got another thing coming. It's not going to work."

Chris's closed his jaw and lifted both hands in front of him. "Listen to what you're saying. It doesn't make any sense."

She laughed. "Oh yes. Of course it doesn't. I'm not thinking straight, am I? Of course you're going to say that.

Well you can just shut up. I'm not going to listen to this shit any more and I'm not going to play your little power games."

She pushed passed him, stalked up the corridor and pounded upstairs.

Chris stood for a few moments, still rocked by her reaction. Licking his lips, he followed. The bathroom door was closed.

"Stase, are you in there?"

"Go away," she said. "I don't want to talk to you."

He tried the door, but it was locked.

"Just go away. Leave me alone."

Chris slowly withdrew his hand and headed reluctantly back downstairs. He stood at the backdoor for a long time, looking out into the garden. He'd tried. She was due a check-up in about four weeks, but in the meantime ...

He didn't really understand where all this stuff about power games had come from. He didn't force her. He didn't push his points too hard. He was the more passive one in their interactions most of the time. If he didn't agree with something he found it easier just not to say anything. Sure, he tried to steer her in more sensible directions, or so he thought, but more, he just wanted her to get on with it when he saw that whatever he thought was not going to change her mind—and that happened more often than not. In some ways, he had learned just to shut up and take it.

He sighed and headed back inside, resigning himself to waiting until she decided to emerge of her own accord. There was just nothing he could reasonably do to force it.

CHAPTER TWENTY-ONE

APPEALING

They spent the next few days filling in the paperwork. Michael came round and suggested that they seek independent advice to help with the process at the local authority. The plans and details filled Stase's head once more, and her focus refined, narrowed and the appeal became virtually her sole topic of conversation. The words swept over Chris, battering him with the constant repetition, the same questions over and over again. Sometimes, he just felt like screaming: "Enough. Do we have to talk about this again?" He held his tongue. In a way, it was as if he felt culpable for the whole cancer thing, that her accusatory glance in the hospital had squarely apportioned the blame on his shoulders for everything the world had conspired to do to Stase. This was what she wanted, so this was what she'd get.

Looking ahead, he could see more plans, builders, dust, architects and more invasions into the little world that hung together in a fragile net around him. Secretly, he started to hope that their appeal would be rejected, not that he'd ever dare voice it. Stase would get over it and start to look at the whole thing sensibly. They'd do up the house as it was, maybe make some more modest alterations and then sell it and reap the benefit. Those thoughts came often while he watched her making her plans.

Stase asked around, and they found an independent town planner and asked him over for a consultation. Peter

173

McNally turned up in long hair, old army pants and checked shirt—not what Chris had expected at all. He brought a stack of papers with him and a pad and pencil on which he took notes as they went through all the existing paperwork.

"Yes," he said, finally. "I think you've got a good chance. The local authority inspector they sent, well, he shouldn't have said what he did. That puts them at fault immediately. You might want to consider some other options though."

"Like what?" Stase asked.

"Well, you might want to put together some lesser plans. Something not quite as contentious. Then we can use those as a bargaining point."

Inwardly, Chris sighed with relief. Stase shook her head. "No way." Her jaw was set.

"You have to consider the possibility," said Peter.

Stase shook her head again. "No chance. It's this or nothing."

Chris's inner sigh became a sigh of something else entirely.

"Okay," said McNally, looking slightly doubtful. "We'll do what we can."

What else was McNally going to say? He was going to get paid for whatever fight Stase wanted to embark upon.

He pulled a small camera out from his bag. "Can you show me out the back? It's best if I can have some images to support the arguments when we put in the paperwork."

Stase led him outside while Chris sat in the kitchen watching them through the window. There wasn't a lot he could do out there anyway. The pair of them walked around the backyard and Peter took photos from several positions while Stase talked animatedly, pointing out either this or that.

Chris happened to glance up at the next-door neighbor's rear side window; he could just see it from where he sat. He thought for a moment that he saw the shadow of a face up there. The pale shape was only there for an instant, but it was enough. Notice had truly been served, he thought.

McNally and Stase finished what they were doing and came back in through the back. Stase was still animated, excited, more than she had been for weeks.

"Okay," said Peter, packing his things away. "I'll be putting together the arguments over the next few days. I should have a draft for your approval by early next week. Of course I'll want you to read through it before we submit anything so we're sure that we are in total agreement; that we're all singing from the same hymn sheet."

Stase nodded, her eyes shining.

"What about the architects?" she said.

Peter shook his head. "No, we should keep them out of it. It creates the wrong impression, especially with a firm like that."

"What do you mean?"

"Well," he said slowly. "They're going to think that you're throwing money at the issue and you just want to make a quick profit. You don't want to look like developers, do you? Remember, you're up against the common people, your neighbors, the locals. They're going to be looking at it from that perspective."

Chris shot her an accusing glance.

"But I don't see what—"

"Trust me," said Peter. "I've seen a lot of these. It's better this way."

Stase nodded slowly, thoughtfully, and then saw him out.

The paperwork arrived the following week and they looked through it together. Chris thought it looked like a cogent and well argued case. They submitted the complete set of forms, photographs and supporting papers, then settled back to wait. They received a letter a couple of days later, telling them that interviews would be occurring with the neighbors and there'd be room for any formal objections to the appeal to be lodged over the following four weeks. One by one, the letters rolled in. The neighbor had hired her own expert, and it appeared she'd also been busy, talking to other neighbors and voicing her concerns. There were letters from people who hadn't even bothered before. The objection period came and went, and they could do nothing other than wait. It was another three weeks before their case even came up before the authority.

As the days passed, Stase became more drawn and nervous. One afternoon, she came home, a look of fury on her face. "Have you seen it?"

"What? What is it?" said Chris.

"The bitch is selling her house. That's what it's all about. She was going to sell her house all along. I bet she thought that if she had building going on next door, it would reduce her chance of selling it, maybe affect the property value."

"Are you sure? You're reading a lot into it. Perhaps she's just giving up. Perhaps she's simply had enough."

"No. She's doing this deliberately." Stase dumped her bag and stalked out into the backyard. She stood there in the middle staring up at the blank windows, her teeth set, a visible snarl etched across her features.

Chris headed for the backdoor and stood there. "Stase, come inside. That's not going to do anything."

"No," she snapped. "This time, the bitch is really going to know."

The ritual occurred every night for the next ten days. Nothing Chris said would change her mind. He'd sigh, prepare dinner and wait for her to tire and come back inside. When she spoke to him, it was only to snap responses through closed teeth, not prepared to enter into conversation. He couldn't understand where so much anger and resentment had come from.

The capper came two weeks later. Chris came home to find an official-looking letter in a brown envelope. He hesitated

before opening it, thinking that he ought to wait for Stase
to get home, but then thought better of it. He wandered
into the kitchen and tore open the envelope.

It was the letter from the local authority. Their appeal had
been denied. They were welcome to submit modified, more
modest plans, but in the case of what they'd submitted, they
were "not approved." He put the letter down on the table,
turned it over and went to make himself a cup of coffee.
While he fiddled with the jars and the kettle and mug, he
tried to analyze what he was feeling. There was trepidation,
but that was about how Stase was going to react to the news.
Apart from that, it was simple relief. Perhaps now, they
could put this madness behind them and get on with their
real life. He glanced out at the empty house next door—the
neighbor had moved out the week before—and then back
down at the letter lying face down on the table. There was
something positive, with the neighbor gone, at least. Perhaps
the next person wouldn't be so protective about the whole
thing. They'd be in a position to plan something that was
more in keeping with the size of the house and realistically
more in keeping with their budget.

He heard the key in the front door.

"Chris?" Stase called from the hall.

"In here," he called back.

He heard her dump her bag, get rid of her shoes and head
in his direction. She appeared in the doorway a moment
later. "What are you doing in here?" she said.

"Come here, Stase," he said, pulling out a chair.

"What is it?"

She didn't take the proffered chair; rather she stood in the
doorway leaning slightly, one hand supporting her, a frown
flickering on and off on her brow.

"It's come."

"And ...?"

Chris turned to face her. "We've been knocked back."

Her face blanked. She stood there for a moment, and then simply collapsed in the doorway. It was as if her legs had just crumpled. She huddled there in the doorway in a heap. Chris had no idea then how similar that action would be to something that would come later, be so important for him, for both of them, but then none of that stuff had happened yet.

"Nooooooooooo." Long and low, the sound came from deep inside her.

"Stase?" He pushed back his chair and quickly moved across to crouch down beside her. "Stase, it's not the end of the world, baby. Listen."

Her face was hidden by her hair, but her shoulders were shaking. He put out a tentative hand to touch her arm. She lifted a hand to ward him away. Again he touched her.

"Listen, Stase. We have other options. It's not all that bad. Look, we can do the place up; we can sell it. We can move somewhere else. It's not the end of the world."

She shook her head without looking up, her body jerking. He didn't know what to do. This reaction was more than he expected. He'd expected tears, screaming perhaps, shouting, but not this. He put an arm around her shoulders and tried to ease her to her feet, but she slumped within his grasp like a sack of bones. He got a firmer grip and tried to pull her upright.

"Come on, Stase. I know you're upset. Come into the lounge and I'll make you a cup of tea."

Again, she shook her head.

Finally, he managed to encourage her to stand and steer her gently into the lounge where he positioned her on the couch. Her shoulders were still shaking and she refused to look at him. He stood looking at her, and then went back into the kitchen to do just that, to make her a cup of tea. There was really nothing he could say.

When he came back into the lounge, she was still sitting in the same position, gently shaking, her hair falling over her face.

"Stase, listen, drink this. You'll feel better." He placed the mug gently down in front of her.

She looked up then, fixing him with a look of total hostility. "What the fuck would you know about what would make me feel better. Nothing will make me feel better," she spat. "Nothing!"

"Jesus," he said. "It's a house. It's a fucking house, Stase."

She shook her head and burst into tears. "But it was our house," she said between the sobs.

Looking at her sitting there sobbing, the way each breath wrenched through her, he understood. She really had believed they were going to win this. For the first time, Chris recognized with an awful certainty exactly how important Stase's plans were to their life together. He stood watching her, helpless, knowing he was unable to say anything that might possibly help.

CHAPTER TWENTY-TWO

GROWTH

After their planning appeal was rejected, Stase refused to talk about the whole thing. She shut down any discussion of the house, the planning permission or anything, and over the next few days, she carefully filed all the paperwork, the documents, the photographs and architectural drawings in lever-arched files and packed them all away. After a couple of days had passed without a single mention of what had happened, Chris tried to broach the subject. It was a Saturday afternoon, the sun streaming in the back windows. The seasonal change was almost upon them, but the afternoon felt like a mild spring day, warding off the knowledge of the impending cold and gray damp to come.

"Stase," he said. "Can we talk about what we're going to do?" He'd been busying himself in the back garden, just for something to do. He desperately wanted to do something inside the house, something that might improve their living conditions, but every time he even mentioned it, she would cut him off with a simple hand gesture, telling him that he knew what they had decided. He leaned against the backdoor, wiping his hands on his jeans.

She stopped in mid step and slowly turned to face him. "Going to do about what?" she said. She'd been occupied in one of her cleaning frenzies and was wearing the yellow rubber gloves, carrying a cloth, her hair held back with a scrunchy. A couple of strands of dark hair trailed across her forehead and down across one cheek. He'd caught her on the way to the kitchen to get something.

"About the house, Stase. What do you think?"

She sighed and wiped the back of one yellow-clad hand across one cheek, disturbing the strands of hair that hung there. Here in the light, the red slash of her scar, now fading, was plainly visible. Chris forced himself not to focus on it, not to let her find him looking. She was still really self-conscious about it.

She pressed her lips into a tight line. "I've told you already. There's no point. If I can't have the house the way I want it, then there's no point in doing anything."

"Come on, Stase. Don't you think you're being a little bit unreasonable about it? We can still do things. If you're worried about increasing the property value, then there are still things we can do. Look at the state of the place—the walls, the floors. What do you want?"

"It's not the same," she said flatly.

"Jesus, Stase. Show a little common sense will you? It's not lost. There's still plenty to do."

She glared at him. "There you go again. I'm not thinking rationally, am I? Stase is unbalanced. Stase is losing it. Well, I'm not listening to your shit any more. You can't control me like that. I'm not going to listen to you."

"What the fuck are you talking about?" he asked, his exasperation bursting from him.

"Yes, that's it. Shout at me why don't you? Enforce your domination. Be the big man. It's not going to work."

"I'm not shouting."

"No, of course you're not," she said.

He stared at her incredulously. She turned away and headed into the kitchen, forestalling any further discussion. When she reappeared, she stalked past and refused to look at him.

He had no idea where she was getting this stuff. He rubbed the back of his neck and stared up the hallway after her.

He followed her into the lounge to try and talk to her again, but it was clear from the set of her shoulders, the furious way she was straightening things, rubbing at small spots on the table where there was no real visible mark that needed rubbing, that he wasn't going to get anywhere.

The distance between Chris and Stase was palpable. Her responses were curt, and every time he caught her looking at him there was a sheen of hostility, almost accusation, in her expression. Chris busied himself, staying late at the office and working on projects, or bringing presentations home to fiddle with while continuing to wander through the pantomime that their relationship had become. He was still not convinced that her medication levels were right, but every time he tried to broach the subject, Stase flew into a rage and accused him of trying to undermine her. Partly because of the hostility, partly because of his own perceived inability to do anything about it, Chris withdrew from the problem. Things might have been better if he tried to do something more proactively. But it seemed that everything that had happened had also drained his will to take those few steps. Stase, on the other hand, obviously aware too that everything wasn't rosy, compensated in her own ways.

Over the next couple of weeks, her circle of friends seemed to expand mysteriously. From the little he could glean from their conversations, terse as they were, there were new names, people he didn't recognize coming up in the offhand comments she dropped. Suddenly, the number of work parties or drinks seemed to escalate. For some reason, Stase was feeling a need to be social, to mix with crowds of people, or at least that was the story. She never invited Chris, not that he asked. She was clearly looking for something that he was incapable of giving her right then, or that she wouldn't let him give her because she had identified him as one of the root sources of her problems.

It was only much later that he found out she was having bi-weekly counseling sessions as a response to how she felt about the disease and she'd kept them from him, going either at lunchtime or after work. Later, looking back, it would make a kind of sense. She was desperately seeking someone or something to blame and Chris was the closest thing to her, or had been. That was the only real thing he ever saw her getting out of those sessions, a directed capacity to blame.

Chris wasn't fooling himself that he didn't have problems too. Everything was starting to seem pretty meaningless. There was work, but that was little more than an automated routine. It was a persona he pulled on day after day, comfortable in its familiarity, but deadening in its sameness. There was nothing new or exciting there, and somehow, it was like being alone in a crowded room, no real connection, because he wasn't really there after all.

Chris began to realize that he had spent so much time imprinting his life and his identity on Anastasia that with her turnabout, he had been cut adrift, and if he couldn't regain some semblance of his life with her, he wasn't left with very much at all. Unless he could cross that bridge between them and rebuild some sort of connection, then he, as an individual, almost had no identity left of his own. It was a hard realization and one he would have rather denied.

He made a decision to monitor what she was doing. He wouldn't broach the subject of the house, not yet. He wanted, rather, to find some common ground with which he could build a platform to reconnect with her. He knew he had to tread carefully, skirting the hostility that sat festering between them, but he had resolved to take some action. Every night, when she came home from work, he'd ask her how she was doing, what her day had been like. She was sparse on details, and Chris was becoming frustrated. She rarely asked him what was happening with him. And still, underlying it all was the touch of accusation lying beneath her brief and inconstant gaze.

A few days after the encounter in the back hallway, she announced that she had found something new to do.

"I'm going to this thing tomorrow night," she told him. "Are you going to be okay on your own?"

"I guess," he said. "It's not going to be much different from normal, is it?"

She almost glared at him. "Anyway, I think this thing's going to be good for me."

"What is it?" Chris asked, leaning forward and clutching at some hope that there might be something there he could become involved in with her.

"It's a self-development seminar. I heard about it from one of the girls at work. They teach you how to take control of your life. Teach you empowerment and how to be assertive about yourself."

"Are you sure?" he asked.

Again the look of hostility.

"Okay, listen, how much do you know about it? There are a lot of suspect outfits out there."

"It's legitimate. You don't have to worry about that. It's called the Root Network. They call it that because it lets you get to the roots of your inner strength and helps you grow."

Chris sat back. "Um, okay … does this cost anything?"

She shook her head. "Anyway, that's not the point, whether it does or not. It's something I want to do. The girl from work loves it. It's only an introductory seminar anyway. If I don't like it, I don't have to go back. There's no commitment."

Already there were faint alarms going off in Chris's head, but if he mentioned anything right then, he knew Stase was just as likely to leap down his throat and accuse him of trying to undermine her again. It was just too much of a familiar pattern of late. He couldn't seem to question her about anything. The fact that the 'girl from work' was nameless too did nothing to ease the concern. He shut up and went back to watching the television. It was a weekly soap that Stase liked to watch. A couple on screen were having an argument. Chris barely saw them. Seemingly satisfied, Stase settled back to watch the show as well.

The next night, when she was out at her 'introductory seminar,' Chris decided to do some research. He got online and typed in: "Root Network." The results were immediate and manifold. There was a website devoted to the organization, but there were other things too. He briefly scanned the website and then hit the back button on his browser to follow the other links. Entry after entry followed and very few of them were good. Many of the links pointed to cult warning sites. He leaned in closer to the screen, frowning. After following a couple of the links, he was frowning even more. A number of the sites went so far as to discuss brainwashing techniques openly.

"Jesus," he breathed and sat back from the screen. He paced the room for a while, deciding what his best course of action was. It was the standard stuff. Where they talked about self-development and empowerment, they were really setting things up to bleed as much as they could out of their potential victims. The root structure was evident. It was based on a principle of pyramid selling: their members were encouraged to proselytize, gaining status points for helping to induct new members. There was a series of ranked seminars, each one costing more than the last, eventually getting to a point where members were supposed to contribute a proportion of their income to the group. Meanwhile, they battered your self-confidence, looking for targets to blame, then rebuilt and refocused it. Their program had a history of turning its participants against wives, against families, against loved ones, until they gained support only from the organization itself. Why would she want to get involved in something like that?

He returned to the screen and followed a few more of the links, finding out all he could, including the fact that their founder had been arrested on fraud charges more than once and been forced to change his name, as well as the name of the corporation.

He found a few select entries and printed them out. If Stase wouldn't listen to him, she might just listen to something in black and white.

Chris waited patiently for her to arrive home.

He met her at the door, a sheaf of papers in his hand.

"So, how was it?" he asked.

She was visibly glowing. "It was great, wonderful," she said, putting down her bag and actually smiling back at him for once.

"Um, okay, Stase, that's great," Chris said hesitantly, "but I think you need to come in here and sit down with me."

He led her into the lounge and steered her to the couch. She was looking at him with a puzzled expression, but there was none of the hostility he had seen of late. Once she was seated, he handed her the papers. "I think you need to read this," he said.

She started scanning the first page then slapped the papers down on the couch beside her, glaring up at him. "Typical. This is bloody typical Chris. I find something that I like, and the first thing you do is try and find some way to get at it, to turn it bad for me."

Chris held up his hands. "Stase, it's not like that at all. Listen to me. I've heard about this sort of stuff before. I was worried about you. I really think you need to read what's there."

She narrowed her eyes and lifted the pages again. This time she read them more slowly. "Okay, so what?" she said after a few pages.

"Can't you see what they're doing? Look, a number of groups like this have been banned. It's bullshit, Stase. They fuck with your head and take your money. That's how they work. It's no better than a bogus religion. We don't need that kind of shit right now. You don't need that kind of shit right now."

She kept reading, not saying anything.

After a while, she put the papers back down, more gently this time. Her shoulders slumped. "But they were so good," she said. "I felt great. There was no hard sell. I know other people who swear by them, say they're great."

"But that's how they work, baby. Don't you see that? Suck you in, then suck you dry. I really don't think you should have anything more to do with them. Really."

She turned slowly to look at him. Her eyes were shining moistly. "Okay, I'll think about it, Chris."

"You promise?"

"Yeah, I promise."

He thought he'd dealt with that one, until they got a phone call a few nights after from a male voice that Chris didn't recognize. Stase took the call and spoke in low tones for a while before returning to the lounge. She didn't volunteer anything, so Chris asked.

"Who was that?"

She shrugged, reaching for the remote and switching channels. "Oh, that was just Asid."

Chris had never heard the name before. "Who the hell is Asid? And why so secretive?"

She shrugged again. "He's just a guy I know."

"From where?"

She flipped the channel again. "I met him at the seminars."

"Jesus, Stase. What are you doing?"

Still she didn't look at him, seeming to have settled on a television channel and settling back on the couch. "He's fine. He's just a friend."

Chris clamped his jaw shut, took a breath and then continued. "I thought you were done with all that bullshit."

She turned quickly to look at him. "He's just a friend, all right?" She turned back to the television.

Chris closed his eyes and fought to keep himself calm. Okay, he was just a friend. Maybe he was. Maybe she was done with the seminars. He'd give her the benefit of the doubt for now. It just wasn't worth the hassle otherwise. He opened his eyes and sat watching her. Just once or twice while she was watching whatever was on the screen, her eyebrows flickered up and down, almost a semi-shocked reaction, one of startlement. There was nothing on the screen that should invoke a reaction like that, and he wondered where it was coming from.

Chris noted it and put it away, but something he'd deal with later, maybe. It was as if the world, everything she looked at, was surprising her from moment to moment.

For the time being, his life together with Stase, finding some common thread between them and building on it was Chris's only focus. But then he saw the fat man on Sydney Street, the girl in the bus shelter, and the world decided to take him to a totally different place whether he was aware of it at the time, or not.

CHAPTER TWENTY-THREE

THE COMMUNE

About halfway through Stase's final year, Chris came over to the flat she shared with the other girl, Barbara. She let him in, stopping him at the door and putting a finger to her lips.

"What?" he asked.

"Come in really quietly. I've got something to show you."

Chris followed her on tiptoe into the living room. Stase gripped his upper arm, stopping him before he went any further.

He gave her a questioning look.

"Over there," she whispered and pointed.

Sitting on the couch, staring up at them with big, wide eyes gazing out from a ball of fur was a black and white kitten. He laughed.

The kitten backed away at the sound, hair fluffing up, a hiss issuing from its mouth.

"Where did you get that?" he said. He didn't wait for her answer, but stepped over to the couch and crouched down, reaching out a hand. The kitten backed away further into a corner of the couch. Gently he stroked its head. It trembled, but let him touch it.

"I found it," she said.

Chris turned to look at her back over his shoulder. "What do you mean? Where?"

Stase moved over and crouched down beside him, reaching out to stroke the kitten too.

189

"I was out for a drive," she said.

"A drive? Where?"

"Oh, I was down at the beach. I'd just gone for a drive. It was down there on the beach alone. There was nobody around, so I brought it home."

Chris kept stroking, but what she had told him worried him. "How do you mean, you just brought it home? Maybe it belongs to someone. Did you look?"

She shrugged. "There wasn't anyone around. Isn't it cute?"

"I'm not sure you did the right thing just bringing it home, Stase. Don't you think it might be someone's pet?"

She gave another little shrug. "It's mine now." She leaned in closer, putting her face right next to it. "I need to think of a name for it."

Chris stood back up and looked down at her. She seemed totally enamored with the small furry ball. It was purring now.

"Okay, if you're sure you know what you're doing ..." He wasn't feeling comfortable about the whole thing. But he could see the look on her face and he knew better than to raise any real objection right then.

The funny thing was, it was gone in a week, nameless, apparently forgotten. Her housemate, Barbara, announced two days later that she was dropping out of university and moving back to the town she'd come from. Stase decided she had to find somewhere else to live, as the apartment was in Barbara's name and changing everything over was just too much hassle. It was also too expensive to try and keep on her own.

Chris was over waiting for her to finish getting ready before they went out somewhere, and he noticed the lack of the kitten. "Stase, what happened to the cat?" he said.

"Oh, I took it back," she said blithely.

"You what?"

"Took it back where I found it. I let it go."

"Where?"

She looked at him as if she didn't understand what his problem was. "Back on the beach, of course. Back where I found it."

He just stared at her. And that was the end of it. Stase didn't talk about the nameless ball of black and white hair again and nor did he. It was just another one of those things he filed away with his incredulity. Not everything was black and white, not even a kitten.

She found somewhere to live within the week. There was a large cream condominium down by the beach, a tall corporate-looking affair that had its own name. It was the sort of place designed for businessmen and the up-and-coming wealthy. Three other students from her old social group were planning on moving in and they asked her to join them. Chris was baffled by the fact that someone would even rent those places to students, let alone a whole group of them. It was right out of their range, out of their lifestyle, out of everything that made any sense to university life. He could see why Stase was attracted by it though. It looked good from the outside in a sort of slick, modern way. It was another external skin for Stase to wrap around herself.

There was something else about it that was worrying Chris. Stase had moved out of her own social circle as much as he had, and he didn't feel comfortable with the fact that she seemed to be slipping back into it. He was threatened. Added to the fact that she was going to be sharing with two guys as well as another girl, he was distinctly uncomfortable. It was a two-bedroom apartment. Sure, it had plenty of space, all the modern facilities—Stase had taken him to have a look at it once the decision was made—but it was still going to be close quarters for four of them. Yes, he was threatened.

One of the guys who lived in the place, Jim, was a big Marilyn Monroe and Beatles fan and as soon as you walked into the place, there was a huge floor to ceiling black and white poster tacked to the wall, the standing-above-the-subway shot. Marilyn's image was reflected from the large built-in mirrors at every angle as you walked in. It just seemed so unlike Stase, so outside of her reality. Jim was a good looking man, high cheekbones, a mop of curly hair, strangely reminiscent of Jim Morrison. Chris noticed immediately the way he followed Stase around the room with his gaze. The other male resident was called Alex. He was tall, loud, a hard drinker and smoker and seemed to spend little attention on his personal hygiene. It looked like he hadn't cleaned his teeth for years. Chris suppressed his shudder with some difficulty when they were first introduced.

The other girl wasn't there the first time he came to visit. Her name was Delores. Chris had had her in one of his classes once, and he knew her to be a poor performer, more interested in partying with the boys than any academic achievement. And this was the girl that Stase would be sharing a room with. It didn't make sense. He knew she aspired to more than that, but he put it aside, telling himself that she'd be spending more time at his place anyway.

Stase moved her stuff, the things that weren't already at his place, into the apartment, and he sat back in numb acceptance. Chris didn't like going there, but the times he visited Jim was easy-going and friendly, if slightly reserved. Alex, on the other hand, was aggressively friendly. Much shoulder slapping and loud laughter ensued. Chris was convinced that Alex really didn't like him. The couple of times he turned up and Alex wasn't there, he felt relieved.

The residents of this new apartment didn't seem to do much. Every time he came over, Chris found them sitting around listening to music, smoking and drinking. Every time Stase dragged him over, he quickly found excuses to get out of there as soon as he could, generally trying to coax Stase to come with him.

She started spending more and more time at the apartment. They had parties and they had people over and Chris's resentment grew. He just wasn't a part of that circle and yet Stase seemed to want to cling to it, as if she could cultivate a whole other world that was separate and beyond what she had together with him. One day, when they were driving back to his place, he voiced his concerns. He was driving. She almost always got him to drive, even when it was her car.

"Stase, how come you spend so much time at that place? I thought we were supposed to be living together, well, at least during the week."

"Oh, come on," she said. "They're my friends. Besides, I have to study. I can't study when I'm with you. We have other things to do." She turned and gave him a half-suggestive grin.

"I don't know. I don't like the place. You know that. And I don't like you spending so much time in close proximity to Jim, either. He follows you around like a puppy dog."

She laughed. "Oh, don't worry about him. He's harmless."

"Yeah, well, he may be harmless, but I've seen the way he looks at you."

She pulled her fingers through her hair, looking back at the road. Clearly, she didn't mind the concept that Chris was a little uncomfortable with her relationship with her housemates.

"And as for Alex, the guy's a pig."

"Alex is just Alex. He's okay."

"Oh come on, Stase. The guy's an animal. Why do you want to be living with losers like him anyway? I didn't think it was your sort of thing."

She shrugged.

"I really wish you wouldn't spend so much time there. What's wrong with being with me? I have work I have to do. You can study when I'm working."

"All my books are there. Anyway, I like it there. I don't know what your problem is, Chris. I've already said that if I'm with you I can't work. I love that apartment. It's a great place to live."

She wasn't going to change her mind about it; that much was clear. He closed his jaw tightly and gripped the steering wheel, concentrating on the road ahead.

The problem was he had given her something she could use without his realizing it and without realizing that she would in fact use it. She liked the fact that he was jealous. She liked the fact that Jim threatened him, and she played on it over the next few weeks. She dropped little mentions about how Jim had given her a massage, or Jim and she had spent an all-night session studying together. She rarely mentioned the other two residents from then on. Little by little, it started to work away inside him. He felt even more uncomfortable every time he visited and he started avoiding it as much as he could. It meant that he and Stase were spending less time together and that started gnawing away at him as well. Gradually he started to feel almost like a small cat, taken in and then dumped by the wayside.

CHAPTER TWENTY-FOUR

ANOTHER PLACE, ANOTHER TIME

At the end of that final year, Anastasia moved back in with her parents, back to the city. Chris was still based at the university, teaching part time. Somehow, her parental home, was strictly out of bounds to him and always had been. She'd made that clear in no uncertain terms. He questioned her about it, but she wouldn't be drawn. He knew that meeting the folks would be a big thing. There was significance in that simple act. It was incursion into ground that belonged exclusively to her, and Stase was very protective of that which was hers, and that extended to Chris. For that reason he was prepared to let it lie for a while. Not only was she protecting her space with them from him, but also guarding her time with him from them. The unfortunate side-effect was that their actual time together was limited, rationed. He wondered if perhaps that was the plan, the old principle of partial reinforcement being the strongest form of conditioning. Or maybe it really was just her way of maintaining her independence.

But the problem was, when people become part of a relationship, they cease being true individuals; their characters, their beings merge into one another in such a way that they start being perceived as a joint entity rather than two individuals bound together by their choice to be with each other They had ceased being Chris and Anastasia. They were Chris-and-Anastasia or Anastasia-and-Chris depending on who knew them first. Chris was reasonably comfortable with that notion, but he failed to notice that the circle of friends that were his alone was dwindling. They started spending time with Stase's friends and going out to things that Stase wanted them to attend. Andy and Bill had long disappeared from his life, except for passing chance meetings, and then they were brief. Moving away had done a lot to settle that.

Partly in an effort to be closer to her, partly because a personality clash had developed with his current supervisor, he decided he'd transfer to another university, back to the city. It didn't take long to find the opportunity. As a transitional step, he moved in with his mother—temporarily.

Chris and his mother were close, but living together was difficult. He was grateful for the space and the opportunity, but there was attendant baggage. There was an underlying tension between them that always grew larger when they were living in close quarters. It didn't mean that they were any less close; it was just that they were better off not living in the same place. Both of them recognized the tension, but the needs of circumstance allowed them to put it aside for the time being.

Still Chris was not allowed to visit Stase's place. She said it was the parents. He didn't know whether somehow they would find him unacceptable, or whether it was still more protection of those things that were hers. There she was, and though he was closer, he felt more removed. As a result, Stase and he spent a good deal of time either in her car or in the front room of his mother's house, the room that had become his in the interim. That did little to help the tension, as both his mother and Anastasia clearly saw each other as a threat. Words that passed between the pair were courteous but curt and no more than were absolutely necessary. Their territoriality wound the tension more tightly. Chris decided he'd sit back and let nature take its course, hoping that they'd grow to accept each other, but things got no better. He was working at the City University, studying part time, and seeing Stase whenever he could. She too was working now, had a steady income stream, but still seemed to manage to maintain the parent-child relationship with her parents that meant they did everything they could to keep her happy. Chris, too, found himself desperate to keep her happy. More than once, he'd seen the look on her face when things weren't going her way. Besides, he loved her, wanted to please her. She seemed to fill him with a power that he'd never known before her.

As it became apparent that Anastasia was not going away, his mother became cooler in the already chill environment that drifted through the house whenever Stase was there. Finally, it became too much for Chris. Taking the gentle route and letting them work it out for themselves just wasn't succeeding. Chris decided he had to do something.

He found his mother in the kitchen.

"Ma," he said. "I want to talk to you about something."

She was washing up. "What is it?"

"It's about Anastasia." He stood at the kitchen table with his hands on the back of a chair. His mother had chosen the rustic look. A long wooden table made from thick beams of aged pine, a pale wood Welsh dresser, wooden chairs and slate tiles. Her plates were hand-made, thick, chunky pottery thrown on a wheel. She stacked a plate in the rack above her head and reached for another without saying anything.

"Did you hear what I said?"

"Yes, I heard what you said," she said.

"Well?"

"What is it?" she said with a sigh, turning around and wiping the backs of her hands on her hips and then the palms on the front of her thighs. She fussed with things on the table, not meeting his eyes.

"I can see what's happening and I need to tell you something. I want you to listen to me now. Anastasia is not going to go away."

Her hands stopped in mid action and she looked up. "What are you trying to say, Chris?"

He pulled out a chair and sat. "Things aren't great between you two and I feel like I'm stuck on the middle," he said. "It simply can't go on."

His mother shook her head and went back to adjusting things on the table.

"I'm serious," said Chris.

There was a long silence. "You're sounding as if it's my fault," she said, finally.

"Well, I think it is, at least in part. I think you could make more of an effort."

Her mouth worked and she turned back to the sink.

"Well?" said Chris.

"Who does she think she is?" she said without turning around. "She waltzes in here as if she owns the place, says barely a word to me. It's as if I don't even exist. How do you expect me to react? This is my home."

"Well, you've hardly made her welcome, have you?"

She gripped the edge of the sink with both hands. "It's not my fault. She was like that from the start. I welcomed her as soon as you brought her here and she treated me as if I was a servant in my own house."

Chris rubbed the flat of one hand over the table surface. "I know, she can be a little cool, but that's no excuse. You can at least make an effort."

His mother spun to face him. "I don't like her. I don't like the way she reacts, the way she treats people. What do you expect me to do?"

Chris took a breath before continuing. "It's simple," he said, summoning the strength for the words he knew he had to say. "You make a choice, right here, right now. Stase is part of my life and she's not going away. It's time to understand and accept that. Either you change the way you react to her, or I walk away. It's as simple as that. You can either have me as a part of your life ... with Stase ... or you don't have me at all."

His mother narrowed her eyes slightly. That was the only change in her expression. She stared at him for a long time, looking as if she was about to say something, then turned away, back to the sink.

Chris sighed. "Okay, I've said what I was going to say. I guess I'll leave you to think about it."

He pushed back the chair and stood. Still she hadn't moved. He left her standing there at the sink and headed back to his room.

"Shit," he thought he heard her say quietly just as he left the room, but he couldn't be sure.

Chris knew that wasn't going to be the end of it, but at least he felt like he'd done something, and in so doing, he himself had made a choice.

In the days that followed, he avoided being at home, encouraging Stase to go with him to other places. He wanted the matter to settle in his mother's mind and he wanted to test it in small stages rather than all at once. He knew everything wasn't going suddenly to change for the better in her mind, but at least he had to give her space to be able to work at it.

Meanwhile, his life at the university continued, but he just didn't feel he was getting anywhere. Stase was out, earning good money, but she'd always wanted to make good money, and somehow, with what the academic life had to offer, he felt like he was letting her down. There was no way he was going to build the sort of income stream that could match hers, not for years yet, if at all. Anastasia wanted things and Chris was in no position to help provide the things that she wanted. The whole living at a distance circumstance was becoming unbearable. She came back a few times to his place and the relationship between she and his mother was strained but cordial. Stase would bitch to him as they drove away, or just whenever the opportunity seemed to arise, but he refused to play that game with her. There had to be a better way. There just had to be.

He'd been tossing the concept around in his head for about three weeks, not wanting to mention it and slightly afraid of even going where his thoughts were taking him. He didn't know how she'd react. He knew that he wanted her there with him, all the time. Just to be with her, to feel her there when he woke in the morning, to slide in beside her and feel his stomach against the curve of her back. To cup her body, his arm encircling her breasts, their forms molded to each other, breathing in the scent of her hair. They'd been spending so much time together anyway, that it just seemed to make sense. He was comfortable when he was with her, and when he wasn't, there was a hollow nestled deep inside him, knowing that something was missing. But still he didn't know. She seemed perfectly content to keep their spaces separate, and maybe that was important to her, that particular, peculiar definition of boundaries and what did and did not belong to her.

They spent a lot of time in Anastasia's car those days. It had become a surrogate apartment in the absence of anything they could share. So they drove, or they sat and talked, or they were passionate, all in the tight confines of the car. The tensions between her and his mother didn't help. Stase was reluctant to spend any real length of time at his place. Perhaps Chris simply constructed the belief in his own mind, but he became convinced that there was only one solution. They were parked in a side street, creamy orange light illuminating the darkened space within the car. Chris was behind the wheel, and he looked away, looking out at the naked street, at the police station opposite where they sat. It was vaguely surreal, painted in the artificial streetlight colors. The urge suddenly welled up inside him and he turned to look at her.

"You know, I'm going to marry you," he said. He felt a wash of trepidation as the final words left his lips. Had he really said that?

"Oh, baby," she said and reached across to take his hand.

"No, I mean it," he said. And he really did. That surprised him a little. He hadn't quite expected to mean it, really.

Later that night, he announced it to his mother.

There was a mix of emotions on her face as she listened. "Are you sure this is what you want?" she finally asked.

"I'm sure. Stase gives me the support I need. She's always going to be there for me. I really believe that, Ma," he said, completely convinced of what he was telling her. "She's my world."

His mother became very quiet. She turned away and busied herself with tidying things up around the kitchen.

CHAPTER TWENTY-FIVE

THE BRIDGE

The time came when Stase could avoid it no longer. Chris was finally going to meet her parents. They set out together in her car, Chris doing the driving as usual, Stase's expression fixed and her hand creeping up to flutter nervously at her chest.

"What is it?" Chris asked.

She didn't look at him. "You don't know how nervous I am," she said. "You don't know my parents."

The statement hung heavily between them. No, he didn't know them, he thought. And that was the whole point. He couldn't see what she could possibly be afraid of. There was nothing in anything she'd ever said to make him believe they were ogres. Perhaps it was something else entirely. He had more reason to be nervous than she did.

"More to the point," she said. "You don't know my father."

Stase gave directions in a quiet, hesitant voice as the pulled into suburban tree-lined streets. Chris had some idea of the locale, but it wasn't quite what he expected. Somehow he'd presumed the area would be grander, more upmarket. They pulled in to her parents' street and headed for an unassuming house, a garage by the side, all done in unflashy subdued brick. There was a veranda out the front and a large, old tree in the front yard.

"Pull in here," said Stase.

"But shouldn't we park in the driveway?"

"No." She shook her head. "Here is fine." It was as if she wanted to scope the place as they approached, checking for hidden traps. It was a quiet street, although Chris imagined it was noisier during the day. He'd noticed a large high school as they'd rounded the corner at the end of the street.

Stase led the way, pushing open a metal gate and checking the mailbox on the way in. She took the two steps leading up to the porch, and stretched one hand out for the front doorbell. He wondered briefly why she didn't use her own keys, but maybe this was some sort of protective ritual, the necessity to be invited in to her own house now that Chris was with her. Her hand was held pressed against the base of her throat as they waited.

The sound of footsteps came from inside and the door swung open.

"Hi," said Stase.

Within the doorway stood a middle-aged woman. She was stocky, her hair black, dyed, Chris presumed. She had some of Stase's looks about her. He could tell immediately where most of her looks came from. Her mother could have been a younger version of Anastasia herself, if perhaps a little more stocky and round of face. She wore a simple floral-print dress and a single strand of pearls around her neck.

"Hello, Anastasia," she said. "And you must be Chris. Welcome. Please, come in."

Stase swallowed and stepped past her mother into the house. Chris gave a polite smile and followed.

"We're in the lounge," said her mother as she closed the door.

As Stase led him down the hallway, Chris, dealing with his own nervousness about the meeting, still managed to take in some of the details. There was nothing special or particular about the trappings. The house had everything he'd expect from middle-class suburbia: neat, plain decorations, a couple of tasteful paintings and one or two family photographs affixed to the walls. He was led into the lounge. Her father sat in a large armchair, perched right on the edge expectantly.

"Ah, so I presume you're Chris," he said and stood, extending a hand.

Chris crossed and shook the proffered hand. "Pleased to meet you," he replied, assessing the tall, thin, graying man before him. He could see nothing that warranted Stase's previous comment. Her father was all smiles, if a little reserved.

"Please, please, sit down," he said.

Chris took a place on the couch and waited, giving his own hesitant smile as the women appeared. They'd obviously been discussing something in the hallway.

"Now, Chris, what can I get you?" asked her mother. "Tea, coffee? What's your preference?"

"Perhaps the boy would like something else," said her father. "What about a beer, Chris?"

Chris lifted a hand. "No, no, coffee will be fine," he said.

There were a few moments of uncomfortable silence as Stase's mother disappeared to elsewhere in the house. Stase was hovering in the doorway, almost as if she was reluctant to cut off her escape route.

"Come and sit down, Anastasia," said her father.

She nodded and crossed to a chair, and sat, clearly ill at ease. By now, her father had relaxed back into his own chair, watching Chris, still with a half smile upon his lips.

Chris took the opportunity to take in the room's furnishings. A couple of armchairs, two couches, a low table and a nice dark, patterned rug in the center. No television. A pastoral scene on one of the walls. A tall vase of flowers stood on a corner table. This was clearly a room for meeting and greeting. Moments later, Stase's mother appeared carrying a tray, carefully set it down on the central table, and looked up at him while she was leaning over.

"How do you have your coffee, Chris?"

"Um, just white thanks. Milk, no sugar."

She poured some milk into a cup with the coffee already in it and handed it to him. She offered him a small plate with neat little pastries on it, but he held up a hand again. Stase, her mother, and her father, all had tea.

"So, Chris," said her father, holding his saucer in one hand and gently resting his cup on it as he spoke. "You work at the university."

"Yes. Well, part time. Teaching. I'm working towards my postgrad degree at the moment. Once I'm fully qualified, I intend to get a more permanent post there."

Stase's father nodded. "Hmm, it's a good job to have. A nice life if you can get it."

"Yes, I like to think so," said Chris. "And you, Mr. Robins?"

"Call me Alex," he said. "No need to be so formal. Me, I'm a laborer." He laughed. Chris must have shown traces of his surprise. "I push paper for a living," he said. "No, seriously—middle management for a retail chain, but I'm surprised Anastasia hasn't already told you that. Frances here works at the local hospital in administration. Both of us are hidden away in offices."

Chris nodded slowly. He glanced over at Stase, but she refused to meet his eyes.

"So, have you been here long?" he asked. "I mean, here, in this house."

It was her mother's turn to answer. "Oh, we've had this place about twenty years now. It's a good house. Probably getting a little big for us now, with the children moving on, but you become attached, don't you?"

Chris knew that Stase had an older brother, but she didn't talk about him. All he knew was that he was married with kids of his own. He guessed he'd meet him in due course as well. He nodded again and took a sip of his coffee. It was pleasant. They were pleasant. The whole thing was simply pleasant.

Stase's father, Alex, leaned forward in his chair, placing his cup and saucer gently down on the table.

"So, do you love my daughter, Chris?" he said, folding his hands together in front of him.

"Dad!" It was the first thing Stase had said since they'd entered the room.

Chris looked at her, at what he presumed was feigned shock on her face, then looked back at Alex and smiled.

"Yes, I do," he said. "Very much."

Alex leaned back in his chair nodding.

"Would you like some more coffee, Chris?" said her mother. "Perhaps you'd like one of those pastries now."

The whole thing had been completely untraumatic. It was nothing like the expectation that Stase had built in him. After the polite conversation petered out, Stase announced that they were going for a drive together to drop Chris back at his place and she'd be back in a while. They bid their farewells and headed out to the car. As they pulled away from the simple, comfortable house, Chris turned to Stase, a look of slight puzzlement on his face.

"Okay, now that wasn't so bad," he said. "God, they were nothing like you led me to imagine. I was expecting something scary. They seem like really nice people."

Stase just shook her head. "Well, at least that's done," she said. "We can get on with planning what we have to do."

They were at an intersection, and he had to concentrate on the traffic for a moment before pulling out. "Wait," he said. "What do you mean?"

"Well, that's the whole meet-the-parents thing over and done with. We don't have to do that again."

"I can't see what your problem was," Chris told her. "Why the big mystery? Why has it taken so long for this to happen?"

"Simple," she said. "Their life has nothing to do with what we're going to do together. It's my life, not theirs. It just wasn't relevant to us, Chris. And now we can get on with things."

He chewed that over for a while in silence as they drove along. He still couldn't quite fathom what it was, what had driven her to keep that whole part of her life away from him. Sure, it was a simple uncomplicated background with parents to match, and perhaps that was part of it. It was probably nothing like the image that Stase wanted to project to the world, about herself, about her life. It still felt uncomfortable though. This was the woman he was going to marry, and she was not only projecting something to the world, but she was projecting something other than the reality of her own life to him, her intended partner, as well.

CHAPTER TWENTY-SIX

A NARROW PATH

Of course, they spoke about the wedding in more detail. There were plans, things to arrange and organize, guest lists to deal with. When it came down to it, there was actually not that much for Chris to do. Stase took control of the whole thing with a firm hand. No expense would be spared. Anastasia was going to have a fuck off wedding at the best place available and the best photographer and the best string quartet and the best reception.

She was going to impress the hell out of her family and friends and anyone else who cared to look. She was going to show them that she was somebody, and she told him so in no uncertain terms. She also told her parents, but most of those conversations happened in the privacy of her family home while Chris was elsewhere. This was Stase's wedding and she didn't want anything to interfere with her plans, not even Chris.

As the planning progressed, Chris still being kept somewhat on the sidelines, Stase started making other gentle suggestions. At least, they were gentle at first. If they were going to have a proper life together, they had to be able to get a house and furniture and all the other things that went with being married. His part-time work at the university wasn't going to sustain that. He had to think about what he was doing, assess what he really wanted. The frequency

of the hints and subtle suggestions grew. Chris had to get a
proper job. He protested that he had a proper job, a future,
though inside he knew he was just really spinning his wheels.
He argued that there was nothing wrong with university
life. It wasn't enough for Anastasia. She needed more from
him. Chris didn't have time to think about it. Events and
Anastasia's plans were sweeping him away. At the same time,
they were also sweeping with them the bits and pieces of
what Chris had imagined for himself.

The marriage finally came and went in a blur that was
almost too much to remember. Everything was happening
too quickly: a sea of faces he didn't know, introductions, being
on show every moment with barely space to breathe. Chris
spent half the wedding night hunched over a toilet bowl,
his best man's hand on his shoulder, unable to eat, unable to
do little more than stand as the whole night swirled around
him, watching and feeling as if he wasn't even really there.
Chris had a small selection of friends and his mother at the
wedding, but his side was far outweighed by the friends and
family that Anastasia owned. And as she owned them, they
in turn owned the entire evening.

They spent their wedding night in one of the top-class
hotels with Chris staring at the ceiling wondering what the
hell he had done. They didn't make love; he just felt too ill.
But then marriage wasn't what it was before. There was no
first night, not in the traditional sense. They'd had their first
night over three years before and the wedding night was
little more than a rubber stamp of what had already been
and become.

Chris was out in the real world now. He'd made the
transition from academic life, looking for something that he
could use to find a place in industry. His teaching experience
held him in good stead, and the English actually added value.
Eventually he found a job doing marketing in a small systems

company. It may have been commission based, but Stase approved. It had the potential to generate the income stream they'd need. They found a house—ideal for the first home buyer—a small cottage that was enough to start, borrowing from both her parents and his mother to have enough funds to be able to make the purchase.

Gradually, Chris made the transition from friend to boyfriend to husband. There's a progression there. Boyfriend or partner, to husband, and then back to partner again. Partly, it was a reflection of the way changes occurred around them— the acceptable labels applied by society, but it was more than that. It was a mark of Anastasia's own transition as she moved out into the world and wanted to establish her identity properly as an individual, an identity of her own rather than one bound to Chris or to her family as it had been. He didn't realize then that there was another transition yet to make. Life itself got in the way of subjecting the real future to true scrutiny. Suddenly, there was just too much to do and most of it was guided by Anastasia's formative vision of where they were going to be. First thing was buying the house. It wasn't going to be perfect, she knew, but it would be a launch platform to what they really wanted, and Anastasia had already decided what they really wanted.

CHAPTER TWENTY-SEVEN

CONFIDENCE

One of the things about being a man is you can't talk about stuff. You're trained to it from the point where you first start being socialized. It doesn't matter what generation you're from, there's still that socialization aspect, regardless of the trends that come and go. New Men aren't much different from Old Men when it comes down to it. That social schooling is definitely a man thing as opposed to a woman thing. Women seem to be able to talk about anything with each other, the most detailed intimate particulars.

Stase had told Chris a couple of times about things she had talked about with her girlfriends and he'd been horrified. Not only horrified; it had also left him feeling naked and exposed. The thought of revealing the sorts of details that Stase and her girlfriends seemed to discuss with ease just filled him with chill blankness. Chris had his own conception of what constituted privacy, and most of that stuff just didn't fit within those boundaries.

Stase seemed to have eased off on the whole seminar thing, so that was a partial relief, but some things still concerned him: her new circle of friends, the people who kept calling, the succession of parties. None of it included him and he could feel the void between them starting to expand. Once or twice over the past few weeks, Stase had talked about joint counseling sessions. The mere prospect filled

Chris with another form of dread. He wanted nothing to do with some know-it-all social worker or psychologist who would fill the pair of them with a succession of platitudes. To his mind, counseling was a band-aid. It didn't do anything to get to the real root of the problem. It was like the counseling sessions Stase herself had undertaken since the operation. He was convinced that they were more likely a cause of her new attitude than a source of any real help to her.

When he thought about it, her seemingly desperate need to put something new in her life, whether confidence, self-esteem, or a new social circle, was a reaction to what had been taken away from her. Her dreams had been unfulfilled when the initial planning proposal was denied, and then the whole cancer thing had swept over her; then, shortly after, her dreams and plans had been dashed once more when their appeal was lost. Though she'd had a surgical excision, they hadn't really solved the real problem within her. He wondered if perhaps the cancer had been some perverse joke, trying to fill her with something where she had been left hollowed by what the world had thrown at her. When they'd taken that away, she'd been left uncomfortably void without being able to explain it. Chris, distanced as he was from her, was unable to fill that void. Sometimes, the universe conspires within us and without us in weird ways.

Intellectually, rationally, Chris could cope with being the target of Stase's resentment, but every time he tried to do something that he thought might help her and thereby help their relationship, he was seen as the aggressor. Yet, at the same time, she sought out complete strangers to help her. After all, he was the one who lived with her, spent time with her, had shared things for years, who knew her. He thought that perhaps she could more easily shape the perceptions of virtual strangers to her version of her own perceived truth.

Not long after she'd made her real recovery from her radiation therapy, Stase announced that she wanted to go off to a health spa and undergo a detox program. Chris didn't think that was a very good idea at all. To go away to a country house and live on a diet of cabbage soup didn't seem very smart for someone whose metabolism relied upon a finely balanced chemical input that Chris wasn't sure was right in the first place. He was still wary about discussing that, but made his best efforts to bring up the subject and address the wisdom of what she was planning. She didn't listen, wouldn't listen, and within days, the whole thing was booked and paid for. He had no idea whether she'd informed them about her medication and really couldn't ask. He drove her out to the place in the new car, an old country house set in its own grounds. A discrete sign sat at the edge of the highway, pointing to a small dirt road leading back over the hills. Chris nearly drove past it on the way up. As they negotiated what looked like a private road, eased through the narrow inner farm gate and headed up a long tree-lined drive leading to a graveled parking lot inset with a fountain, Chris cast a doubtful and speculative gaze over the whole place. He was put strangely in mind of country retreats for celebrities, the sorts of places where stars went to dry out.

Inside, the place was just what he expected of a converted country house, except for the Laura Ashley wallpaper and the Scandinavian furnishings. The workers all wore white coats as if they were medical staff, but whether they were or not, Chris didn't know. More likely, they were dieticians and massage therapists and group activity coordinators and all that sort of thing. He looked at it all with jaundiced eye. He knew precisely what they were there for, to milk as much as they could out of the prospective returning client. This was like the weekly visit to the day spa gone mad.

He accompanied Stase to her room and helped her get settled in. It was a small room with the same floral wallpaper that stretched throughout the facility, but the tall single bed and the lounge chair beside it looked comfortable enough. Stase had brought a stack of magazines with her and there was a television on a bracket on the wall, enough to keep her relatively amused for the time she was there. Still skeptical, but reconciled to letting her get on with it, he said his goodbyes, headed out and got back in the car for the long drive back home.

As the miles of highway slipped past beneath him, he thought about the way she was reacting to him. All of it was starting to weigh heavily: the resentment, the refusal to listen to anything he had to say, her determined commitment to reach out and beyond anything that seemed entirely reasonable in what she wanted and what she wanted to own. It was as much owning as anything else, and more and more, Chris was becoming convinced that he himself was like an object, a possession rather than a partner. He was certainly no longer a confidante. And clearly, she no longer trusted him other than as a place to rest the culpability. The way she was shutting him out seemed like he was no different from an old toy that had somehow become broken and was still around more because of familiarity than anything else.

The worst thing was, that as a man, as was his proper station in life, he had no one with whom he could really discuss it. Even if he had had any real remaining friends, he couldn't really talk to them about this stuff. It just wasn't right.

By the time he pulled up into his street he was tired from the long drive, but he'd come to a decision. As soon as he got in the door, he headed for the telephone. There was one person he could still talk to, but then he guessed that's what mothers were for.

He called her, slightly relieved that she was there to take the call.

It was a hesitant, halting conversation, one in which he was forced to ask her not to say that she had told him so more than once. When he was all talked out, the conversation trailed off into a succession of long pauses punctuated with innocuous statements that meant absolutely nothing.

"So, what are you going to do?" his mother asked eventually after another dragging silence.

"I don't know," said, Chris. "I wish I did."

"Well, whatever you do decide," she said. "You know you will have my support. Just be careful. I'm worried about you, Chris. You've been through a lot over the last few months."

"Yeah, I know," he said. "I'm worried about me too."

"Well, you take care of yourself and let me know if you decide to do anything."

"Yeah, Ma, I will. Thanks."

As he put the phone down, he knew he hadn't really achieved anything or moved any closer to a solution, but the unburdening had made him at least feel a little better.

When the phone rang two days later, he thought it might have been his mother again to check up on how he was doing. Instead, it was the retreat.

"Mr. Baron?" said the woman at the other end of the phone.

"Yes?"

"We need you to come and get your wife."

"Huh?" said Chris, blinking a couple of times. "What's happened?"

"We don't want you to worry, but she's had a bit of a collapse."

"What do you mean 'a bit of a collapse?' What's that supposed to mean?" His head was racing with possibilities.

"She's okay. She just went a little too far with the detox diet. She became a little dehydrated and fainted. We think it's better if you take her home and she doesn't finish the program at this stage."

"Jesus," said Chris. Talk about I told you so.

"Can you come and collect her, Mr. Baron, or should we try and make other arrangements?"

"No, no. That's fine. I'll be up in a couple of hours."

He was shaking his head as he grabbed his car keys and headed for the door. Once again, Stase's utter determination had led her to places that she wasn't really ready to be.

CHAPTER TWENTY-EIGHT

ON A SEA BECALMED

On the ride home, Chris didn't say 'I told you so.'" He didn't say very much at all, just the passing query as to whether she was all right. He helped Stase into the house in silence, got her bags out of the car and set her up on the couch with a cup of tea. He stood watching her from the doorway, the only noise the sound of the television washing over their mutual silence.

Despite having moved on from that place in their lives where the planning approval and renovations were everything, Chris and Anastasia were growing even further apart. He could feel it, not only when he analyzed their reactions to one another, but the subtle awareness of something else deep in his gut. He knew it was happening, but he didn't know what he could do about it. How do you mend something if aren't sure exactly how it's put together or precisely how it is broken? He wasn't even sure whether he wanted to stop the gradual decline from happening any more.

The conversation he'd had with his mother had been good in more than one way; it had allowed him to use her as a sounding board, as a means of testing what he was really feeling and what he really wanted from his life together with Stase. He wasn't convinced that he wanted them to drift apart completely, and yet he wasn't so sure that he didn't.

Some days after that, on the night of that first real confrontation when the violence burst furiously between them, the worry and concern, the simple frustration, became tinged with fear—but there was more. There was the simple veiled knowledge that he couldn't yet allow himself to believe, that they'd gone to a place that he no longer wanted to be. That was the hardest realization to make.

Chris had confronted her in the kitchen, finally determined to do something about the widening chasm that yawned between them. He'd wondered to himself if he even loved her any more, and that was a big question for him. He knew for certain that he wasn't in love with her. There was just too much trial and pain. They may have moved beyond the things that caused those feelings, but it was embedded now, stuck in uncomfortable places that he couldn't really reach. Though he kept telling himself that he had to do something to make it right, there was another part of him warring with the concept, battling silently within. And all the time, he could not allow her to see his inner conflict. To admit it to her, would be to admit it to himself.

"Stase," he said. "We have to talk."

He had to be sure.

She turned to look at him, resentment already building on her face. "What about this time?"

"About us, about your attitude towards me, about everything. About what we're going to do with this place and with each other."

She turned away again. "There's nothing to talk about."

"How can you say that?" he said. "There's plenty to talk about." He was fighting to keep his voice level.

"Damn it, Chris, no. You're just going to tell me that everything's my fault again, that I'm not thinking straight. I'm not going to listen to your undermining bullshit any more."

He sighed, his teeth firmly clenched; trying not to let the spark of anger ignite and flame within him, he leaned back against the counter. "Listen, I don't know where you're getting this crap, but for once will you put whatever's being fed to you out of your head and listen to me?"

She said nothing. Her shoulders were tight and hunched. She kept looking down at the table and shaking her head.

"For fuck's sake, Stase. Will you turn around and look at me?"

She stayed where she was. If anything, her shoulders became tighter. He took the couple of steps that separated them and stood behind her.

"Stase? Why are you doing this? Don't you even care about what I have to say any more?"

Her silence was working in his jaw, worming away under his skin. He reached out, grabbed her arm and spun her around to face him.

"For Christ's sake, look at me!"

As he swung her about, her other hand came up, clenched into a claw, her nails out. She bared her teeth and dug her nails into his cheek, raking down.

"What the fuck!" he said.

His hand flew to his face and he drew it away again, looking at the red brown stripes across his palm. He pressed the hand quickly back to his face. His rage was incandescent, immediate. He lashed out with the palm of his other hand and slapped her. In that instant, he realized what he had just done and his eyes went wide.

"Jesus. Fuck!" he said through clenched teeth.

There was rage there, there was horror and at the same time, there was instantaneous shame for what he had just done. For just a moment, he didn't know which one took precedence.

Anastasia stepped right up close to Chris, her cheek red from the contact of his palm. His other hand was still pressed up against the now stinging wounds on his face.

"That's it," she said. "That's it, big man. Go on, hit me again. Go on. Show how strong you are. Come on, beat me up."

Chris backed up a step. She followed, her eyes hard, glittering. "How many other ways can you prove your dominance, hey? That's it. So, go on. What are you waiting for?"

"Fuck it, Stase. What are you doing?" He tried to step past her, away from the threatening anger, but she followed, pressing right up against him. He couldn't deal with the hard, sharp anger in her eyes. She put her face as close as she could to his.

"Come on, big man."

He pushed her away with his free hand and took two steps back into the doorway.

"I don't know what you want any more." The anger washed up in him again. "But I know what I want. I want a fucking divorce. I've had enough of this. I've had enough of you. Is that what you want? Well I'll tell you something—it's what I want."

There. He'd said it. He didn't know whether he wanted it or not, but there was something in the words that held a ring of truth. Even if he didn't, it might give her something to think about. It might even prompt her to reconsider what was happening.

She stared at him, folding her arms across her chest.

"Is that what you want Chris, is it?" She nodded her head, her expression dead calm, her voice steady. "Sure you don't want to hit me again? Let's add some physical abuse to the mental and emotional abuse. You can't undermine me, so you'll assert yourself physically, will you? So, come on."

He turned away from her. "I'm not going to play, Stase. I'm not going to listen to this shit any more. I don't know where it's coming from, but I'm just not listening to it anymore. I've had enough. You don't know what you're saying."

"Yeah, that's right. I don't know what I'm saying. I can't think for myself, can I? It has to be coming from somewhere else. You don't know what the fuck you're talking about. And I've had enough of you trying to diminish my worth."

He shook his head, frowning, and left her there. He knew they weren't her words. They didn't even sound like her. There was not a trace of that driving confident force that he'd fallen in love with. He almost didn't recognize what had become.

He slept on the couch that night, and he was gone before she was up in the morning. That was the first day, the day he saw the fat man on Sydney Street.

Chris tried to apologize when Stase came home that evening, but though he felt the shape of his own fault and his complicity in it, his heart really wasn't in feeling sorry. It was a shared blame that lay between them, and he didn't see why he needed to be the one that owned the culpability. She didn't respond, but gave a barely detectable smirk as her eyes flickered to the marks on his face; the look was gone as quickly as it had appeared. She didn't talk to him for the next three days; when she finally did, it was in a voice that radiated nothing but chill.

Over the next couple of weeks, as Chris's own obsession began, as he began seeking out those hollow shells of humanity that he'd started to discover, Stase became even more social in her endeavors. She wanted to go out to parties, and drinks, and dinners with friends, and spent very little time at home with him. There was a clear and uncomfortable space between them, and Stase was filling it her own way. Chris, though, was feeling less than social. He had little interest in the shallow public interactions that Stase was currently drawn to. He sent her off with his blessing, as if she needed it.

Chris had other things to attend to, convenient things. He was working up to broaching that place within himself where he could properly understand what was happening with them, summoning his internal energy so that he'd be prepared. Finding out about those empty hollow people in bus shelters and on the street became a kind of displacement activity in itself, keeping him occupied in a mental and emotional space where he didn't have to address the issues between them. In that sense, their relationship simply took a backseat.

Wryly, Chris imagined that it was little different from the obsession Stase herself had shown with the house and their inevitable social climb over the past few months. He was aware of what he was doing, his avoidance, but wasn't yet ready to deal with it properly.

Finding an answer to the van, the clean-cut guys, would mean finding a solution to what was going on inside him; then, if he was lucky, he might be able to use that knowledge to address what was happening with his life. His own life and what remained of his life together with Stase.

The sudden respite from anger and hostility that came just a couple of weeks later was a balance he didn't yet feel like upsetting. It was a welcome relief, but one that was counterbalanced by the knowledge that something had happened to him, something that had occurred without his knowledge or permission. He suspected that he shouldn't let Stase know about all of it. With that suspicion he decided it was better to keep the van, what he was doing, and everything associated with his quest secret from her for the time being. Her reaction the last time he had tried to discuss the woman in the bus shelter would have been enough to make him wary on its own, even without the doubt that he now carried. He already had his confidante, his partner in crime, in Jason. When Jason and he discovered what was going on, then and only then would be the time for expanding the knowledge to his broader world. Then and only then, he suspected, Stase would be one of the first he told. And when he did, it would be a revelation.

CHAPTER TWENTY-NINE

THE CATHEDRAL

Chris was ready. His trepidation still lurked—what if he really was just imagining the whole thing?—but he was committed to doing what he and Jason had planned. He picked the day and gave Jason a call. He suspected that doing this whole thing on a weekday was the right decision. Most of what he'd already seen had occurred during the week, and besides, there were many more people around during the working week. It would mean more difficulty with city traffic and they might end up having to drive around for hours, but city traffic was slow enough that he wouldn't be forced to race through the city streets in his car, missing whatever there was to see. He saw Stase off, made a show of getting ready for work himself, but lingered, waiting for the right moment. Very occasionally, they left for work together, but more often than not, Stase was out of the house before him. Recently, over the past few days, she'd been dragging, as if she were reluctant to go in, as if she wasn't looking forward to the work day. Before, she used to love being in at the office.

At last she walked out the door, closing it firmly behind her. He heard the brass knocker bounce and thunk against the door from the force with which she slammed it closed. He waited for about ten minutes to be sure that she hadn't forgotten anything and then headed for the phone.

It rang about eight times before Jason picked it up. For a moment, Chris was afraid the answering machine was going to kick in and he was going to end up frustrated once again. He just didn't need any more frustration at the moment.

"Hello, Jason. God, I thought you weren't going to be there."

"Yeah, hi. Sorry, I was doing something out the back."

"Well, anyway. How are you set for today?"

"Yeah, no problem."

"Great," said Chris. "I'll be over in about half an hour."

He put down the phone and nodded to himself. Good, that much was set. He pulled off his tie and hung it loosely over the back of a chair. He wouldn't need it today. He looked around the kitchen as if he might have forgotten something, but there was nothing really for him to forget. Grabbing the car keys and pulling on his coat, he headed out the door.

As he walked out of the house and pulled the front door gently shut behind him, he looked up and down the street. It was a good day, bright, with a few high clouds making lighter streaks across the pale blue sky. A gentle breeze stirred a few leaves in the gutter. He walked down the four steps to the front gate. He was pulling it shut behind him when some sense made him look up. A dark-eyed form was watching him from the guttering of the house next door. A motion from further up the roof, and it was joined by another. Two large, black birds sat on the edge of the roof next door, looking down at him. He swallowed, feeling a sudden chill, stopping with his hand on the top of the gate.

"What the fuck do you want?" he said quietly between closed teeth.

One of the birds tilted its head to look at its companion, and then turned its head back to look down at Chris. The other one fluffed out its feathers, making it look suddenly larger. A ripple of green-black shimmered in its wings. At that moment, the breeze picked up, rustling through the leaves of the trees opposite.

"No," said Chris and shook his head. He palmed his car keys and headed for the car, parked a little up the street. Refusing to look back up at the roof, he got into the car and started the engine. As he pulled out from the parking space, despite himself, he glanced up through the sunroof. They were still there, clearly watching him. He gritted his teeth and accelerated up the street. He was going to do this. He wasn't going to let a couple of bloody birds distract him.

With the morning traffic, it took him about twenty minutes to get over to Jason's. He found a parking spot a little way up the street and wandered down to collect him. He stood on the front step, rocking back and forth on his heels as he waited for the door to be answered. Jason finally appeared, looking a little disheveled, a big dark blue bulky sweater on, his shirt hanging out from beneath it.

"Hi guy," he said, looking past Chris and up and down the street. "Good day for it."

"Yeah, you set?" asked Chris.

"As ready as I'll ever be."

Chris nodded. "Let's go then."

"Hang on. Let me just lock up inside. I'll be with you in a sec."

Chris walked down the front steps and leaned on the gate post while he waited for Jason to do whatever he had to do. It really was a good day. Jason appeared a few moments later and bumbled down the steps. He stood in the entrance and looked up at the sky then back at Chris.

"Which way?"

"Yeah, sorry," said Chris. "I'm down this way."

"Heh, look at that," said Jason. "It's almost prophetic."

Chris turned to look in the direction that Jason was looking. Sitting in the branches of a small tree a few houses up was a large black bird, preening its feathers.

Chris swallowed. "Jesus. That I did not want to see."

Jason gripped his shoulder. "Come on. We have things to do, don't we? The game's afoot."

Chris shook himself and nodded. They headed up the slight slope to where the car was parked, Jason scuffing at the ground with his casual brown loafers as the walked. He wandered around to the other side of the care and stood bouncing up and down on the balls of his feet as he waited for Chris to open the door.

"It's open," said Chris.

Jason grunted and clambered in, reaching down to adjust the seat. As soon as he had everything to his satisfaction and his seat belt on, he leaned over and started rooting around in the compartment between the seats, pulling out a CD, then slotting it back again, then pulling out another.

"So what are you in the mood for?" he said.

"Hmm, nothing particularly," said Chris, pulling out and heading down the street. "Whatever you want."

Jason picked out a CD, slotted it into the player and looked out and around, watching the passing scenery as they started the drive into town. "Nice car," he said, nodding his head in time to the music. He seemed blithely unconcerned with what they were doing, more interested in what was passing outside the windows. Chris was still feeling the chill the unwelcome avian visitors had left with him.

The traffic swelled as they got closer to the center of town, Chris leaned forward and shut off the CD player.

"Hey," said Jason.

"Sorry, we really need to concentrate."

"So, exactly what are we looking for?"

"Hmmm, anything like a white van. If you can keep an eye out for things that look like white, square ice-cream vans."

"With or without the cone?"

"Yes, very funny. Without, of course. The other thing is

people sitting in places, just staring into space. I know that might be a little harder to spot, but it will be easier for you to see something than it will be for me. I'm going to have to concentrate on the road."

They turned into one of the main routes into the city center. Jason craned at the front window and back through the side windows, turning his head to follow things he'd spotted. After a while, he turned to Chris.

"Any idea what make this van is supposed to be?"

"No, sorry. I just have a rough idea what it looks like. There are things about that memory that are still pretty foggy."

"Uh-huh." Jason turned back to watch the outside.

They cruised the streets for about half an hour without seeing anything. Once or twice Jason tapped Chris on the arm and pointed.

"Van, there."

Chris would look and shake his head. "Nope. Not right."

For another hour they simply drove around and around, up side streets, down main thoroughfares, along streets with lots of people and areas with only a few, down narrow shadowed byways, across bridges and through underpasses. Nothing made itself apparent, or at least nothing that Jason pointed out. After a while longer, Jason started to become fidgety.

"Man, I'm parched. Can we stop for a coffee or something?"

Chris sighed. "Yeah, okay." He headed into the center of town again, with Jason looking for a parking spot. Eventually he spotted one and Chris reverse-parked in. They got out of the car and headed towards the intersection, looking for a coffee place. There was one every couple of streets in this part of town.

Chris barely glanced as they passed a newsstand and the headlines shouting at the passers-by. Big black letters announced an embassy bomb in the Philippines. Some extremist group had targeted the American Embassy again. 23 dead. Chris sighed and shook his head.

"So much for the War on Terror," he said.

Jason shrugged. "Yeah. Same old, same old. Can you see a coffee place?"

"I think there's one up here."

Jason nodded. "And not before time," he said.

They wandered in, ordered, and took up seats facing the window. After they'd sat in silence for a while, watching the people walking by outside, Jason asked, "So what are you hoping to achieve here?"

"Well, I'm hoping we can spot one of these vans and follow it, see where it goes. Not only will that be confirmation, but it might give us a chance to work out what's happening to these people."

"What is it with you and Stase, Chris?"

Chris frowned and turned to look at his friend. "What do you mean?"

"Oh, Claudia's mentioned a couple of things. Girls talk, you know. I usually don't pay much attention, but you know those two."

"Why, what's she said?"

Jason watched a girl walk past outside, assessing before answering. She was cute, and Chris followed her with his gaze too.

"Nothing particularly," said Jason, still tracking the girl. "Just that things might be a little tense between you two."

Chris rubbed his fingers up and down on the outside of his tall, white latté mug. "Well, you know. Things haven't been great. The operation, the house, all that stuff. Yeah, things have been a bit tense, if you know what I mean."

"I can imagine."

"Doesn't seem I can do anything right at the moment. Of course, she won't talk to me about it, not that I'm that keen on beating the whole thing to death, but it's almost as if she blames me for everything. Yeah, of course she's going to talk to her girlfriends about it. I can never understand that whole thing. Can you? The sort of stuff they're prepared to talk about. The intimate details."

Jason watched another girl walk past as he sipped at his coffee. "No, not really. Jesus, can you imagine if we talked about that sort of thing?"

Chris shrugged. "Yeah, well. It's private isn't it? I'm amazed at some of the things she talks about with her friends."

"Yeah, I know what you mean."

They lapsed into silence again. Chris toyed with his now empty mug.

"So, shall we get back to it?" he said, looking at Jason.

"If we must."

They headed out to the car and started driving around again. It was slow going and they seemed to be getting nowhere. About 3:00, Jason wanted to stop for another coffee and something to eat. He suffered from low blood sugar and it was beginning to take its toll. Chris spied a likely looking spot and slowed to a crawl, looking for somewhere to park. They'd just got out and were heading towards the place when Chris stopped in his tracks. He grabbed Jason by the arm.

"Do you see that?"

"What?" said Jason. "Listen, man. I really need to get something to eat."

Across the other side of the road, a narrow underpass covered some concrete steps that led up to a broad, flat, paved open space on an upper level, a place where office workers all clustered to eat lunch. Chris could see the space was pretty empty at the moment, being mid-afternoon, but there, in the shadow of the small ascending tunnel was a man, sitting, huddled. He was maybe mid-thirties, well dressed, with light brown, receding hair. Chris had seen that blank expression before.

"Look, over there, in the shadow of that archway."

Jason frowned, looked in the direction that Chris was indicating, frowned again and shook his head.

"Listen, Chris, I'm serious."

"Jesus, Jason. Concentrate. Think about what you're looking at. Study it."

Jason looked up and down the street as if looking for assistance, then back over to where Chris was pointing. He squinted across.

"I don't ..."

Chris gripped his arm more tightly. "Concentrate, goddammit."

"Ow." Jason shook his arm free. He leaned forward, narrowing his eyes even further pulling his arm free from Chris's grip.

"Wait ... ah ... okay. There's a guy over there, right?"

"Yes. Look at him carefully."

Jason frowned with concentration. "Yeah, doesn't look right, does he?"

Chris was disturbed that Jason seemed to have so much difficulty even seeing the man let alone maintaining his concentration. At the same time, he was relieved that Jason could see him. Chris grabbed Jason's arm again.

"You wait here. I'm going to get the car."

Jason frowned at him, having a little shake of his head. "Listen, Chris, I really do need to—"

"No time! Wait here. I'll be right back."

Chris dashed down the street, heading for where he had parked the car. He fumbled in his pocket for the car keys as he ran, managing to snag them and pull them free. He pointed the electronic key at the car when he was still a hundred yards away from it, desperately listening for the alarm signal that would tell him the car was unlocked. He raced the last few paces and wrenched the door open, bundling himself in, strapping on the seatbelt and shoving the key into the ignition. He had no idea how long the guy had been sitting there. He only hoped he could trust Jason to stay in place until he got back.

Quickly, he touched the button that wound down his window, and looked out, seeking an opportunity to pull out onto the street and do a u-turn.

"Come on, come on," he muttered under his breath as one, two, three cars decided to take that moment to pull around the corner and head his way. Finally, there was a break, and he managed to turn the car and head back down the way they had come. Just as he was reaching the end of the street, the lights changed.

"Dammit," he said under his breath, giving the steering wheel a quick slap. He drummed on the top of the wheel impatiently, waiting for the lights to change again, watching the traffic passing either way on the adjoining street, praying that he would see no white van, at least not yet.

The lights changed and he turned, driving slowly up the side of the road towards where Jason was standing waiting for him. Thankfully there had been nothing behind him. He drew up beside Jason and hit the hazards. He glanced up in the rearview mirror as Jason leaned over and opened the door.

"Don't get in," Chris told him.

"What?"

"Just stand there with the door open looking as if you're talking to me and keep an eye on the guy over the other side of the road."

"Hmmm." Jason didn't look impressed.

Chris looked up in the rearview mirror again and then into the wing mirror, checking what was coming. He didn't want a police car to suddenly turn up and move him on. The traffic flow had started again. Dammit, they could put up with him sitting there.

"Can you see any sign of anything?"

Jason glanced around and shook his head. Chris was starting to feel uncomfortable and exposed.

Just then, Chris glanced in the side mirror and felt a rush of nervous excitement. There, coming up the street behind them was a white van. It looked the right shape. From what he could see with his limited viewpoint, it looked like there were two men riding in the front.

"Shit, this is it," he said quietly.

"What?" said Jason, one hand on the car roof, leaning over inside.

"The van. Can you see the one I mean? Keep an eye on it, in case I have to deal with something."

Jason stood up and looked in either direction, then leaned back in. "I don't see what you mean," he said.

"Shit!"

The van swept past them and Chris kept watching it. It started to perform a wide circle, through the traffic, performing a maneuver that would turn it to come back the other way. There was no way Chris could perform a stunt like that. How far was it to the next intersection?

"Jason, quick, get in."

"What?"

"Fuck it, man. Just get in will you?"

Jason had barely half closed the door when Chris took off, racing for the next intersection. As they were turning, he remembered the hazards and flicked them off. He glanced over at Jason, who was looking less than impressed.

"Listen," said Chris. "For some reason, you're having problems seeing what I'm seeing. You saw the guy in the archway. Well, the van's here now. When we get back on to the street, you're going to have to concentrate again, actually look for the bloody thing. It's there. I just hope to hell we're fast enough."

He threw another u-turn and ended back at another set
of lights, rocking back and forth in his seat, willing them
to change. Finally they did, and he tore around the corner,
then immediately slowed. The van's backdoors were open,
and the two clean-cut guys were just in the process of closing
them. He slowed to a crawl.

"There. Look. Can you see them?"

Jason craned forward in his seat, putting his fingers up to
his temples, frowning ahead at the road.

"Shit. Yeah. I see it. Damn. It was as if I were seeing
it but not seeing it. I could see it was there, but ... Christ,
what's going on?"

"Keep your focus," said Chris. "We need to follow these
bastards."

The two clean-cut men, white coats and everything,
climbed back into the front of the van and it slowly pulled
out from the curb, gently accelerating down the street. Chris
sped up in pursuit, receiving a blast from somebody's horn
behind them for his efforts.

"Oh, fuck off," he said, not even looking to see who had
blasted him. He had the van in his sights now and that was
all that mattered.

"You can see it, right, Jason?" he said.

"Yeah." Jason was still frowning. "Though it's kind
of strange."

"How do you mean?"

"I'm finding it hard to maintain concentration on it. I have
to really work to keep my attention there; it's as if it keeps
wanting just to slide off and away to something else."

"Uh-huh." But thank God he was actually seeing it now.

They followed the van for about four blocks before it
turned off. Chris almost lost it then. An unfortunate snarl
in the traffic, another set of lights and he was cursing. He
accelerated into the side street, just in time to see the van

turning another corner towards the end. Jason seemed not to see it at all.

"Is it still there?" Jason asked.

"Yeah, just turned into a side street, but I need to hurry."

He accelerated up to the corner and took it, the tires squealing slightly as they rounded. Jason clutched for his seatbelt, but said nothing. It didn't take Chris long to catch up.

"There, do you see it?"

"Oh, yeah. Right."

The van led them on a route chasing through back streets and major roads. There seemed to be no particular pattern to the route they were following, but it was heading somewhere. It wasn't too long before they were out of the city proper and into the sprawling suburbs. The streets became wider, tree-lined, and there were fewer other cars on the road. Chris wondered where they were going.

The van slowed, and Chris eased off. Nearby, a large building, fenced off from the rest of the surrounding area loomed through the trees. Large, pale stone blocks formed flat blank walls. The van pulled through a gate and Chris stopped, pulling to the side of the road.

"What do you think it is?" he said.

Jason leaned to one side, trying to get a better view. "Something big."

"Well, yeah. Tell me something I don't know."

"You want to take a look?"

Chris nodded. He engaged the parking brake, gently opened the door, stepping out and closing it just as quietly. He stood beside the car waiting for Jason to join him.

"Damn," he said. He could see what it was now. "It's a church."

"Hmmm. Bigger than a church," Jason said. "You want to take a closer look?"

"Uh-huh. But let's try and keep out of sight."

They quickly hurried across the road together, looking both ways and keeping to the concealment of old, gnarled, broad tree trunks as much as they could while they moved closer to the side of the church. Jason was right. It was bigger than a simple church. It was huge. A graveyard sat at one side, old stones arrayed in lines, marked with lichen and old trailing vines. The moss-covered ground appeared well tended. There was no sign of the van.

It took Chris a moment or two to notice it in the shadow, but atop one of the slightly leaning old stones, perched a large black bird. The cool, dark shadow reached out tendrils to Chris's chest and he sucked in his breath.

"What is it?" asked Jason.

Chris shook his head. "Let's take a look." He turned away from his winged adversary, turning his face away from its clear dark gaze. They walked along the front of the ground; tall sandstone posts inset with arrow point barred iron fencing separated the roadside from the churchyard. There was nothing Catholic about the church itself. It was Calvinist in design: austere, pale stone, no adornment. Large double wooden doors sat at the front above wide stone steps. A simple grassed lawn was broken only by a simple blacktop path from the front gate.

A wide lettered sign sat next to the gate, supported by twin posts. The faded lettering had once been in gold, but was now gilded black atop the flaking cream paint beneath. The name was indistinguishable, but Chris could barely make out the last word: "Cathedral."

Farther down, another gate led into the churchyard proper. It sat open and twin muddy tracks led in from the road, divided by clumped and dirty, spattered tufts of grass. This driveway had seen lots of use, and recently, through all weather by the looks of it. They walked slowly along the fence and down to the open double gates. The back of a single white van poked out from behind the rear of the building. Even farther back, the grounds looked slightly overgrown; a profusion of weeds clustered in the rear corner, their tops sprouting pale white flowers. Chris stood at the gate, scanning the grounds, looking for any sign of life. Apart from the bird he'd seen in the graveyard, there seemed to be nothing. Another large tree shaded the muddy ground at the rear, obscuring it from direct sunlight. A scattering of old brown-gray leaves littered the ground below.

Jason was watching him, leaning against one of the gate posts. "What do you want to do, Chris?"

Chris chewed at his lips. "I don't know. Hang on."

He scanned the grounds again. The large, wooden front doors of the building were firmly closed. There was no way in there, not without alerting anyone inside. Jason had turned and draped his arms over the top of the stone gatepost. He was resting his chin on top of them, alternating between squinting his eyes and frowning, then opening them wide again.

"Damn," he breathed. "The bloody van still keeps slipping out of focus."

"Wait here," said Chris.

With a quick look in either direction, then one more assessment of the unmoving grounds, he dashed towards the back of the cathedral down the central strip between the muddy ruts leading around to the rear. Tall plain windows were set at regular spaces down the building's length. They were constructed of smaller multiple panels of slightly opaque glass, revealing nothing within. Set in the standard cruciform, the building jutted out in front of him. The path curved around, behind, and he slowed to a quick lope, rounding the edge of the corner. As he reached halfway, he saw the complete side of the van. He drew up short, and slipped to the side, pressing himself against the wall and sidling along it until he could poke his head around the corner.

There wasn't just one van. Three more sat parked in the shade, all identical. Chris sucked in his breath, his heart pounding now. A strange floating feeling nestled in his stomach. Nothing moved. Nothing. There was no sound, not even a breeze rustling the leaves. He could smell the damp ground and something like mold mixed with mud. He tried to still his breathing, struggling to work out what he was going to do next. He didn't have a plan. He had no idea what he was going to do.

Any idea of making plans was suddenly whipped away from him. A loud squawking came from the branches above him, again and again, loud, beating down across the damp empty space. He heard the sound of a door.

"Shit!" he said, tore himself from the wall and dashed back out to the gate. "Jason, quick. Let's get out of here." He waved one hand in the direction of the parked car. "Move it!"

He didn't dare look around. He didn't want to see those faces, that clean-cut blandness. He just wanted to get out of there.

Jason stumbled from the gate. "What?" he said. "What?" "Just move!"

They reached the car and piled in. Chris slammed his foot down on the accelerator as soon as he got the car started, skidding from their standing position, jerking them out onto the road and away.

"Jesus, Chris, what are you doing?" said Jason, his breathing heavy, his features pale.

"That was too close. Way too close." He eased off on the accelerator and slowed to an acceptable rate. "Sorry. I got scared. That's all. I just realized back there I didn't have any idea what we were going to do. At least I know now where it is." He kept driving, noting landmarks as they went.

"So, what next?"

"I don't know. I need to think about it. Sorry, Jase. Fuck."

At least he had the confirmation now—he wasn't going mad after all.

"You believe me now, don't you?"

Jason took a moment before answering. "Yes. I suppose I have to. Very strange the way things keep on sliding in and out. Hmmm. I don't know if I believe quite everything, but there's definitely something going on. I want to look some things up tonight, see if I can come up with anything."

"Yeah, okay, but that's not necessarily going to help, is it?"

"No, but it might give us some idea."

"Yeah, maybe. Listen, I've got an idea. Are you up for an excursion on the weekend? Maybe Saturday?"

Jason thought about that for a couple of moments. "I guess so. I was just thinking about Claudia."

"Yeah, well, Stase often goes out and does stuff on a Saturday. Beauticians and shit like that. I'll just tell her I'm going over to see you. Shouldn't be a problem."

"Okay, I can work something out."

"Good. Anything you can find out in the meantime would be great."

They lapsed into silence. Chris felt better about having some sort of plan, but the traces of fear still wormed inside his chest. Now, at least, he wasn't alone.

CHAPTER THIRTY

SOMETHING FOR THE WEEKEND

Chris picked Jason up from his house on the Saturday afternoon and, not without some trepidation, they headed off for the cathedral. Jason, as usual, was decked out in a bulky sweater and corduroy pants. Jason looked nervous, a little unsure. He'd come up with nothing from his research effort over the past few days, and that also unsettled him. He'd been looking for things associated with vans and strange periods of blankness in people's lives. He did research, he was good at research, and yet he'd drawn a blank. All he'd come up with was the usual rubbish about abductions.

They had to cross the town to get to where the cathedral sat, but traffic was light, and apart from weekend shoppers, the streets remained free-flowing.

"So, where's Claudia?" Chris asked him.

Jason chuckled. "Funny you should ask that. She's gone off to meet Stase to do some shopping."

Chris gave a short unamused laugh. "Huh. I knew she was meeting a girlfriend, but she didn't bother to say who."

"Well, that's the girls for you."

They drove on in silence for a while.

"So what do you expect to find there?" asked Jason after a while.

"I don't know. Some way to get in and see what they're up to. Everything I've seen happens during the week. I'm hoping they have less activity on the weekend. Maybe we'll get a chance to sneak inside, have a quick look and get out again. Enough for us to develop a proper strategy. What do you think?"

Jason nodded, his eyebrows beetling. "Uh-huh. Sounds like a plan."

"You thought any more about this stuff?"

"Jesus, man. I've thought about nothing but. I don't like the idea that something's screwing with my head. Not at all. My head's my most important asset, apart from my sylph-like frame and animal magnetism." He chuckled at himself, tapping with one hand on the dash. "Can I put some music on?"

"Yeah, sure," said Chris. They didn't have to concentrate on anything particularly yet.

"Thanks. Just want something to steady the nerves. Keep my mind off it, so to speak." He pushed in a CD and drummed on the dash with his fingers in time to the music, singing wordlessly under his breath as he watched the passing streets.

"Jason, listen," said Chris. "I really appreciate this."

"Shit. Nothing. Happy to be along." He didn't look it.

As they neared the area of the cathedral, Chris slowed and killed the volume. He recognized the streets now, having imprinted them firmly the last time he was here. A couple of times he'd pulled up maps on some of the search programs and studied the street layout so he knew exactly where he was going. He knew his way around, but just needed the confirmation to be clear in his own mind. Stase never even bothered disturbing him when he was online. She seemed to have no interest, except when she had something very specific to look up, and then she got Chris to do it for her.

He slowed still further, leaning forward in his seat and studying the road, the surrounding houses, the trees along the side of the road, even the sky above them. He kept on being afraid of seeing some large black flying thing tracking them as they went. Jason was still drumming gently with his fingers.

They turned into the street containing the large building that was their destination. Chris frowned, in spite of himself. The street was packed with cars. Something appeared to be going on. Deciding that caution was the right course, he decided to cruise past the cathedral, have a look, and then park somewhere beyond it.

As they reached the cathedral grounds, Chris sucked air through his teeth. "Shit," he said.

In the front of the cathedral steps sat a couple of large black cars, ribbons draped from their hoods to the top of their windows. A crowd of people stood on the steps and arrayed out in front of them. The wooden doors were wide open. It was a wedding. It was a bloody wedding. But that didn't make sense. How could there be a wedding here if this was supposed to be the place where things happened? Chris cruised past slowly, turning his head to look. It was real enough.

"So, what do you make of that?" said Jason.

"Shit," he said. "I don't know. Damned if I know." He shook his head and sped up and away.

Scratch that plan. He had to think of something else.

He'd dropped Jason off at his place with the agreement that he'd give him a call as soon as he came up with any real idea what they needed to do next. At the same time, Jason agreed to continue his research, not that he seemed very hopeful that he was going to come up with anything.

On the way home, Chris decided that he could at least swing past the cathedral on the following day, Sunday, and see what was going on there: whether the place did more than service bridal parties. He didn't need Jason along for that particular excursion.

In the morning, he gave Stase some story about going out to get a few things from the store, leaving her half asleep and still in bed. She liked to sleep in on the weekends and had been staying in bed later over the past few weeks. He figured he could pick up the papers and perhaps some breakfast things on the way back, enough to make his story credible.

Sunday morning, it was a quick run across town to the cathedral, and he was there in record time. As with the previous day, he drove slowly past, looking not only to see if he could spot the vans, but also for any other activity. As he neared the cathedral grounds, he was surprised, and at the same time unsurprised to see a cluster of cars around the area, and again, the doors open.

He chewed at his lip, trying to decide what he was going to do. He glanced at his watch to make sure of how much time had passed and how much time he might have left, though the way Stase slept and kept going back to sleep during the weekend, she was not likely to be unaware of how much time had actually passed since he left. Setting his mouth firmly, he located a parking space and pulled up to the curb. He may as well find out what was going on there.

Chris walked back to the cathedral's front, his hands shoved deep into his pockets. He slowed as he reached the front gate. A quick look had revealed no sign of the vans out the back, and for the moment, he didn't think that was a very good sign. He was almost starting to think he was imaging things again. But he couldn't be. Jason had been with him. He'd seen them too. Where did they put the things on the weekend? He stood at the gate, watching and listening. There were unmistakable sounds coming from inside the building, floating down the path towards him on this bright, crisp morning.

"Damn," he said quietly to himself. He knew what the sounds were, but he didn't want to admit it right now. It was singing. The sounds of multiple voices blurred by the building itself and the distance at which he stood, joined together in song and underneath it all, the sound of an electric organ sounding more like a 70's rock band than real church music.

Chris slipped through the gate and walked nervously up to the front steps. If he could just get a look inside ... .

He took the steps slowly, one at a time, pausing with each new level. The voices were clearer now. Definitely singing. Definitely singing a hymn. They were having a service inside.

He took the last step and crossed to the side of one of the doors, gently leaning his face around the corner so he could see inside. He got a good view of the back few rows. People stood, prayer books in hand, belting out the chorus of an old standard, the mix of good voices and others making the kind of amateur swell of noise that came with public services. He pulled his head back, thinking. If they were holding a church service in there, how the hell could this be anything else but a functioning church? Though he had often wondered what happened to these places most of the time when there weren't services in progress. Did they just gather dust in the hollow spaces that echoed between the walls?

He ducked his head around the corner for another look. Long lines of pale, polished wood pews, scattered with people in groups, or individually, stretched up to the front, where a pale stone altar sat beneath an unadorned window. A tall crucifix was affixed to the wall beneath the window, pale polished wood, almost matching the pews, but not quite. A brown stone floor, matt and smooth, echoed the sound of the congregation, sending it bouncing back from light stone walls. The interior was simple, unaffected, strangely unlike what he had imagined for the interior of a cathedral. It was big enough; there just didn't seem to be any of the trappings of high religion. A couple of flag-like devices were affixed to the walls, one burgundy, one green, with gold letters embroidered into them, but they looked dull and faded.

He pulled himself back and stepped quickly down the stairs and out to the street. He didn't want to be caught hanging around here, and he wasn't keen on being seen. He walked quickly back to the car, a new plan starting to form inside his head.

CHAPTER THIRTY-ONE

WHAT HAPPENS INSIDE

Chris was ready, well, just as ready as he was going to be. He'd picked the night with care, a Thursday evening when Stase was going out for drinks with the girls. He'd given Jason a preparatory phone call from work, checking that it was going to be all right with him. Jason was a little bemused when Chris had asked him if he owned a crowbar, but then it was the sort of thing Jason would own. It wasn't the fact of asking for it; it was what he wanted it for. He also suggested he bring along a flashlight. Chris had one of those big heavy-duty black numbers from the tool cupboard downstairs, and he'd checked that the battery was okay and everything was working correctly. He'd shoved the flashlight, a hammer, and a pair of pliers, in a small black bag in preparation, not one hundred percent sure exactly what he needed to take, and stashed it in the cupboard from which he'd taken the flashlight. He wasn't worried about Stase finding it and asking any potentially awkward questions. He had never seen her open the cupboard once. All it held were tools and old cans of paint.

He'd also asked Jason about Claudia.

"No, no trouble," he'd said. "You know the little woman. Works till all hours. She'll get home when she's ready and if I'm out, well I just got bored at home. Simple."

"Okay, if you're right then, I'll pick you up around six thirty."

He grabbed the bag from downstairs, headed out to the

car, and got in. He sat for a few minutes, just staring ahead, his hands on the steering wheel, wondering if he was doing the right thing; finally, convinced he had little other choice, he kicked the engine into life and pulled out onto the street. He'd come this far; he might as well go all the way.

When he rang at Jason's door, it took only moments for a shadow to darken the glass from the inside and the door to swing open. Jason nodded to him and stood there looking back as if waiting for something. Chris glanced down, and piled on the floor to one side lay a crowbar, a hefty flashlight and a pair of bolt-cutters.

"Aren't you going to put those in something?" he asked.

Jason grinned sheepishly. "Oh yeah," he said. He disappeared back down the hall and left Chris standing on the front doorstep rocking back and forth on his heels. Jason reappeared a few moments later with a battered black canvas bag, dropped it on the floor and crouched down to shove all the things inside it. He stood, rubbing the palms of his hands together. "Let's hope we don't get pulled over," he said. "Anybody'd think we were off to do a spot of housebreaking. Not that we aren't."

"Yeah, okay," said Chris, not in the least amused. Jason seemed to be taking this awfully lightly.

Jason lifted his eyebrows then stooped and hefted the bag. "Okay. Let's go then," he said. "I hope you know what you're doing."

"Yeah, so do I ..." said Chris.

When they got to the car, Chris opened the backdoor. "Shove that stuff on the floor back there. We need to keep it in easy reach."

They both climbed in and Chris started the car. Jason was chewing at his lip.

Chris turned to look at him.

"You're okay with this, aren't you?" he asked.

"Yeah," said Jason. "Just a little nervous, I guess."

Chris was too. Breaking into places wasn't something he exactly made a habit of. Jason had been good enough to agree to come though, so he wasn't going to try and unsettle him any further than he already seemed to be.

They drove in silence across to the other side of town, Jason not even asking to put on any of his habitual music.

Chris pulled up a little way down from the cathedral, killed the engine and the lights and waited. He wanted to see if there was any kind of activity around the place, if there was anything that might give them away. It was a quiet, mainly residential street. A couple of cars drove by in quick succession, and then everything was quiet again.

Jason cleared his throat. "Um ..."

Chris held up a hand. "Hang on, we need to be sure."

He'd been thinking about this. The cathedral grounds had enough trees to provide a fair bit of covering shadow. There were a couple of nearby streetlights, but they didn't cast that much illumination into the grounds. With the trees lining the street, which still hadn't lost their leaves, the grounds and building itself were further obscured. If the pair of them kept low enough, what with the surrounding walls, they should be able to avoid immediate observation.

Chris was just about to reach for the door handle when he saw an old figure, long coat, walking slowly up the street towards them.

"Shit," he said. There was no way the old guy could miss them. Maybe it was dark enough, and what with the shadow of the trees around them, if they sat very still, he might just walk past without even seeing them. "Don't move," he said quietly.

"Wha—?"

Chris cut him off with a quick wave of his hand.

The old man kept coming, walking slowly with a slightly uneven gait. His neck was bent forward, watching the pavement as he came. Chris held his breath. A small white dog pulled on a leash in front of him.

The old man walked slowly past, seemingly intent on his own feet, or at least the ground beneath them. He didn't even look up.

Chris let out a long, relieved breath.

"Thank God this is a quiet neighborhood," he said. "I'd rather we weren't seen."

Jason nodded.

Reaching over the back, Chris pulled up Jason's canvas bag, juggled it over the seat back and dropped it into his lap, then reaching over again, felt around and snagged his own bag.

"Okay, hang on a moment," he said, checking the front and all of the mirrors. "Right, it seems to be clear. We'll just get out, walk quickly but calmly across to the gates and then straight inside. Once we get behind the front fence, keep low and we'll head for the back. We can't very well go in through the front door."

"Sounds like a plan," said Jason, reaching for his door and pausing.

"There's got to be a back way in somehow," said Chris. "Okay, let's go."

As they both stepped out of the car and gently closed their doors, a slightly curious thought came to Chris. It was the most definite action he'd taken about anything for a long, long time. In everything, with the house, with the relationship, he'd just been sitting back and watching, letting it happen. Even looking for the hollow people wasn't real action. It was just more of the same, standing back and watching. This was actually doing something.

They made it to the gate and further with no problem. Chris, keeping an eye out for other people, dashed along the side of the cathedral, Jason beside him, their bags barely above the grass that whipped past their feet. They rounded the corner to the back and Chris held up a hand, stopping Jason in his tracks. They were in deep shadow here. The branches of the nearby tree blocked the sky above, and Chris pulled them in close to the wall. His breath was coming quickly and he could hear Jason breathing rapidly beside him. He took a couple of moments to slow his breathing, looking around, seeing if he could spot anything of use.

All was still. Not one, not two, but five white vans sat parked in a line back from the building itself. He swallowed. Okay, the vans were here. They definitely hadn't been on the weekend, or not that he could see. He listened. A faint breeze stirred through the leaves above him, seeming to whisper caution.

"Do you hear anything?" he breathed, close to Jason's ear. Jason shook his head and Chris nodded.

Step by careful step, he moved further around the back of the building, Jason following close behind. He could smell the dampness, the mud, the thick earthy scent of moldering leaves. He put out a hand, feeling the cold rough stone of the cathedral's wall. Every couple of steps, he paused looked around, checked behind him, but apart from the slight motion of the leaves above, everything seemed still.

Along a facing wall, right near the corner was a small door that Chris presumed must lead inside. It probably didn't give access to the body of the cathedral proper, but it was a way in. Whatever lay behind it must give entry, or at least a route to what sat beyond. He indicated the door with a tilt of his head and Jason nodded and took a few quick steps over to it. Chris kept watch and then trod rapidly over to join him. Jason was running his hand slowly over the door's flat surface.

"Well, it's an ordinary door," he whispered.

Chris made as if to cuff him and shook his head. Jason grinned, his teeth looking unnaturally white in the gloom.

"I feel like I should have a black woolen hat pulled down over my ears," he said.

"Oh, shut up," whispered Chris. He pressed his ear against the door. He could hear absolutely nothing. He pulled back from the door and gently lowered his bag to the ground. Jason did the same. There was a slight clank of metal on metal as Jason's bag met the ground and Chris winced. He looked quickly around, but there was no cause for alarm.

"Now what?" Jason asked.

Chris leaned down and pulled the crowbar out from Jason's bag. "Go back there and keep watch. I'm going to open up."

He waited till Jason had walked quickly back to the building's edge and then hefted the crowbar, examining the locks. They were simple. No need for the bolt cutters or anything like it. He just hoped to hell the place wasn't alarmed. He looked over to Jason, who waved a hand to indicate that everything was okay. Taking a firm grip, he inserted the edge of the crowbar between the doorframe and the door, near the locks and pushed. There was a slight give, but that was it. Putting his back into it and gritting his teeth, Chris gave a hefty shove. With a splitting of wood and a loud crack, the door swung open. Chris sucked air through his teeth, looking around nervously. Jason looked back over his shoulder then back around the corner. Gently, gently, Chris dropped the crowbar back into the bag. He gestured for Jason to come join him.

What lay revealed behind the door was a small dark room, windowless and featureless in the lack of light. Chris picked up his bag and rooted around for the flashlight.

"No lights till we get inside," he whispered. Jason nodded in response.

They slipped into the room and Chris pulled the broken door shut behind them before hitting the flashlight.

He played the beam over what turned out to be a simple narrow side room containing a desk, a closet, and some shelves, all in dark polished wood. There were a few papers in the desktop and Chris stepped over and started riffling through them, holding his flashlight aloft and pointed down at the table surface. There seemed to be nothing of immediate interest. He glanced around. There was another door set into the wall almost directly opposite where they had entered. He shone his flashlight at it then stepped over to it and listened, but there was no sound from the other side, though the noise of his forcing the outside door would have alerted anyone who might be lurking on the other side. He waved Jason over, killed the flashlight, and slowly turned the handle. He eased the door open a crack and tried to peer beyond. It was gloomy, open on the other side; clearly this door led into the cathedral proper. Swinging the door open a little wider, he verified that there was no movement from that dark, chill space.

Chris chewed at the inside of his bottom lip. This was not what it was supposed to be like at all. He didn't know what he'd expected—medical equipment, a lab?—but it was just as he had seen it before, only draped in semi darkness. Enough light filtered through the plain glass windows to touch the tops of polished wooden pews with a hint of silver light. The same for the dull floor.

"Shit," he said under his breath.

"What is it?" whispered Jason beside him, craning over his shoulder to get a look.

"It's not supposed to be like this," he said, still whispering.

"What's it supposed to be like?"

"I don't know. I don't know. Come on. This doesn't make sense."

Chris stepped into the vast echoing space of the cathedral itself. His footsteps were clear and unnaturally loud in the dim, empty space. He walked up the central aisle, looking carefully at either side, looking for some clue, for something that would tell him he hadn't been imagining it all. He stopped right in the center. Jason stood at the other end of the aisle watching him. There was no need for the flashlights here; it was dark, but still light enough to see.

"Jesus," he said.

"So what now?" said Jason, his voice sounding distorted as it echoed from the walls and floor.

"Shhh," said Chris, holding up two fingers in a gesture bizarrely reminiscent of a religious benediction.

"What?"

Chris gestured for quiet. He had heard something, a vague whisper of something. He was sure of it. There it was again.

A gentle rustling sigh stirred through the space. He couldn't tell where it was coming from.

"Listen," he said. "Do you hear that?"

It rippled around the walls, the floor, the ceiling, seemingly from all directions at once.

Jason cocked his head in a way that Chris would have found comical in any other situation.

"What?" he said.

The sound insinuated itself around them. Chris looked up. It was coming from somewhere above them. He narrowed his eyes, trying to focus on the source of the motion, peering into the darkness. At first, he wasn't sure, and then the hint became a certainty. There was something moving up there. He tilted his head back, trying to maintain his focus, his attention. There was something wrong with what he was seeing, an almost wavering flowing in slight ripples, distorting the beams above him, wavering across the darkened ceiling vaults far above. He stared, hard, concentrating.

There was movement up there all right, movement above and along the vast wooden beams, dark night shapes jostling each other for position. Black shapeless forms shifted and stirred all along the beams and around the edges. There came the sound again, louder, and this time it was accompanied by a low murmur.

As he concentrated, the amorphous shapes started to resolve themselves into individual forms.

"Oh Christ," he said.

All along the beams, clutching to the ceiling arrayed along the edges of the walls, were crows, gently shifting one against the other. Chris's heart went cold. One of the birds croaked and then another, the sound echoing around the empty space, chilling him.

He couldn't move. His breath was suddenly tight in his chest. He tore his gaze away from the creatures still there above him and glanced around.

Jason stood where he was, just staring blankly ahead, a slightly puzzled expression on his face.

"Jason?" Nothing, not even a flicker. Jason appeared stuck in place.

Chris forced himself to look up again. Black eyes were looking back at him, glittering, even blacker in the darkness.

One of the black birds detached itself from the rafters and launched itself into space, quickly followed by another. The first beat its wings against the air, slowing its descent, heading towards him, the other circling behind it. Chris swallowed, overcome with the image of hundreds of beaks rushing down upon him, tearing him to pieces. He couldn't move.

The flapping bird came closer, but as it reached almost head height, level with Chris's eyes, it seemed to lose form, becoming insubstantial, changing, reshaping. Its color faded, washing out and becoming paler and paler. And then it was past him, wings beating the air in cleanly defined strokes. A feather drifted down in front of him, spiraling lazily in the darkness, black against deeper gray.

Chris was having difficulty coming to terms with what he was seeing, what he'd just seen. It was as if he wasn't there, not conscious and aware. This wasn't what it was supposed to be like at all.

"Gaaah," he forced out between his lips with every effort of his elusive will.

Any moment, he expected to feel the weight of sharp claws landing on his shoulder. Stray dust motes caught the light of his flashlight beam, floating in seemingly random patterns. He pulled his attention away from Jason, trying to focus on them, trying to fix his concentration on something small and insubstantial, but his vision kept slipping in and out of focus. He couldn't do it.

From above, came the sound of constantly shifting and rustling feathers. He tried to swallow, and couldn't. He tried to close his eyes and couldn't. Right then, right at that moment, he felt drained, felt as if all feeling had simply flowed out of him and away.

The hollow-eyed people he had seen, immobile, scattered in various places. And as Chris thought about that, he remembered. He remembered that night when Stase and he had argued, when she had simply drained away to collapse on the kitchen floor. He remembered the men coming in the white van, pushing past him in the doorway without a word and taking her away. Somehow, some way, they had screwed with his memory too. They'd come back and taken him and done something to make his memory other than it was. They were screwing with him now.

That didn't explain who they were and what they were doing. Was this some vast experiment? Some cosmic joke? Were people really little more than hollow vessels that could be filled with whatever thoughts and memories that could be thrust at them from without? Or maybe it wasn't that at all. Maybe they were just manipulating the thoughts. Chris was struggling with the ideas. Patrick. Patrick could be one of them. Did these people, whoever they were—or were they even people after all? He couldn't tell. He couldn't even rely on what his eyes were telling him. Did they just batter away at you through everyday life until there was nothing else, sensations, impressions, thoughts, memories, everything that made you what you were, gone? Or perhaps the people, these beings, were benevolent, monitoring what went on in the world every day, watching the media barrage—that much at least was clear from this place—and fixing the problem of perceptual overload when it all became too much.

Chris fought with himself, fought with the paralysis overwhelming him, summoning every ounce of his will, scrunching his effort into a tight ball that he thrust up and out, exploding into three simple words.

"Who ... are ... they?" he cried.

Chris's perception started blurring then.

There was a hand upon his shoulder, and he jumped.

"Chris, what is it?" said Jason's voice. "You okay, man?"

CHAPTER THIRTY-TWO

THAT WHICH LINGERS

Chris sat in the car, looking down at the keys held in his hand. He had been going somewhere, or perhaps he had been somewhere. He closed his fingers around the keys. Strange. He knew he should know. He opened his palm again, looked at the keys and was just about to lean forward and push them into the ignition, when he noticed the black bag on the seat beside him. He didn't remember putting it there. He put the key in the ignition and reached over to the bag, pulling it to him. It was heavy. He frowned, opened the bag and looked inside. There was the big flashlight from downstairs and a pair of pliers and a hammer. What the hell would he want those for? Perhaps Jason had asked to borrow them. There was dried mud on the bottom of the bag. He ran his fingertip over it. But if he was dropping the stuff off to Jason, what the hell was the mud doing there. Maybe he'd dropped the bag somewhere. That's the only thing he could think of.

He shoved the bag onto the floor in front of the seat and leaned back, resting the back of his head on the headrest and rubbing his forehead with his fingers. There was the hint of a weird buzzing noise in his head, barely beneath his perception. He ran his fingers through his hair and gently massaged the back of his neck.

Putting his arm in that position fired a painful sensation on the top of his shoulder. That was strange too. He reached beneath his shirt and felt along the skin of his shoulder, probing for the source of the pain. His fingertips encountered something and he sucked air through his teeth. Three raised ridges sat there, painful, like scratches. As he felt, he noticed a similar slight twinge in his other shoulder. There were more scratches there. What the hell had he been doing? It was probably something he'd done while attempting to clear out the garden, but what on earth had made marks like that? Had he been pushing through bushes or something? But that didn't make sense either. He simply couldn't remember. He shook his head, as if to clear it.

He wasn't going to find any answers sitting in the dark in the car. He pulled the key out of the ignition, reached for the bag and stepped out to the roadside. He stood there for a couple of seconds, remembering something—or rather, half remembering something. It had to do with birds. He struggled with the memory for a couple of seconds then shook his head. It simply wasn't going to come. He wished he could get rid of the buzzing sensation in his ears. It was like it was deep within his head, rather than something he was really hearing. He glanced over at the house. The windows were dark. It looked like Stase wasn't home yet, or else she'd got home and had already gone to bed. Glancing down at his watch, he realized that that couldn't be the case. It was only 9:30. With a brief shake of his head, he locked the car and headed for the front steps.

Once inside, he headed downstairs, dropped the bag in the cupboard where the stuff belonged, and went back into the kitchen. He looked around, seeking a clue, seeking ... he didn't know quite what he was seeking. He stood staring at the fridge, at the notes and photographs held in place with small round fridge magnets for a while, running the day's events through his mind, but they kept slipping away from him, oily, sliding through his mental grasp. He frowned, walked out of the kitchen, passing the phone on the way and suddenly having second thoughts, he turned back to it. The only thing he could think of was that he was taking those things over to Jason's. He picked up the phone and dialed.

The answering machine kicked in, but just as it was starting to grind out its message, someone picked up the phone.

"Jason?"

"Ah, Chris. What an unexpected surprise."

"Hope I didn't catch you in the middle of something."

There was a chuckle from the other end. "Not something I can't talk about," he said. "No, I was just fiddling with one of the doors downstairs."

Doors? There was a brief flash of something. A door. Darkness. A crowbar.

"Um, right," said Chris. "Listen. You didn't ask to borrow anything did you? Some tools? A flashlight, maybe?"

"Chris, now why would I do that? Think about it, man. Or is this some sort of trick question?"

"Yeah right, sorry." It was stupid. Jason had enough tools to set up a building company. Why would he want to borrow tools? "Sorry, I just forgot something and I was trying to work out what it was."

"You're getting old, young man." Another chuckle.

"Yeah, right. Well, sorry to drag you away from whatever you were doing."

"Not a problem. So, how's the little woman?"

Stase. Something about Stase. Confusion passed across his brow. "Yeah, um ... yeah, she's fine." He struggled to remember where she was. "She's out at the moment. Some work do or other."

"Well, give her my best if she's in any state when she gets in."

"Yeah, I will do. Same to Claudia."

There was a sharp intake of breath at the other end. "Ow."

"What?" asked Chris.

"Oh, I don't know. I've done something to my shoulder. Caught it on a nail or something I suppose. Damned if I can remember doing it."

Chris reached for his own shoulder, frowning again.

Birds. Black birds. Big ones. The white noise in his head, buzzing behind his eyes. He winced.

"Right, well you take care now, Jason. You ought to be more careful. Hey, listen, it's been ages since we've seen each other. You want to catch up for a drink some time when the girls are otherwise engaged?"

Jason chuckled. "Sounds like a plan," he said.

Sounds like a plan. That meant something. Chris frowned. "Okay, I'll give you a call," he said.

"Sure. Later."

Chris gently put down the receiver and stood staring at the phone. After a while, he stepped back into the kitchen, dropped a couple of painkillers and wandered back into the living room and flipped on the television. He didn't really care what was on. He sat there in the darkness, watching the moving images without really seeing them, letting the noise simply wash over him. Occasionally he'd feel his eyebrows twitch, and then he'd blink involuntarily. There was a strangely empty feeling inside at the top of his abdomen for most of the night, and though he tried to think, his head fogged the process, so he let it slip away.

Stase arrived home around midnight. She'd clearly had a couple too many, a little unsteady and giggly, still in her work clothes. She barely spoke to him and was up in the shower and to bed within half an hour. Chris sat there for longer, much longer, not motivated to do anything, let alone go to their strangely distant bed.

Chris never got the chance to set up his drinks date with Jason. Four days later, Stase came home and announced that Claudia had accepted a position overseas. Both she and Jason were going to be moving within the week, permanently. It was something they'd been negotiating for a few weeks, but they'd kept it quiet in case it hadn't come off. It was an amazing opportunity and Claudia was going to be getting stacks more money, better conditions, a full relocation package thrown in. Stase was clearly envious, but more than anything, she was sad to be losing one of her closest girlfriends. Of course, she'd go and visit, and Claudia and Jason would probably be back from time to time, but it wouldn't be a regular event. They had so much to do before they left that there was little chance to spend any real time together.

Chris couldn't quite focus on Stase's announcement. In the past few days, things had been occurring in Chris's head, strange things, unexpected things. Brief flashes, images. He kept seeing these very conservative-looking faces, leaning in close to his own, and always, always, he'd be thinking about something and a quick sharp image would form in his inner eye—feathers, wings, beaks, eyes. He wondered if he might be starting to develop a morbid fear of crows.

On Tuesday, he was on the bus into work, when he saw the old guy who hung around the local shopping center, walking up the road carrying a couple of plastic bags. His breath caught in his chest.

"Patrick?" he said quietly.

"Excuse me?" asked the person sitting next to him.

Chris apologized and looked out the window, watching as the man called Patrick hobbled along, the bus quickly leaving him behind. He'd talked to him, talked to him about ... a van? Something like that. He shook his head and went back to vaguely watching the world passing outside.

That night, he was in front of the television when another image swept over him, blocking all other thought. Some program by HBO started and the screen full of white snow leaped out at him from the set. Ranks and ranks of screens floated before him, covered with images, newsfeed, webpages. His entire consciousness was swimming with it, filling his head with details and titles, pictures of everything he could imagine. It rocked him back on the couch, his eyes wide, staring at the phantom picture in front of him.

"Jesus," he said, involuntarily, gasping for breath.

"What is it?" said Stase, reaching for the remote, looking for something else to watch.

He shook his head, quickly, half trying to shake away what he was seeing, half as a response to her question.

"Nothing," he told her. "Nothing at all."

In dribs and drabs, more pictures came over the next couple of days, floating up into his mind at work, in coffee shops, on the bus to work and home again. He saw a collection of black birds lining a rafter, an empty church, clean-cut faces and white coats and vans, hollow-eyed people sitting motionless in different places, and one by one, little by little, they started to slot together into a coherent whole. Every evening he looked at Stase with slightly new eyes. Every evening he looked at the house, at everything they did, at everything they had done with new eyes. And every night he dreamed. He'd forgotten what they'd done and what they'd been through. Those nameless constructions he'd built within himself had forced him to forget, but he was remembering now.

The final jolt came a couple of days later, when he was walking home. There, at the end of his street, sitting at the corner and watching him approach, perched a large, black bird.

Chris's breath went completely from him, and a shaft of cold sliced through his spine. His vision clouded, became dark, and then was full of light. The remaining memories came rushing back to him, a mental cacophony and he stopped in his tracks, unable to move.

The bird stepped along the fence, dipped its head, and then turned one eye to look at him.

He regarded it suspiciously, standing where he was, not wanting to move, wanting desperately to bolt, but not letting himself. All the time, battling against that inner struggle, was the knowledge of what it was that stood before him, perched so innocuously on the top of a fence. There was no innocence there. Not a shred of it. Not in the gaze, not in its stance, not in the mere fact of it being there.

Mustering as much calm as he could, he said slowly, deliberately, quietly, "Leave me alone now."

The bird turned its head as if listening, and then, seemingly in response, suddenly took to the wing, black feathers beating strongly against the cool night air.

He was probably crazy for talking to a bird, but then again, he might not be. He was probably just crazy.

Chris watched it as it soared above the rooftops till it was no more than a speck against the twilit, steel-blue sky.

Then he walked slowly home.

CHAPTER THIRTY-THREE
SEVERANCE

Five days after he saw the crow, he came home after work and Stase's things were gone. Chris stood there staring at the empty spaces not knowing what to do, not quite believing what was plainly evident in front of him. At first, it didn't really make sense. He thought maybe the place had been burgled, but then rationality took over and he saw that all the portable stuff that a burglar might take was still there. All his things were still there too. He walked from room to room, mentally cataloguing, struggling to understand, and refusing what he was seeing. And then, the bleakness washed down upon him in a wave of realization and emptiness. He just stood there.

Though he looked, knowing what had happened, there wasn't even a note. Had she thought so little of him that she could just walk out without a word? He kept telling himself that there was some other explanation for what he was seeing.

For a while, he sat on the bed, staring blankly at the wall and wondering what he was going to do. There was no point calling her parents. She wouldn't be there, and even if she was, they wouldn't tell Chris. He knew that they tolerated him at best, despite the congeniality of their meetings. Stase only saw them maybe once a year now, the dutiful annual visit, so it was a fair bet she wouldn't be there. They were too much a reminder of her old life, and in a way, she tolerated them in the same way she had tolerated things about their own relationship. She would have found someone, somewhere, away from him and difficult for him to trace.

He cursed himself for allowing her to be so secretive, perhaps for not taking enough of an interest despite the distance and the fights. He should have forced himself to bridge that space between them. She had kept so much from him. But them she always had. In the beginning, even later, none of it had mattered because she was with him, part of him, and whether separate or apart, we all have holes in our memories that we gloss over. Just in the same way that we all have parts of our shared existences that we gloss over because it's convenient. The things that we want to remember. The things we don't.

His despair turned to cold rage for a moment. He felt abused. How could she have left him without a word? It was gutless. If she'd cared, she would have told him something, but to sneak out while he wasn't there ... He looked around the bedroom, impotent with his anger. There wasn't even anything of hers left to throw. He punched the air, but it did nothing, and he swung at the emptiness again, even though the gesture was pointless.

One more time, he walked around the room, opening drawers and closing them, opening the wardrobe and looking at the empty hanging space. He went into the bathroom, but all her toiletries were definitely gone too. Empty shelves stared back at Chris accusingly. He glanced at himself in the mirror, and his image stared back with hard hostility, then afraid, then with a haunted, hunted look. He turned away from the mirror and went back into the bedroom and checked again. No matter how many times he looked, the evidence didn't change.

"Shit!" he said, and sat slowly on the side of the bed, his forehead resting on his hands. What was he going to do? He massaged the top of his head with his fingers and then looked up again. He had to approach this rationally. He looked around the room seeking something, checking that she'd left nothing, but there wasn't a single thing out of place, not a thing that didn't belong there by rights. Not a trace of Anastasia remained. Oh, there were their personal things, their joint acquisitions, those things purchased in deference to a certain conception of taste, but clothing, toiletries, jewelry—all gone. The worst thing was that he knew there was nothing he could do. Maybe she had gone to stay with one of her new friends, but the problem there was that he didn't really know who those new friends were. There were snatches of names, semi-remembered in his own obsession with solving the mystery of what had happened. He didn't ever really know where any of them lived.

Was this a punishment for what he'd done in chasing the answers to what had been happening to people, to what had been happening to them? Was Anastasia's departure linked to what he had done? He knew there was no real answer in the asking, but he had to find somewhere to begin apportioning blame.

There was no one he could really tell.

He paced from room to room again, trying to find some confirmation that the whole thing wasn't really happening, knowing in his guts that she had really gone. She hadn't even talked about it as far as he could remember, but memory these days was a strangely insubstantial thing. He didn't feel like tears. He just felt numb.

He sat for most of the evening staring at the wall, powerless. The least she could have done was leave him some confirmation of what she'd done. Twice more he wandered from room to room, looking at everything, seeking a message, a note, anything.

The phone rang about 11:00.

"Chris?" Her voice was hesitant.

"Stase? Where the hell are you?"

"That's not important."

"What do you mean it's not important? Of course it's bloody important! Where are you?"

There was long silence. He could hear her breathing at the other end of the line. "I'm not going to tell you. I think it's better that way."

Chris forced himself to keep his breathing, his voice, steady. "Why are you doing this, Stase?"

Again a pause. "I just think it's better. Let's just call it a trial. I think we need some time apart."

"Why are you doing this, Stase? Why are you fucking doing this?"

"Chris, I don't want you to get angry. I just want you to listen to me, okay?"

He held his breath.

"Okay?" she said again.

"Yes, but I don't understand. Couldn't you have talked to me about it first?"

Her breathing was close to the phone. "If I'd talked to you about it," she said quietly, "you would probably have talked me out of it."

"Christ! How long have you been planning this?" His breathing was faster now, shallow.

"Listen, Chris. I don't want you to get angry, okay? Just listen to me. I think this is for the better. We need to have this time apart. I need to work things out, and I can't do that if we're together. I need time alone by myself. I'll call you in a couple of days."

She hung up the phone. She hadn't even given him a chance to respond properly.

He stood with the receiver to his ear for several seconds, waiting for her to say something else, to pick up the phone, to do something.

"Shit!" he said, slamming the receiver down into its cradle. "Shit!"

Rage washed up first, and then dissipated just as quickly to be replaced by cold emptiness. It was impotence. She had made him totally powerless. He had a quick thought and quickly keyed the last caller number. It hadn't sounded like the call had come from a cell. He waited, tapping his foot and closing and unclosing the fingers of his other hand. Number withheld.

"Shit!"

He paced the room, looking for something to do, something to fill the void he was feeling. He went outside, out into the backyard and stood there in the darkness, breathing shallowly.

The night was chill and there'd been rain earlier. In their tangled backyard with the piles of rotting vegetation, the smell of corruption rising damply into the air around him, he stood, feeling totally isolated from reality. There was nothing he could do. He went back inside to the lounge, switched on the television, but couldn't watch it. There were moving images that just wouldn't resolve into anything meaningful. He stared at them, not really seeing them, hoping somehow they would make everything all right. The sound was a meaningless blur. He sat staring into nothing, hearing Stase's voice, and her breathing on the end of the phone.

He finally slept in his cold bed alone, strangely having enough presence of mind to set the alarm, but he awoke still feeling hollowed and impotent. He had to go to work and he had things to do. He would try to call her during the day at work. He knew she was going to be there; she'd already said that she couldn't afford to take time off at the moment, but it was little consolation. As he drank his morning coffee, Chris was still trying to come to terms with the resentment and the sense of fragile powerlessness warring inside him. He was dreading work. What if anyone asked? What would he say? He decided to deal with that the only way he knew how; he'd just say nothing. It was like that time he'd been forced to try to disguise the marks on his face. He dreaded the looks, the knowing glances. After all, he was basically a private person and the last thing he wanted was his life on full show.

An odd thought came to him then. Stase had always wanted their life on show, as long as it was under her terms. Chris had been along for the ride, sitting back and letting her shape those terms. He thought it was a fair price to pay for what he was getting in return.

He just never expected her to leave ... ever. He could hardly believe it. He didn't really believe it still.

Any thought of doing something about the cathedral and the clean-cut guys in the van had slunk away looking furtively over its shoulder. He had more important things to worry about now, like trying to re-find what was left of his life.

People left other people, not Chris, and not Stase. Not Stase and Chris.

As he walked out the front door, the hollow walked with him. A motion over the other side of the street caught his attention. Perched on the fence across the street sat the black bird. He stopped on the top step, staring across at it accusingly. He frowned. It could have been any bird, but somehow he was convinced it was the same one, the one that had been haunting him over the past few weeks.

He called her as soon as he got to work. She started early and was always there first thing. He got her voice mail. An hour later, and he got her voice mail again. Around lunch, he huddled over the phone, not wanting anyone to overhear and he tried through the switch, but they just put him through to voice mail again. On the fifth attempt, he left her a message.

"Stase, call me please. I need to talk to you."

For the rest of the afternoon, his phone failed to ring,

and in desperation, he sent her an email. That drew no response either.

Going to her office would be pointless, he knew. She worked on the tenth floor, and she'd probably left a message with security to not let him up, not that her employers appreciated people turning up on personal business anyway. Her corporate security had built extra walls around her, walls that he knew he'd have little chance of getting through, and he wasn't about to turn up and create a scene. He had only one choice, to go home and wait for her call. Just as he had controlled their life together, she was now controlling their separation, on her terms.

Three nights, he waited, fragile and tense. Twice during those three days he cried alone. Anger had turned to loss had turned to sorrow, then to frustration and back to sorrow again. He kept turning around to say something to her and then he'd catch himself and realize she wasn't there. At work, he was tense and on edge, reluctant to engage in any conversation that wasn't directly related to work, and he was noncommittal when his workmates asked about how things were going.

On the fourth day, he got her call.

"Chris, can we meet somewhere? Maybe for a drink?"

She sounded calm, and he frowned at the question. It was a strange thing to ask. Or maybe it wasn't. Somewhere public, somewhere safe, though he couldn't imagine what she thought he might do. Perhaps she expected retribution. Was she feeling that much guilt? He chased away thoughts of what she might have been doing in the meantime.

"Sure, where?"

She named a bar and a time.

"About seven? Sure. See you then."

✦ ✦ ✦

Chris wandered into the bar feeling a mix of emotions, looked for her, but she hadn't turned up yet. He ordered a drink and found a solitary table by the door. She arrived about fifteen minutes late and didn't notice him as she walked through the door and looked around the bar.

"Stase, over here," he called out to her.

She was looking slightly nervous as she walked up to him and planted a kiss on his cheek. "Hi," she said. "How are you?"

Small talk.

"Yeah, I'm okay, I guess. You?"

She nodded.

"Can I get you a drink?" Chris said.

She started removing her coat, putting down her bag and pulled out the stool to sit. "Yeah, thanks. A gin and tonic."

Chris watched her as he made his way to the bar and got her drink. She was looking at the other patrons, around the room, everywhere but at him. She pulled out a cigarette and lit it, drawing deeply. In her other hand she kept hold of the lighter, tapping it briskly on the table in a regular, nervous rhythm. She looked drawn and ill at ease.

Chris carried her drink back, pulled out his stool and sat opposite, his elbows on the table, not bothering to reach for his drink.

"So," he said.

She sipped at her drink and took another drag of her cigarette.

"So, how are you doing, really?" he said.

Stase looked at him, a brief, glancing look, and then looked away again. She shrugged. "It's okay."

Chris picked up his drink and took a sip. He'd been hoping for something else, not this.

"What did you want to talk about?" he said quietly.

There was hesitation before she spoke again. "I need to come round to the house and get some things. I wanted to sort out a time with you."

He frowned. "All you had to do was come over, Stase. Why the need for all this? Why don't you stop this nonsense and just come back home? I don't know why—"

She held up a hand. "I didn't want this. I just wanted to see how you were, have a quiet chat and work out a time when I could get the things."

"You can come over any time."

"No, I want you to be there. It's better if you're there."

"What's better, Stase?"

She shook her head and took a drag of her cigarette. "So when can I come over?"

"Whenever you want. Thursday. Is Thursday okay?"

She nodded. They both sat, saying nothing, not meeting each other's eyes, sipping at their drinks. Chris's glass was getting empty, and he turned it around and around on top of the table, waiting for her to say something else. She stubbed her cigarette out in the ashtray, and took a last sip of her drink.

"I'll always be your friend, you know," she said.

Chris just looked at her.

"Okay," she said, reaching for her coat. "I've got to go."

"Is that it?" he said.

"I'll see you on Thursday evening," she said, reaching for her bag. Then she was gone, leaving Chris staring at the door. He looked down at his glass, pushed it across the table with one finger till it stopped, resting against her empty glass in front of where she had been sitting.

"Is that it?" he said quietly to himself, knowing the answer without even thinking about it.

CHAPTER THIRTY-FOUR

SECRETS

Anastasia turned up on the Thursday evening as agreed. Chris was sitting inside, waiting nervously, unable to settle. He paced the empty house a few times, looking for something to do, but he couldn't concentrate. The doorbell rang and he started, then gave a sigh of mixed relief. He headed quickly for the door, trying to maintain the impression that he was casual and relaxed, that there was nothing unusual going on. He took a few deep breaths, then opened the door, forcing himself to smile.

"Hi," he said.

"Hello," said Anastasia. She wasn't alone. Behind her was a woman he didn't recognize.

Anastasia headed up the stairs, beckoning the woman to follow her. "This is Sam," she said as Chris stepped back to let her pass, holding the door open with one hand. The other woman gave him a brief nod and followed Anastasia inside. Chris was left looking stupidly after them, holding the open door. It took him a moment to regain his composure; then, he shut the door and followed them into the living room.

"What do you need?" asked Chris.

Sam was a shorter woman with dark hair and Mediterranean features. She stood in the background, behind Anastasia; unobtrusive, but obviously there. Chris glanced from her to Anastasia and back again.

Anastasia was looking around the room.

"You've unpacked some things," she said.

"Yeah, well, there seemed little point in keeping everything in boxes still."

Anastasia nodded.

"Stase?"

She shook her head. "Not now," she said, glancing back at Sam. "I need some things from the kitchen and some bedding. That's about it for now. We can sort out other things later."

He looked at her, not quite understanding what she meant by sorting other things out. What other things? He moved over to the lounge and sat, looking up at her, holding his hands clasped together in front of him. He sighed.

"Take what you need," he said.

He sat there listening as Anastasia and Sam wandered into the kitchen, taking what he presumed were pans, cutlery and plates. They moved upstairs to the bedroom next. There was the sound of opening drawers and cupboards. Chris sat there, helpless, listening to the creak of floorboards as they moved from room to room. Finally, they appeared to be done. There was the sound of feet coming down the stairs and then Anastasia appeared in the doorway.

"I'm done," she said.

Chris stood, feeling awkward. Anastasia seemed fixed, intent on what she was doing.

"Can we talk?" he asked.

"No, not now," she said. "I want you to come and look at what I've taken."

"What for?"

She looked slightly exasperated then. Her voice was snappy. "Because it's just better if you do. We need to agree what I've taken."

Chris frowned. "Okaaay. I trust you. Why is this necessary?"

"It just is." She disappeared back into the hallway.

Chris followed. Lined up against one wall were three large, black, plastic bags. Sam stood at one end of the hallway, not looking at him. He opened the first bag and looked inside. There were some sheets, a couple of pillow cases, a bedcover. The next bag had towels and some knives and forks. The last one had a couple of pans and some mugs.

"Okay," he said. He didn't quite know what else to say.

"All right," Said Anastasia. "We'll be going now. I'll give you a call in a couple of days."

"Let me give you a hand," he said.

"No, it's okay. We can manage," she said.

Sam opened the door. Anastasia lifted two of the bags and Sam picked up the other. Chris stood watching, shoving his hands into his pockets. Anastasia put down one of the bags on the front step, pulling the door shut behind her.

Chris stood in the hallway a long time, just staring at the door. He felt the house around him, empty, hollow like the way he was feeling. There was growing understanding forming in the back of his head, but it wasn't anything he was prepared to deal with in detail right then.

Finally, with a sigh, he turned back into the lounge, returned to the couch and sat, resting his head in his hands. He sat like that for a long time. Every couple of minutes, he expected the phone to ring. It didn't.

Anastasia called him once or twice during the next couple of weeks. She was still blocking his calls at work and blocking the number she used to call him from. Chris tried to do things to keep himself occupied. He unpacked the remaining stuff from boxes in the house and put them away. He started painting the inside, just to keep himself occupied and to freshen up the environment a little. It remained empty, however. At work, he kept as much to himself as he could. He avoided talking about his private life—not that he did that much anyway, but now, he deliberately said nothing about home. A couple of times people asked after Anastasia, and he shrugged them off with non-committal answers that would steer any further questions away. It was a place of solitude, of frustration and of a ringing hollowness that shadowed every action. He'd asked her to come home a couple of times when they spoke, but she wasn't having any of it, not then.

When he came back home one Friday and found the letter, it was like a body blow, but a blow that he'd been expecting. Anastasia was initiating divorce proceedings. He read the letter over three times, then placed it gently down on the kitchen table and stood staring down at it. It was there in black and white, undeniable.

She must have been planning it for ages, just like she planned everything; and yet, she had kept it from him. She hadn't even bothered to discuss what she was going to do.

She had been in control of it. She always had. Chris, in many ways, had been just along for the ride, an accessory that suited as long as it was fashionable.

He wondered if there was anyone else—a new, more modern accessory.

He flattered himself that there wasn't, that they'd just grown too far apart, but he cursed himself for letting things get too far away. Anastasia would have probably worked to take them from his grasp anyway, but at least he could have tried.

As part of the final process, he thought about buying out her share of the house, but there was just too much baggage there. The house was part of what had happened and he couldn't really live there any more, not that he ever really had. Houses accumulate memories like places and they stalk the rooms, especially late at night when everything is still and quiet, and there is time to listen to what the walls are telling you. He ended up selling the house and paying her out of the proceeds as part of the divorce settlement. Fees, lawyers, process and waste. The architects and the dreams. The architecture of dreams that came to nothing and it had all evaporated in a pointless antagonism that had no real reason to exist in the first place.

In reflection, there was little he could find that was good or right. They had been driven by Anastasia's ambition, and beneath that ambition, he thought that maybe she didn't really feel or care, that maybe she couldn't. All she'd had was want. It was a desperate driving need that battered at her underlying persona, shaping it to its own desires. He believed that she, the true Anastasia, had perhaps drowned within.

Was that a product of their environment, a symptom of modern life? He didn't know. All he really knew was that every day, every one of us is bombarded with images and thoughts of extremes that pound at us through pictures and movies and news and everything else that assails us through our day-to-day existence. All of it is underpinned by the constant need to consume. It is that production of need that becomes our true role in life. He didn't know whether he wanted a part of that, but within, inside, in that strangely echoing place, he knew it was unavoidable.

Eventually, he reached the point where he was removed enough to really analyze what had happened, not only between them, but to them. Shreds of what had taken place at the cathedral came back to him when he least expected, and though he tried to put them away, still they returned. It was a violation, what had been done to him, what he'd done to himself, but he thought perhaps it was a necessary violation. He even wondered whether he would be better off sitting blank eyed in a doorway and then taken away to refill with something that would wash away the pain and hurt and betrayal, if they could ever do it. Then he would take pause, reflect again, and think that the largest betrayal was probably his own betrayal of himself.

It was a betrayal that had taken years to accomplish.

And after all, the black bird had granted his wish; it had left him truly alone.

CHAPTER THIRTY-FIVE

FRAMING GLASS

You've heard the expression, "the milk of human kindness." Back before there were cartons, tetra packs, plastic containers, milk was delivered in thick glass bottles and the empties were collected every morning. You could hear the milkman clinking and rattling from door to door, a white wire basket held in one hand. He'd grab a bunch of bottles, collecting a handful with a finger shoved down each neck, and one for his thumb, pressing against the others to keep them in place. He'd carry them back and slot them into his basket, ready to return for washing and refilling, and he'd replace them with full ones. Sometimes, the lady of the house would wash them for him, even though they were always rewashed. Often though, there'd be a thin white scum left on the inside of the bottle—perhaps a few drops, or a dead fly to swirl around in tainted milk in the bottom of the glass inside. Sometimes even, there'd be a small shiny piece of thick foil, left from the cap as it had been peeled away, shining dully in the streetlights.

The early morning milkman would carry the empty bottles back to his truck, and they'd be taken away. Taken away to refill.

Maybe sometimes, what they put in the bottles the next time around wasn't quite the same as the stuff they'd put in before. Maybe that's what happened to Patrick, to some of the others. Maybe that's what happens to all of them some way. There are traces of what they were, but the essence has changed. They're tainted, but tainted with vestiges of themselves. Chris continues to tell himself that had to be the explanation for what happened with Anastasia. He wonders if the same thing happened to him.

Over time, Chris decided that there was a possible reason for what happened to him. He didn't live in the particular macrocosm shaped by the media, the images and sensations we are bombarded with every day. He had existed for years in his own microcosm, or rather Anastasia's. He was totally protected from the outside world by a bubble of someone else's construction, and by his own complicity in its design. Perhaps in the end, she left Chris because those strange black birds really were looking after him, but he was not so sure.

He continues to look out windows, on buses, in cafes, in cars, and think about his ex-wife, expecting to see her walking past, or standing on the side of the street, staring at him as he passes, her face turning to track him with a blank expression. He practices his reaction in his head, the expression he'll use, whether he'll gesture, whether he'll stop and get off the bus and try to catch up with her, but it will never happen like that. Occasionally, he even thinks he's caught a glimpse of her in a passing car or through a shop window and his heart and guts grow cold. But it's never her. His memory reaches out and tries to make her there and how she was before. It's a haunting where the ghost is nothing more than his own memories and broken aspirations.

He heard something once, about how it takes you one full year for every four years you've been together to get over a significant relationship. Or was it the other way around? Either way, it was just too damned long. It was always going to be too damned long. He wonders sometimes if she does the same sort of thing, imagining that she'll catch a glimpse of him as he passes. He doubts it. She was always far too bound in her own version of reality and he's no longer a part of that, not that he ever really was.

"You'll always be my friend," she'd said.

Yeah right.

The markers in all of our lives are stuck together in a disorganized collage of memories, abbreviated like street signs, pointing the way, but existing only as self-defining shorthand.

If Chris spends enough time looking at those places, he discovers that there is a taste that comes with that observation. It is a bitter taste that flows through him like a shudder, but it passes, just like everything else. All memories pass and fade with time, blurring and reshaping to our own convenience. Everything passes.

Now, at least, he can remember what it's like.

Down the street, jackhammers are busy making alterations to someone else's life. The builders pound away, ripping apart the old and reshaping it into something habitable. From time to time, Chris gazes out the window of his rented apartment half-expecting a white van to pull up and two clean-cut guys in white coats to step out. It hasn't happened yet; perhaps it never will.

He thinks he's safe from his own mental constructions ... for now.

And the cathedral? The place or places where he thought it all happened? There were wisps, fragments that floated up when he was thinking about nothing in particular, painting cinematic images on the inner screen that tells him what has been. But that's just memory. And really, it doesn't matter, because memory is transitory too. He avoids other people's memories, and he doesn't watch television very much any more.

He's the one in control.

Chris scrapes his things together, ready to head out the front door. A flicker of dark motion over the other side of the street catches his attention. Perched on the fence across the street sits a black bird. He stops on the top step, staring across at it accusingly. He frowns and the accusation fades. It could be any bird, but somehow he is convinced it is the same one, the one that has been haunting him over the past few weeks and months.

"Just fuck off," he whispers at it. "I don't need you any more."

As he wanders down to the bus stop, there's the hint of a smile on his lips.

END

About the author

Jay Caselberg is an Australian author based in Europe. His work has been nominated for multiple awards and is generally on the darker side. He has short fiction recently or forthcoming in *The End of the Road, Halloween: Magic, Mystery & The Macabre, Extreme Planets* and *Airships & Automatons* to name but a few. Occasionally his poetry will also appear in print. More can be found at http://www.jaycaselberg.com. This is his seventh published novel.

www.ingramcontent.com/pod-product-compliance
Lightning Source LLC
Chambersburg PA
CBHW051248260626
47162CB00002B/670